THE
PATMOS
DECEPTION

THE
PATMOS
DECEPTION

DAVIS BUNN

BETHANYHOUSE

a division of Baker Publishing Group
Minneapolis, Minnesota

© 2014 by Davis Bunn

Published by Bethany House Publishers
11400 Hampshire Avenue South
Bloomington, Minnesota 55438
www.bethanyhouse.com

Bethany House Publishers is a division of
Baker Publishing Group, Grand Rapids, Michigan

Printed in the United States of America

Library of Congress Cataloging-in-Publication Data is on file at the Library of Congress, Washington, DC.

ISBN 978-0-7642-1228-4 (hardcover)
ISBN 978-0-7642-1139-3 (trade paper)

Scripture quotations are from the Holy Bible, New International Version®. NIV®.
Copyright © 1973, 1978, 1984, 2011 by Biblica, Inc.™ Used by permission of Zondervan.
All rights reserved worldwide. www.zondervan.com

This is a work of fiction. Names, characters, incidents, and dialogues are products of
the author's imagination and are not to be construed as real. Any resemblance to actual
events or persons, living or dead, is entirely coincidental.

Cover design by Kirk DouPonce, DogEared Design
Author photograph by Angel Grey

14 15 16 17 18 19 20   7 6 5 4 3 2 1

This story is dedicated to
Renée and Allen Johnson.

In countless ways, your love
and generosity enrich our lives.

1

Carey Mathers arrived in Greece in a state of breath-less exhaustion. She had passed through five different airports in four different countries—Dallas to Chicago to Toronto to London to Athens. For a girl who had never traveled farther than Austin, Carey thought she had managed pretty well. The reason for her roundabout trip was money. As in, Carey didn't have any and never had. Which was okay. She had never been too worried about what her grandmother called the store-bought life. But this trip was different. Her journey to Greece was all about dreams coming true.

So when the check had come from the prestigious Athens Institute for Antiquities, Carey spent days researching the cheapest possible way to arrive at her new home. The funding was supposed to cover her flight plus a week in a hotel while she found an apartment and settled in. Carey planned for the sum to go a great deal further. Nana Pat always said Carey knew how to make a nickel complain over being pinched too hard and too long.

Carey had never much liked the term *orphan*. Even as a child she had refused to be classed as one. To her ear, the word sounded too much like *alone*. And she was far from that. Soon after her father died from an early heart attack and her mother in the tragic car wreck, Carey's life became filled with grandparents and aunts and uncles and cousins, some of whom she had never met before then. An animated discussion started between them at the funeral over who was going to give Carey a home, and continued until she went off to university.

Once again Carey unfolded the letter from Dr. Adriana Stephanopoulos, the Institute's vice director. It was smeared now, but that hardly mattered since Carey had read the invitation to come work in Athens so often that the words felt tattooed on her brain. She had anticipated this moment for so long, her jet lag and her headache were nothing more than a minor nuisance. She stood by the Athens airport terminal windows, mesmerized by the view. Beyond the landing strips and the tower and the main satellite building loomed the Parnitha Mountains. Their upper slopes glistened with an early October snowfall. The famous forests of Greek pines, described by poets for four thousand years, spread like emerald quilts over the lower reaches. Carey took a breath as deep and delicious as a dream come true. She was in *Greece*.

She took the train from the airport to the Athens central station, then rolled her suitcase to the taxi stand. The sky had darkened, and she was slapped by a blustery wind and accompanying rain. And it was *cold*.

Carey decided not to open her case and drag out her coat for fear of getting everything inside wet. She stood in the taxi line arguing with herself. She would have preferred to take a bus. Her thrifty nature disliked the extra expense, but the

8

Institute's location was just some address on a scrap of paper. She could read a little Greek, yet it was *ancient* Greek, and the spoken language was well beyond her. She would never be able to figure out the bus markings.

The taxi driver looked to be about eighty, with a three-day stubble and clothes that smelled of cigarette smoke. He stood by the taxi's rear and stared mournfully at Carey's suitcase. She got the message and lifted it into the trunk herself. She set her backpack on the rear seat and grimaced at the tobacco stench. The driver accepted her sheet of paper, squinted at the address written in Greek, said something, and shook his head. She pointed to the address and spoke one of her few Greek phrases, "I want to go there."

The driver grunted a response, which launched a coughing fit that lasted through starting the engine and setting off.

As he drove around the square fronting the station, she noticed the beggars. They didn't swarm like the ones she had seen in documentaries about Africa or the Indian sub-continent. These people held to a grim sense of place, sitting or squatting along the curb and the benches and the empty fountain. They lifted up packets of tissue or gum or single cigarettes. They were clumped together by race and culture. Africans formed a colorful mob, dressed in rainbow hues of mismatched jackets and trousers and mittens and scarves and caps. The Greeks were mostly old, with faces so seamed their eyes vanished in the folds. Then came the largest group of all, swarthy and dark-eyed and bleak. The taxi driver scowled through his side window as he waited for the light to change and pretended to spit. "*Gyftos.*"

She recognized the word for Gypsy, and at the same moment she noticed the pendant dangling from his rearview mirror. It was stamped with the political symbol for Golden

Dawn, the neofascist organization that had pushed its way into parliament with the last elections. Carey huddled deeper into her seat, stared at the rain-swept world beyond her window, and grimly held on to her dream.

She was so glad to step out from the taxi that she didn't even flinch at the cost. She paid the man, ignored his frown over the lack of a tip, and hauled her case from the trunk.

She recognized the Institute immediately. The stone building matched the image on their website. The taxi had already driven away by the time she noticed the chains wrapped around the gates, locked in place.

The front drive passed through the stone pillars where she stood, swept through a front garden knee-high in weeds, and circled a dry fountain. Two of the Institute's ground-floor windows were broken, revealing internal bars. A trio of papers in transparent folders, lashed to the front gates with plastic ties, flapped in the wind.

Carey stared through the gate at the broken windows and watched her dreams trickle away with the cold, wintry rain.

Carey was shocked from her stunned immobility by a voice demanding, "What are you doing, standing here?"

Carey swung around. "I have a job—"

"Here?" The young woman gestured angrily at the locked gates. "No, no. You *had* a job. Your job is no more."

Carey turned back to the gates. Her mind simply could not take it in. "I don't understand."

"Of course you don't understand. How could you? I am Greek and I have lived here all my life, and I understand nothing." The woman was about Carey's age, small and narrow, yet strong enough to grip Carey's arm and turn her about. She grabbed the suitcase handle and wheeled it behind them. "A generation from now, I will gather with the other old women, and we will quarrel over how this happened."

"I can't . . . There has to be somebody I can talk to."

"Certainly, yes. There is me. Your name, it is Mathers, yes?"

"Carey Mathers. How did—?"

"You think you are the only person who has been hit by the lightning bolt?" She waited for an opening in the traffic, then pulled Carey across the six-lane road. "Look at the people there. See them in the doorway?"

Four young men huddled before a rusting accordion security door. They shared a cigarette and the shelter of the recessed doorway. The showroom windows to either side were shuttered as well, the steel covered with angry graffiti. "They worked for the Institute?"

"No, no, you are not thinking. The lightning bolt, it did not just strike the Institute. It is *everywhere*. It is *Greece*."

The young men watched as the woman drew Carey into a *taverna*, the Greek version of a neighborhood restaurant. The men's dark gazes followed her with weary disinterest.

"Here, this is good." She steered Carey into a booth by the front window. "You can sit and look at what is no more and decide what to do. You are hungry, yes?"

"I . . . No, thank you."

"But of course you are hungry. And tea, yes? You sit and wait." She started away, then turned back and said, "I am Eleni."

Only as Carey watched her depart did she realize the woman wore an apron over her jeans and sweatshirt. Her thoughts were sluggish with shock and jet lag. She looked out the rain-splattered window at the building across the street, glad that the world wept when she could not.

The woman returned with a steaming glass cup and a towel.

11

"You need to change into dry clothes. You must open your case here. There is not room inside the lavatory. It is back through those doors there, see?"

Carey decided it was easier to agree. No one inside the crowded taverna seemed to find her opening the large suitcase by her table to be the least bit strange. She pulled out the first top and pants she touched, as well as her down jacket. She shut the case, picked up the towel, and headed toward the doors Eleni had pointed out.

Eleni followed, saying, "Here, take the tea. No, no arguing. You must drink the warmth. Give me your pack. I will watch your things."

Carey had scarcely locked the door when there was a knock, and Eleni passed her a comb. "You will need this."

She turned and gazed back at the stranger in the mirror. Carey had often been called a beauty, but not today. She looked like a bedraggled rodent. A tall, sad one. Her hair, normally her best feature, was straggly and limp. The copper coloring had turned a transparent brown. Her green eyes no longer sparkled with the electric hope she had known for the five weeks since receiving the Institute's contract. Instead, they were red-rimmed and blank. Carey stared down at the comb in one hand and the tea in the other, and swallowed against a rising sob. The strange woman's kindness threatened to break her heart.

When she emerged, Eleni hurried over. "Better, yes?"

"A little. Maybe."

"Yes, yes, is a very great shock. You sit. I bring food, take my break. Sit with you."

She had scarcely settled back into the booth when Eleni brought over a brimming plate, then slipped off her apron and seated herself on the opposite bench. "You must eat. Food, it is good for such times."

"I'm really not hungry."

"Take one bite. You'll see."

Carey didn't have the strength to argue. The shallow bowl was filled with a stew of lamb, white beans, and vegetables cooked into submission. The flavor was as startling as an unexpected embrace. Three times she had to swallow around the same sob she refused to release in the bathroom. Eleni watched with satisfaction as Carey ate. "We Greeks, we have come to understand how to cope with the great shocks. We have no choice."

"How did you know who I was?"

"I was the director's administrative assistant. I sat in the meeting when they decided to invite you to undertake this research project. I wrote the letter. I processed your check. You cashed it, yes?"

"I did, yes." Carey looked around the café. "And now you're working as a waitress. I'm so sorry—"

"What, you think this is bad?" Eleni showed genuine surprise. "Do they not know of our situation over in America?"

"Of course they do."

"Listen to me, Mathers. For Greeks under the age of thirty, the unemployment rate is *seventy-four* percent. Do you know what they call us? The lost generation." She flattened her hand on the table between them. "Me, I am the lucky one. Of all my friends, I am the one with a job. But enough of this. What are you to do now?"

"I don't know." Carey could barely get the last word out.

"You have a place to stay?"

"I rented a room in a guesthouse for a week." She fumbled in her backpack for the information.

Eleni took the paper and inspected it. "Good, this is very good. The street, it is safe. I know this family. They are solid

13

people. Some places are no longer reliable. Thieves, they are terrible now. A scourge. And drugs. But some areas, they hire vigilantes. This is a good neighborhood." She handed back the paper. "You will tell your family, yes?"

"Oh, no. I can't."

"You must. Your parents, they will be expecting a call, yes?"

"My grandparents. But my grandmother, she won't understand."

Eleni's features were made for sunshine and laughter, full of energy and life. The somber look and the weary eyes did not suit her. "You must tell them, Mathers. Without delay, they must know what has happened."

"My name is Carey."

"Forgive me. I process your papers as Mathers. The work permit, that was such a difficulty. Bringing in a foreigner when so many Greeks are out of work. But the forensic research you have done, this is very needed. And rare."

Carey stared out the window at the Institute's locked gates. "Lot of good it's done me."

"That is for later," Eleni said sternly. "Now you must call your family."

"I was going to buy a Greek phone. I haven't . . ." Carey watched the young woman slide her own phone across the table. "This will be awful."

"Yes, yes, these talks, they are terrible. Better to do it now and be over."

"You don't understand. My grandmother—you've heard the expression, some people see a glass as half full and others don't?"

"Of course. This is very Greek."

"Well, my grandmother is like, the glass is not just half empty. It's also laced with poison."

Eleni smiled for the very first time. "She must meet my father. He is *exactly* like this. Which is why it is so very hard for me to live back home again."

"Nana Pat is convinced I'm going to be kidnapped by white slavers."

"My father wants to check my arms for needle tracks. Every night." She shook her head. "And your father?"

"Grandfather," Carey corrected. "Papa Grady's favorite expression in all the world is 'I know just the thing.'"

"He lives to make everything better, yes? Him I am liking very much. And your parents?"

"I was raised by my grandparents," Carey replied firmly.

"So. Them you must call." Eleni tapped the phone. "Now, please."

There was probably an absurdity to the moment, being ordered around by a woman who had rescued her. But just then Carey could think of nothing to do save pick up the phone. "I don't know what to say."

"No, no, that is not the problem. You think they will blame you, yes? But this is not happening. They will be disappointed, yes, but what is the problem here? This is your fault? Did you make the Institute go bankrupt? Did you destroy my country's economy?" She nudged the phone closer. "Call."

Carey punched in the number with shaky fingers. She felt the tremors course through her body as the phone rang. Then the most welcome voice in the whole world answered, "Is this my baby bird?"

"Hi, Papa Grady."

"Darling Carey, is everything all right?"

"No. Not exactly."

"How can I help?"

It was just like him to say that. Not ask about the problem.

15

Rather, what could he do to help. Carey wanted to tell him how sweet those words sounded. How much it meant to have him there, as he had been since Carey's mother had died, and he promised to make the world better. For all her life.

But just as she was trying to shape the words, the squall passed, and a blade of sunlight fell upon a hill not more than a mile away. And there rose the image that had hung on her bedroom wall for almost ten years, washed clean by the storm, as fresh as a polished gemstone. The Parthenon.

She couldn't hold the sobs down any longer.

2

"Dimitri, hon, where are you hiding?"

Dimitri Rubinos did not turn from the ship's wheel, not even when the woman stumbled over the top step. Her name was Mavis, or Agnes, or something. The way she had introduced herself, holding his hand overlong when he greeted the arriving passengers, had promised trouble.

By now Mavis or Agnes had downed her share of the heady Greek wine, more than enough to convince her it would be a good idea to enter the wheelhouse and flirt with the skipper. The fact that Dimitri was at least fifteen years younger no longer mattered. Usually he could smile and offer an apologetic word about the mythical woman who waited for him back on the island. But British divorcées like Mavis or Agnes could be very insistent. Dimitri recognized such traits in women from all over the world. Some people knew wine or fine books. With Dimitri, it was women. And for most of his twenty-eight years, the hobby had been more than enough to keep the smile firmly in place.

Mavis or Agnes fumbled with the unfamiliar handle, finally managing to slide the wheelhouse door open. "Aren't you the most *handsome* lad. My friends are calling you a Greek Lothario." She needed three tries to properly say the word *Lothario*. "*I* think you look just like Humphrey Bogart. *He* fell in love with an older woman in some film, I don't remember which. Have you ever—?"

His first mate appeared in the doorway. "Dimitri, would you like . . . ? Oh, hello there."

The British woman demanded, "And who is this?"

"My wife, Sofia," Dimitri replied.

"Your *wife*." The spark that had carried her up to the top deck faded to an alcohol-induced glaze. "Well, I like *that*."

"Careful with the stairs, madame." Sofia watched the woman descend to the main deck, then switched to Greek. "Wife. As though any woman in her right mind would ever marry you."

"You wanted to. You told me. Many times."

"I was twelve years old and didn't know any better. Back when I still thought I could read love and a future in the night sky." She pretended to wipe a speck from the windshield. "Now, what do you say, Dimitri?"

"I owe you."

"You know, my favor bank is growing very full." She leaned against the ship's radar. "I wonder what I should do with all this good fortune."

"Anything you like, as long as it doesn't cost money." He pointed to windward. "We're in for a squall."

"That's why I came up top. There are several customers who look a bit pale."

He changed course, drawing them away from the shelter of one of the small uninhabited islands dotting the Aegean. "Take the wheel and bring us into open water."

"Take the wheel, *please*," she corrected. "You can only be rude when I am paid."

"I am never rude."

"All right. Yes. This much I grant. You are polite and you arc handsome and you have a beautiful smile."

"Careful now, I might think you are flirting with your captain."

Sofia sniffed her disdain. "You are *too* handsome. And you break far too many hearts for any woman on Patmos to ever trust you with more than a stolen hour. Shall I tell my husband, the policeman, you sought to steal time from me?"

"No, thank you very much." He carried his grin down the stairs and onto the rear deck. Today, thankfully, he ferried a dozen or so tourists on a sunset island tour. In the protected space directly below the wheelhouse sat his three usual musicians, old men of Patmos who played the traditional tunes and made the tourists smile. All but Mavis, or Agnes, who was seated in one of the fighting chairs, left in place for the rare occasion when he had a client who paid to go in search of the big fish. She drank more wine and tapped her foot to the music, pretending she didn't notice his arrival. Dimitri spoke to a couple of his guests, and he waited.

Ten minutes later, they emerged fully into open water, and instantly the boat's rocking motion strengthened. The sea rose to jagged peaks and began tossing chilly froth over the gunnels. The party's brittle gaiety was silenced, and the guests turned as one and frowned anxiously into the rising wind.

Dimitri approached his client and pointed at the dark line on the horizon. "It appears we are in for some rough weather, sir."

The man was, as the Brits liked to say, six sheets to the wind. A wave chose that moment to slap the bow, and the man would have gone down had Dimitri not been there to grip his arm. "I say, that's rather unsporting of the Aegean, wouldn't you agree?"

"Absolutely, sir." He pointed to where the next major island was silhouetted by a looming dark cloud. "I said I would take you around Lipsi, but it means we could be caught out when the storm hits. The wind could strengthen, and the waves—"

The client's wife chose that moment to declare, "Harry, I'm feeling a bit squiffy."

The client tried to hide his portliness through an overly erect bearing. He squinted at his watch, which was made difficult by the fact that neither the boat nor his arm was particularly steady. "But we've another two hours on the clock."

"I could take us back to harbor where we'd be sheltered from the wind, sir. We could anchor where the cliffs will protect—"

"Harry, I really am not at all well." His wife's voice rose to a determined whine. "Could we please continue this discussion somewhere *calm*?"

Two and a half hours later, they docked at Skala's main harbor. Dimitri disliked how he had maneuvered the clients. But the cost of diesel had skyrocketed, and his credit was stretched to the limit. The sky was sullen and the wind biting as Sofia adjusted the ropes. The berth had belonged to his family since they had fled their former home in Turkey's second biggest city, back when Dimitri was two years old. The client settled up, and the tourists off-loaded. Dimitri thanked his mate and the musicians, putting as much of his heart into his words as he could manage, since he could not pay them anything. They journeyed with him because all tips were shared equally. Today, fortunately, their take wasn't bad.

Sofia stayed behind to help him clear the drinks and plates, but he refused to let her swab the decks. She was an excellent first mate, cheerful and capable and handy with all things mechanical. She was married to Manos, the island's only full-time police officer. Manos didn't appreciate Sofia like he should. Twice, Dimitri had been blistered for expressing this opinion. So he did not say anything when the dishes were cleaned and she could have departed but instead watched the squall's arrival, so she could pretend her tears were only rain.

He walked the wet cobblestone street into the port of Skala and entered the island's main pharmacy. The only one of his childhood friends who had never left the island now ran his family's business. He had the tank of oxygen ready for Dimitri and accepted the cash with a grimace. Officially, the government's medical program was meant to cover all such costs, but the money wasn't coming in and the pharmacy had been forced to insist on payment—in cash. His friend had the decency to apologize every time Dimitri reached for his wallet.

He climbed the narrow path rising up the hillside and entered his father's home. It was Dimitri's home now as well, ever since he had been forced to walk away from the water-front apartment he could no longer afford. The bank threatened and blustered, yet Dimitri was not the only person on Patmos who had faced foreclosure. "Hello, Papa."

His father was in late-stage emphysema, and talking was a painful effort. Dimitri knelt beside his father's chair and replaced the depleted oxygen tank with the fresh one, then kissed his father's clean-shaven cheek. The nurse assigned to him was no longer paid, though she continued to come twice a week. As Dimitri made them dinner, he described the voyage and the squall and the sea. His father had been a fisherman all his life. He lived for the sea and for his son. They ate a quiet meal with the television for company. Afterward, Dimitri settled his father into bed and kissed the man a second time. As he always did before sleep, his father caressed his son's face and spoke what had become a tradition between them. "I am proud of you."

"Papa . . ." Dimitri started to confess what he had been trying to say for almost four months now, that they might have to sell the boat. If only he could find a buyer. But once again he could not find the air to speak.

His father nodded, as though his son's one word was all he needed to declare, "I am content."

3

Carey's first phone call went so well, she figured the second would be pure misery. Her grandmother had not been home when she'd called the previous day. Which had been a blessing beyond measure, because her grandfather had insisted that Carey rest up and settle in, and give him a chance to break the news. Papa Grady had spent a lifetime spreading his version of peace on Nana Pat's usually troubled waters.

It seemed the most natural thing in the world to take her new phone back to the café where Eleni worked. She had slept for twelve hours and showered in the bath down the hall from her little room. There was no way she would make such a call from the cheerless guesthouse with all the people hanging about, young and old, men and women, all sharing the same blank gaze and muted conversation. Every time Carey walked through the parlor she felt the urge to settle into the patched sofa and swallow her own dose of helpless misery and watch the dust motes dance in the still air.

Outside the guesthouse door was a brisk October after-

noon, with rushing traffic and blaring horns and people
speaking the language of ancient myths. She did her best to
ignore the teenagers huddled in every shuttered storefront,
and the glass vials and drug paraphernalia that scrunched
beneath her feet. She had lived in a big city. She knew she
was in an area that would not be friendly to strangers after
dark. She also knew she could not stay.

The question was where to go.

Carey hesitated outside the café, worried about how the
staff might react. The last time she'd been inside she had
broken down and wept. But there was nowhere else to go,
and so Carey pushed through the swinging door.

Eleni waved through the kitchen window and greeted her
with a "halloo" that drew most of the others around. Carey
recognized half a dozen people from her previous visit. She
felt her face flame with embarrassment and tried to slip into
an empty booth. But it seemed as if the whole café wanted
to hug her. Eleni's boss and his wife and their daughter were
followed by two hefty women and a smiling young man whom
Carey suspected just thought it would be fun to embrace an
American girl. Most of them spoke only fragmentary English, but their sympathetic expressions and loud comments
left her feeling, if not better, then at least a little less hollow.

Eleni arrived with an embrace of her own and another
bowl of stew. She rushed about while Carey ate, later returning with her aunt Kyriaki. The older woman poured
tea into three tulip glasses, motioned for Eleni to slide over,
and settled herself into the booth. Kyriaki had a strong voice
and a commanding attitude, and the fact that she spoke no
English did not slow her down at all.

Eleni said, "My aunt has never met a stranger. She wants
information. She is also my boss, you understand? Kyriaki

says, why you are not married, a beautiful young woman like you?"

Carey stared into a broad flat face the color of old bronze, with eyes that flashed and hair clenched tight in a no-nonsense bun. Her hands were mannish with wrists twice the size of Carey's. But there was something about this utterly alien woman that reminded Carey of home. She said, "I was in love with a man at university. I met him at the beginning of my junior year. A year later he was accepted into a Boston law school. I thought I was going with him. Six weeks before we graduated, he said it had been a lot of fun, and it was time for both of us to move on."

The woman offered a biting pair of words that Eleni did not translate. Then, "How long ago was this?"

"Two and a half years."

"And still your heart is not healed, yes? Still you pine for the lover who crushed your dreams of a life together."

"Not so much," Carey replied. "And not all my dreams."

The woman turned and blasted the young man seated at the next table, who apparently had been paying too close attention. It was the same man who had fitted himself into the line of huggers. He grinned at Carey before turning away. Carey didn't actually smile, but she liked his determination.

Kyriaki turned back, and Eleni went on, "I have told them about what has happened to you. Kyriaki says, so you come here to work on your doctorate, and what happens but your next dream is crushed. And none of this is your fault. Not the man, not the Institute, not the economy of our beloved homeland. So then what do you do now?"

Carey lifted her phone. "My grandmother will say it's time for me to come home."

"Is this what you want?"

DAVIS BUNN

"None of this," Carey said, "is the way I want it to be."

"But you are here, and the question is what do you want?
Yes, the Institute is closed. Yes, the man you loved walked
away from the best thing he will ever know, and he will suffer
bitter regret for all his life long. He will rise up in the law and
he will fail as a human being. He will wake in the middle of
his dark nights and be swept away by everything he lost. He
will see your face on every street, and he will weep tears no
one will ever see." Eleni worked hard to keep a straight face.
"That is what she is saying."

Kyriaki reached across the table. Her grip was as fierce as
the words Eleni rushed to keep up with. "You must decide
what it is that you want. You must keep the flame of hope
alive. Your heart is good. There are not enough good hearts
in this time. Listen to your heart, decide what you should
next do, and be firm when you speak with those who try to
draw you away from your dreams."

Carey felt the burn return to her eyes. "Thank you."

Kyriaki slid out of the booth and made a fist that thumped
against her heart. She turned and swiped at the still-grinning
young man before walking away.

Carey lifted the phone. Eleni watched with overlarge eyes.
"Who do you call?"

"My grandmother."

"The one who speaks of the poisoned well, yes? She could
be Greek, this one. What will you say?"

"I'll think of something. I better."

"I declare, this whole thing was a mistake. Didn't I tell you
that? Didn't I say you shouldn't leave home?"

"Many times, Nana Pat," Carey replied. She stared out
the taverna's front window. Above the grimy city scene rose

the Acropolis, relics of a distant age she had spent her entire adult life studying. "Almost every day."

Thankfully her grandfather had insisted on getting on the home's other phone. He countered, "What Carey did wasn't a mistake."

"Did I ask you? No, I did not. I'm having a conversation with my granddaughter. You can behave or get off the phone."

Grady huffed. "Since when does behaving mean making her feel worse than she already does?"

"The girl ought to feel bad. Carey is six thousand miles from where she belongs."

"Our granddaughter is right where she should be," Grady said. "And you'd know it if you'd just stop thinking the world revolves around Dallas."

"The world doesn't," Nana Pat said. "My family does."

"And they always will," said Grady, "no matter how far they roam."

"I want my baby girl *home*."

"I know you do, sweetheart, but she isn't a baby anymore."

"She will *always* be my baby bird."

"In your heart, darling. In your heart. But we're not talking about that, now, are we? We're talking about the smartest gal either of us has ever met, who's twenty-four years old and counting."

Carey had sat in on a thousand such conversations, when Grady and his loving ways calmed Nana Pat's tempest. She wondered at the man who had spent his life selling and repairing farm machinery while being a friend to all the world.

Nana Pat possessed a whole dictionary of sighs. She could express anger or frustration or displeasure without speaking a word. She sighed now, and Carey realized the conversation was over. Nana Pat had run out of steam.

Grady said, "Tell the girl you're proud of her."

"Well, I never."

"Let her hear she's done the right thing, just like she has her whole life long."

"She misbehaves as much as all my children combined."

"Now, you know that's not true. Tell her, my dear. Go on."

Nana Pat sighed again. "We love you, Carey. And we want you home, just as soon as you finish chasing your dreams."

"There you go, honey," Grady whispered. "There you go."

"I love you, Nana Pat."

"You're my sweet baby bird, and your home is right here waiting for you."

"Okay, is it my turn now?" Grady said.

"Oh, go ahead. I know you're just ready to burst."

"My seams are all strained to the max, I'm so chuffed."

Carey asked, "Over what, Papa Grady?"

"You remember Nick Hennessy?"

"Of course she remembers the boy," Nana Pat said. "Didn't she have a crush on him near about her whole life?"

Grady went on, "Nick needs to talk with you."

The words didn't want to fit together in her brain. "But . . . Nick is in Paris."

"He sure is," Grady said, the excitement rich in his voice. "And he wants to offer you a job."

Carey listened as Grady related what he knew, which wasn't a lot, but enough to cause her heart to soar. "Are you sure you got all that right, Papa Grady?"

"I got enough to know it's what you're after. Enough to know I had just the thing to make my Carey's day."

4

Nick Hennessy sat in the hot seat, hoping his desperation didn't show. Over the past eight months, he had known more than his share of such predicaments. Seated across from the decision makers, doing his best not to beg for a job, or a contract to write an article, or enough money to pay his rent. Sometimes, late at night or while waiting in the reception area for his brief moment before the throne, some of their faces flashed before his eyes. They came in all sizes and ages and races, yet they all had one thing in common: They were experts at saying no.

The woman seated behind this desk, however, was different.

For one thing, she wasn't the editor of a newspaper or magazine. Nor did she run a television news show. Up until this moment, she had simply been a source, one he considered of vital importance. Someone to be treated with respect. Which was easy in her case, since Nick both admired and even liked her. But today's meeting wasn't about information. Today he was after a chance to climb out of the career gutter he'd been in for far too long. Phyllis Karras held the key to what Nick had almost decided would never come. His chance to enter big-time journalism.

If only he didn't blow it.

Phyllis Karras was intelligent, passionate, and unmistakably Greek. She served as the assistant director of the World Heritage Sites, an organization linked with the United Nations. Her immediate responsibility was the protection of the sites and the management of events that took place around the globe. The World Heritage Sites were cities and regions that held exceptional historical and artistic significance, places that literally defined human culture, both now and throughout the ages. Phyllis Karras lived and breathed her work. She took on whatever task was required, whether or not it actually fell inside her area of responsibility. Which was how they had come into contact in the first place.

They had met in Paris at an auction by Sotheby's, featuring classical artifacts. At the time, Nick had been researching another story. Because of his desperate state, he'd been forced to ask the editor for an advance in order to pay his rent. The editor had handed him the check with a full dosage of journalistic cynicism. Nick's hand still burned from taking money he hadn't yet earned, but it was either that or be evicted from his apartment. Paris was a wonderful place for a journalist, but it was also brutally unsympathetic to anyone who could not pay their way.

Phyllis Karras had been a breath of fresh air in an otherwise stifling atmosphere. They had left the auction and taken coffee and talked for over an hour. Phyllis had helped with contacts and made some important suggestions about black-market buyers. Nick's article took on an authoritative and compelling tone.

Nick submitted the piece, and overnight the editor had changed his tune. He praised his work and offered him another assignment. Phyllis had not only returned his second call, but offered even more help. Nick was left with the distinct impression that the woman had an agenda of her own.

Then that morning Phyllis had called and announced she had a story, a huge one, and was wondering if Nick was the person to write it.

Most of the UN's Paris operations were located in a vast modern structure just off the Faubourg Saint-Germain. But they still held conferences in the stately manor on the Trocadero that had been donated by President de Gaulle at the end of the Second World War. Phyllis Karras had asked Nick to come there, as she was speaking that afternoon at an event. She had escorted him into what once had been a side parlor, with an ornate ceiling and crystal chandelier and a parquet floor, and grand windows overlooking the foliage. Pointing him to a chair, she walked around the elegant conference table, seated herself, and said, "Thank you for sending the copy of your latest article. You did quite a good job, especially given your time restriction."

"I followed every lead you gave me," Nick replied.

"How did you manage to identify the team passing the stolen artwork to the dealers?"

Nick hesitated. An investigative reporter was only as good as his sources. None of which should ever be named or shared. Secrecy was a vital component of his work. But the woman across from him was more than a lead. What she had in mind, he had no idea, but he was increasingly convinced that she was sitting on something big.

And he was just the guy to write it, whatever it was.

"I made an ally in the police force," he answered. "The

detective in charge of overseeing the art world used my first article to flush out the middlemen. He was after the next tier. I agreed never to name him."

Phyllis Karras was a brilliant woman in her late fifties, who highlighted her autumn years with a distinctly Mediterranean flair. She rose from her chair and turned to the window. "I find that most interesting."

"May I ask why?"

"Because it is precisely the arrangement I require if we are to move forward on my own issue." The midday light caught a silver thread woven into her blue Chanel suit, flashing like a beacon toward Nick's future. "I have a problem. Actually, the organization does. But apparently no one else around here is concerned. They listen, they nod, and then they point out the risks. Truly they are not interested at all. They simply want it to go away. They keep their heads in the sand, and all the while we move closer to a disaster with global repercussions."

"I am definitely interested in following this through to the—"

"They ask for details. They want to know all the specifics." She didn't appear to have heard him. "But truly they ask their questions because it gives them an excuse not to *act*. How am I to find out the details unless there is an investigation?"

"I'll investigate for you, Dr. Karras. It's what I do."

She turned around and looked at him. "There is an even larger problem. Two, actually. First is the issue of timing, which is crucial. If I am right, which I am, every hour is vital. What are you doing at this moment?"

Nick gave it to her straight. "Trying to find some story that I can sell. If I don't, I lose my apartment."

"You were brought to Paris by the *Dallas Morning News* six months ago?"

"Eight." Confirmation that she had researched him gave Nick an electric thrill. "Actually, the office was shared by four papers. Two of them decided to cut all their overseas reporters. Overnight I was out of a job."

"It is very difficult making a living as a freelance journalist these days."

"Terrible," he agreed. "A nightmare."

"Not to mention the problems you face with the authorities over your work permit. Which I am given to understand will not be renewed."

Nick swallowed against the wrench of defeat. He understood the tactic. She was grinding him into a position where he would accept not just her terms but her demands. And he had no choice but to accept. He nodded his agreement and thought, *Just kill me now.* He said, "You mentioned two problems."

"You lack the necessary expertise."

"I have contacts. I can learn. You've seen that or we wouldn't be talking."

She shook her head. "For this story you require a researcher. Someone who is an expert in Greek antiquities, who can discern art forgeries. And who can be trusted beyond question."

Nick immediately said, "I know just the person." And to his own amazement, he did.

"If I went to my normal connections, the story would fall into the wrong hands." She stared at him. "You know someone?"

"Her name is Carey Mathers."

"An American?"

"From Dallas. We grew up together. She's in Greece now."

Phyllis leaned against the window frame and crossed her arms. "In Greece."

33

"Athens. She arrived yesterday." For the first time ever, Nick blessed the gossip network that his mother was plugged into. "She has a degree in archeology and recently completed her master's in antiquities."

Phyllis frowned. "Then she is perhaps too young to have the required field experience."

Nick persisted, "She's working on her doctorate in forensic archeology."

"There is such a thing?"

"It's brand-new." He knew the hunger was in his voice, but could not do anything about it. "Carey is sharp, she's trustworthy, and she's already on the ground. She has a job with some institute."

Dark eyes probed. "Not the Athens Institute for Antiquities?"

"I think that's the one, yes. Why?"

"It has been shut down."

"But . . . this is terrible. Carey's been working toward this, well, all her life."

"Come." The woman reached for her purse. "Let me take you to lunch."

Phyllis hustled him out the building's main entrance, where a driver sprang from a waiting Citroën and swept them off in a heady rush. Nick started to ask about the gig, but Phyllis silenced him with a single warning glance. The driver dropped them at Fouquet's, a restaurant Nick had passed dozens of times and yet never dreamed he might actually dine there. Phyllis waited until they had ordered, then launched straight in.

"We have a serious problem that soon could grow much worse."

Their table fronted the Champs d'Élysées. As in, they were

34

having lunch on the most famous street in Paris. The outside seating area of Fouquet's was separated from the gawkers and the pedestrians by velvet ropes and brass stanchions. The day was autumn brisk, but the restaurant had upright gas heaters to warm the diners. Behind their table stretched the restaurant's trademark display of fresh seafood on ice. The conversation was musical, the guests at ease with the Parisian elegance. Nick knew he was out of place. His dark brown hair was two months beyond needing a cut and only partially hid the frayed collar of his corduroy jacket. The leather patch on his right elbow was coming undone. His khaki pants no longer had even a hint of a crease. His shoes were scuffed, and his plaid wool necktie from high school hung limply from his neck.

He pushed his concerns aside. Fouquet's was a place of legend. It had been the favorite restaurant of W. Somerset Maugham, Mark Twain, and Ernest Hemingway. The waiter set down the first course with a flourish, filled his glass, asked if madame required anything more, then vanished. The china was finest Limoges. The shrimp cocktail was overly fussy and tasted divine.

Phyllis took a single bite and demanded, "Can you enjoy your meal and still pay attention?"

He wondered what it would be like to dine at such places so often that any concern, no matter how grave, could dim the ability to enjoy the moment. "Absolutely."

"I don't even know how to begin," Phyllis confessed.

"First tell me what you know for a fact. Then what you suspect."

"What I know. What I *know*." She mulled that over as she picked at her food. "Several treasures of national importance have gone missing from various venues. The pieces are priceless and hold a vital position in Greece's heritage. A pair of alabaster vases dating from the time of Alexander the Great. Three of our oldest icons. A gold statue recovered from Thrace. An item from the Etruscan period taken from the national museum. Another artifact from a private collection, one from a university library. And so on. These items disappear, while others of equal value are left untouched."

"So thieves are stealing for hire," Nick said. "This is great."

"Great?" She looked at him askance. "You are calling this a good thing?"

"Of course not." He took the last bite and regretfully slid his plate to one side, planting his elbows on the table. "Look. You have your problems, I have mine. For a story to get out, first I have to sell it. Stealing for hire is a huge issue. If I can manage to lift the lid—"

"No, no, nobody can know about this until I give you permission. That must be part of our bargain."

Nick leaned back at the waiter's reappearance. When Phyllis gestured for him to take her half-eaten plate, he asked if madame was dissatisfied with the food. Phyllis managed a smile and replied, "I am dissatisfied with everything but the meal and my companion."

Nick found himself liking this woman, and not just for how she might hold the key to a brighter future. He liked Phyllis Karras and her intellect and her commitment. He said, "Truth for truth. I can't afford to wait. Holding on to a story means getting kicked out of a country I've fallen in love with."

"Truth for truth. That is very Greek." She folded her napkin. "Very well. I will give you truth in exchange, my hungry young journalist. This matter is both explosive and dangerous. If you succeed in uncovering the mystery, and if you survive, you will be able to sell this anywhere in the world. And I will help you."

"That's all great, Dr. Karras, but—"

"I believe we are now at the point where we should use our first names, yes?"

"Phyllis, I need to eat."

"And I will pay you."

"I . . . What do you mean?"

"I have a discretionary budget for research and PR. I will offer you a contract as a short-term consultant, working on a story of great international potential. In the contract will be sufficient funds for you to hire this young lady—I'm sorry, her name?"

"Carey Mathers. You're serious."

"I have never been *more* serious." Her eyes were dark and piercing and as grave as her voice. "Especially about the danger."

"I hear you. But now I need to ask some basic questions."

"You may ask anything you like. Truth for truth."

"You're bound to have top-notch security within the organization—those who can find these answers better than I can."

She leaned across the table and responded, "Not if one or more of my superiors are involved in these thefts."

5

In Dimitri's view, morning was the most beautiful time of day. The sunrise cast fresh promise in the golden light. The gulls sang the sea's song, and the air was clean and crisp. The port of Skala, capital of the island of Patmos, rested in a broad cove and fronted one of the world's most remarkable natural harbors. The bay was an inlet of crystal waters, protected at its back by the rocky spine that ran the island's length. The highest ridge was crowned by the medieval monastery fortress of Saint John. Dimitri's home was situated south of the harbor, high enough up the hillside for the rising sun to peek through and greet him with a gentle glow. Down below, the harbor remained cast in shadow and in the mystical wonder of hours not yet spent.

Dimitri took his coffee on the stone veranda, wishing he could look beyond the weight this day already carried, and remember how to laugh.

He went back inside, helped his father shave and dress, and settled him into the padded chair by the window. The old man liked to pretend he could feed himself, so Dimitri sat and drank his second cup and helped steady his father's hand when necessary. He was washing the morning dishes when a familiar voice asked, "How are my two men this morning?"

Of all the changes the past two years had wrought, this greeting signaled the most unexpected. Chara, the mother of Dimitri's late mother, entered their home and actually kissed his father on the forehead. She said, "The baker made *bourekas* and *tiropites* this morning. I know they are your favorites. We will have them with our tea."

When Chara entered the kitchen, he leaned over so she could kiss his cheek as well. She was a tiny woman, barely five feet tall, dressed all in black. She had lost her husband and son long ago to a late spring storm, more recently her daughter to a winter chill. With each loss she seemed to shrink further, until she was reduced to the very essence of who she once had been. But she remained a woman of good cheer and unshakable faith. Her eyes were the only remnant of her former beauty. Dimitri knew his grandmother had been courted by every young man in the Dodecanese Islands, as had his mother. The island's older women often mentioned this before covering their mouths with red-chapped hands, laughing at Dimitri—his looks, his charms, and his ability to break every heart within reach. They claimed he carried on a family tradition, but in a style that was all his own.

Chara unwrapped the feather-light pastries filled with goat cheese and set them on a plate. "What is it that hangs around your shoulders like a shroud this morning?"

"It's nothing, I'm sorry, I don't—"

"You don't think I see the shadows in your face? The way

39

you are bowed by the burden you think no one notices?" She wiped her hands on a dish towel. "When was the last time you laughed?"

"I don't remember, *Yiayia*." The Greek nickname for grand-mother was a word meant to be sung. This morning, however, he could scarcely manage a sigh.

"So come sit at the kitchen table and tell me."

"I need to get to the harbor."

"Nonsense. You have ten minutes to share with an old woman. Come."

But when Chara looked at him from the rickety chair, Dimitri confessed, "I don't even know where to begin."

"Tell me the first concern that rises from your heart, my son."

It was easily spoken, words from a woman who had heard much and experienced more. He stared at her seamed features and found the strength to confess what he had not expected to say, not then, not ever. "The life does not hold me any longer."

She settled back and clasped her hands together. "Well, now."

"I wake up at night and think it is all the worry, the econ-omy, the drop in tourism, my father—"

"But it's more. Much more. Isn't it?" Her voice carried the calm creakiness of one who sought only to help. Not condemn. Nor judge. "You hear the cry of hearts you have broken, don't you, my Dimitri?"

Dimitri shivered, then shrugged. "I loved the life, I loved the women, I loved . . ."

"My dear boy, you treat this period as an illness you hope will pass and let you recover. But to do what? Go back to the same life? You have *always* known it was not enough."

"No, that's not . . ."

She let the silence drag on, long enough to ensure he could not finish the sentence. And the lie. "Your good-time friends will laugh at you for listening to an old woman. And here is my reply. It is this same old woman who has prayed for this moment for years. That one day you would wake up and yearn for something more."

When he was unable to respond, she leaned forward and patted his knee. "It is a beautiful first step. Be patient with yourself. We will talk more. Now tell me of the next weight your heart carries."

But he had no interest in releasing any more of the fears that trapped him night after night. So he demanded, "When I was growing up, why did you hate Papa so?"

"What a question. I never hated your father."

"You fought their marriage tooth and nail. It was a favorite topic of my parents, how you hated him."

"I hate no one," she replied calmly. "I simply did not think your father was right for my only daughter."

"They were happy, Yiayia."

"Indeed they were. And I was wrong to oppose the marriage." Her hands were rough from a lifetime of work and oversized for her small frame. Dimitri had never seen them so still. They rested in her lap, ruddy and swollen. "I knew your father's older brother had the restaurant in Izmir. I knew it held the promise of a future our island did not offer. I knew your uncle wanted Adoni to come help him manage the place. I did not want my daughter to emigrate."

"Izmir is only six hours away by boat," he pointed out.

"It might as well have been the other side of the world, as far as I was concerned. I wanted my grandchildren to grow up in my front room. I wanted . . . So many things, I wanted. I was selfish, and I thought only of myself." She said to Dimitri's father through the open window, "Do you hear me, Adoni? I was wrong. I apologize. You made my daughter happy. You did your best by her."

The weak voice spoke from the shadows. "I am content."

"Then you are a fortunate man." She turned back and went on, "This is my penance. I do these things for your father now because I cannot change the past. Before my days are ended, I want my God to see my apology in action."

His father managed, "You may not depart from this earth before me, Chara. I will not lose this final bond to my dear wife."

"That is in God's hands," she replied. The wrinkled face remained directed at Dimitri. Her eyes were almost lost in the folds, tiny slits of gleaming black. Waiting.

He knew she had been so open with him because she wanted the same in return. And through this revelation of her own secret he found the strength to confess to her and his father both, "I have a buyer for the berth."

She shifted, made uncomfortable by what this meant. "Things are so bad?"

"Things are awful."

"And the boat?"

"I will anchor in the harbor. The buyer has promised I can use the spot in the morning and evening hours."

"Who is it?"

"Stavros."

"The head of the family from Kos?" She waved away the invisible insect of his words. "Nonsense."

"Don't trust him," his father rasped.

"He is a thief and a scoundrel," his grandmother agreed. "He and his brothers and his cousins are a gang of thugs."

"I have no choice," Dimitri said, his misery almost strangling him. "I owe money to everyone. Unless I pay the harbormaster for fuel, I will not be able to leave port."

His father's ragged hoarseness was evidence of the strain he shared. "And your boat?"

Dimitri bowed his head to hide the burning in his eyes. Those simple words were evident of how good a man his father was. The vessel had been his father's. The boat had saved the family when Izmir had fallen to the vigilantes. It fed them in the years that followed. Even so, Adoni now considered it Dimitri's boat, no longer his own. The question said it all. Adoni wasn't concerned about the loss of their family's most cherished legacy; he wanted to know how his son would make a living.

"Winter is no time to sell a tourist boat," Dimitri said, staring down at his clasped hands. "Money from the berth will see us through the coming months. In the spring, we'll see."

"Why you waited so long to tell us this, I cannot understand," Chara said.

"I did not want Papa to know I failed."

"You have not failed," his father said through the window. "There. You hear? The whole world is collapsing, and you have done your best."

"It wasn't good enough, Yiayia."

"Here is what I think. We shall pray for a miracle, and then you will go tell Stavros that you need another day."

"But Stavros is coming with the cash. He wants—"

"Who cares what that man wants. He is not to be trusted. You tell him he must wait one day more. And you trust in God."

Dimitri allowed her to take his hand. She rose from her seat, drawing him with her, and together they walked outside so she could grip Adoni's hand as well. As Dimitri held the swollen knuckles and felt the chapped skin, he scarcely heard her praying. What could these two old people do in such a time of crisis and ruin?

Dimitri took the steep road leading from his home straight to the port. The road had been laid in the ancient pattern dating back to the Roman era, with two stone grooves for wagon wheels and broad steps in between. He descended as he had every day since he could walk. Never had his heart been so heavy as today. His only hope rested on an old woman's prayer for a miracle, which to him was no hope at all.

A gleaming yacht was moored in the middle of Skala's harbor, like a pearl anchored in the Aegean blue. It was far too big to lay up alongside the ancient quay. Such vessels normally remained in the more tourist-friendly ports of other islands. The yacht was a Hatteras, meaning it lacked the more streamlined appearance of the Italian vessels. But Dimitri had always considered the Hatteras designs to be an ideal mix of stateliness and functionality. The boat had to be at least twenty-five meters long and would have cost well over three million dollars. Having such a vessel moored here in the off-season was a rarity.

The Skala harbor was centuries old and still remained focused on its fishing fleet. Island officials had gone on for years about building quays for luxury yachts. Hotel and bar and restaurant owners all complained that the money was now going to the more tourist-oriented ports of Mykonos and Kos. The wealthy landowners of Patmos argued that rebuilding the port was only the first step, for afterward would arrive the grand hotel chains and the glossy seaside developments. But all such talk had ended with the economic crash. Now the locals who had resisted the harbor expansion pointed smugly at the skeletons of half-finished projects that tarnished other islands. Not to mention the destroyed businesses and reputations.

Dimitri had always liked the harbor as it was. The stone quayside was over six hundred years old, its broad cobbled expanse still holding nets and beached vessels under repair. Tables from cafés and restaurants extended right up to where the fishermen off-loaded their crates of iced catch. Tourists and locals alike could select their fish, which the tavernas' chefs would then prepare.

Locals in favor of the expansion had accused Dimitri's family of seeking to protect their own self-interests. A new harbor development would have created piers long enough for yachts to dock, and some said this would have reduced the value of the existing berths. Dimitri disagreed. On other islands, such developments had bolstered the value of existing berths.

Dimitri's family had been opposed to the expansion because it went against the island's nature. Each of the Dodecanese Islands held a unique heritage and a flavor all its own. Life on Patmos was dominated by the hilltop monastery. Even for someone like Dimitri, for whom both history and faith held little personal interest, the island's legacy was its greatest treasure.

But this meant berths like his were highly sought after. For six generations Dimitri's family had owned the harbor's largest mooring. What was more, it was situated directly in front of the town's most fashionable hotel and restaurant. For anyone seeking to draw the attention of visitors, the berth was a prize.

Stavros, along with his brother and his brother's son, was seated in the café fronting the fish market. Big and bearded and surly, Stavros and his brother and nephew shared the same scowl. He greeted Dimitri's request for a delay with a roar that drew the entire market to a standstill. "What's this you're trying? We had a deal!"

"I must respect the wishes of my family. They want—"

"They've had a week to object. It's too late now." He brought a heavy fist down on the table. "Today it's about what *I* want!"

Dimitri was aware of all the eyes on them. He also noted the nephew's tight smile. The dark-haired bruiser had come hoping for a fight. Dimitri held his voice calm but firm. "With respect, nothing has been finalized. I am only asking—"

"Nobody walks out on a deal with me!" Stavros leaped up, and his chair tumbled into the group behind them. "This is your last chance. You'll do this deal, or else."

"With respect—"

Then a voice declared in English, "And wouldn't it be a grand thing to just drop this altogether?"

The statement turned them all around. A man in his fifties stood between the café and the quayside, an easy grin in place. Stavros tried to verbally shove the stranger back with his own heavily accented English. "This is no concern of yours."

"Ah, but you're wrong there. As it is, I've business to discuss with the young gentleman here."

"So do I have business. And I was here first, so now you will leave."

"Yes, well, that's reasonable as far as it goes. But it appears the young gentleman has no interest in your manner of business."

Stavros barked in Greek, "Get rid of this scum."

But as the brother and son pushed away from the table, three men rose from chairs to Dimitri's right. They were all dressed the same—dark blue canvas trousers, navy sweaters, and boat shoes. They weren't particularly large men. The tallest was almost a head shorter than Dimitri's six feet. But they all shared the same hard-edged look. Dimitri knew the type from his military service. Such men were the ones selected for special training. They hadn't one ounce of excess weight between them. They also shared the same cold, calm intent. Even Stavros and his bully of a nephew realized they faced a very real danger.

Stavros snarled to Dimitri, "You owe me. And I'm going to collect."

"You gentlemen have yourselves a fine day." The stranger's smile remained firmly in place. "Now, why don't you and these two *boyos* skip on away while you still have legs to carry you."

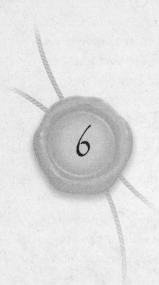

6

Carey found herself adopted by the taverna's great, talkative, excitable family. And she loved it. They did their best to fill the hollow disappointment at the core of her being with their love and their passion and their scorn for the entire Greek mess. They were genuinely thrilled by the call she received from Nick Hennessy.

That evening, over a meal of the taverna's roast lamb, Carey confessed she was anxious about meeting Nick again. Her nerves over Nick's offer of a research job were compounded by everything she had yearned for but never known.

Eleni asked, "Do you two have, you know, a history?"

"No, none at all," Carey replied, smiling. "I'm sorry to say."

Eleni's dark eyes flashed with conspiratorial fire. "You loved him?"

"So much. For years."

"Oh, oh, this is marvelous. And he broke your heart, the cad, the wretch!"

"He didn't even know I was alive."

All of this had to be translated, which resulted in the taverna's service grinding to a halt. The dishwasher and the grinning unemployed youth were enlisted as temporary waiters so the patrons wouldn't go hungry, because Eleni and her aunt and the other waitress were now ensconced in Carey's booth by the front window.

Carey explained, "I was only eleven. Nick's brother was my best friend."

"Nicholas is his name? He is Greek?"

"Purebred Dallas. A shaggy-haired Texan through and through." She smiled at the crystal-clear memories. "I thought he was the most handsome guy ever born. All I wanted was to grow up and be the woman he did not even know he needed. Then the year I turned fifteen, Nick left for university."

"It broke your heart."

"I cried for days," Carey agreed. "You mustn't breathe a word of this to Nick."

"How could we possibly betray your secrets?" Eleni was having difficulty with the translation now, because her mother had arrived and heard only part of the story, enough to know a man who had once broken her adopted Texan daughter's heart was coming to Athens.

And soon every woman in the taverna was dead set against Carey going out to the airport alone.

The debate over who would stay to keep the taverna open took up most of the evening. Eleni's mother worked as an assistant hospital administrator, which kept her busy at all hours and gave her a sharp edge when it came to getting her way. She was definitely coming. Eleni's father was a notary, and his work had dried up to a trickle. But he still insisted on sitting behind his desk for nine hours each day. He arrived, heard what was happening, and insisted that he as a legal official could best represent the entire flock. Yet he was a soft-spoken, retiring gentleman and was swiftly shouted down. Eleni's father, it was decided, would cook in his brother's place for the afternoon. His meager protests went unheeded, and soon he was reduced to a grumpy silence.

That night, for the first time in over a year, Carey dreamed of the other man who had broken her heart.

Carey had only cried over two men in her life. Well, there had been her father's death, of course, but she had been so young she hardly remembered. Nick Hennessy had been a heartthrob, and in many respects her love for him had helped shape who she was today, driven and ambitious and unconcerned about her clothes and hair and such. Just like the girls Nick had been attracted to in high school. And she hadn't been one of them.

Franklin, on the other hand, had been a page from a different book.

She had met Franklin during a college choir competition. He had the finest tenor voice of the entire assembly and was ogled by any number of the female students. Carey had found him easy to talk to, and accepting his invitation to the season's first football game had come naturally. They talked until dawn, and soon they were an item. People considered them a perfect match. Franklin was tall and strong and gifted and driven, just like Carey. She loved him with an easy affection. She wanted nothing more than to spend the rest of her life with him.

Apparently Franklin thought differently. But he neglected to mention that until April of their senior year. The nightmare moment, when all her dreams of love and a family were shattered, had assaulted her for months afterward. She relived the surprise on his face, the confusion, as though he thought it daft that Carey had ever considered this to be something more than a college fling. When Carey bitterly reminded him of all the plans they had made, Franklin had been unable to see how Carey could not move on, like him, to the next phase of their lives.

The memories drove Carey from her narrow bed in the cramped room on the top floor of the Athens guesthouse. She stared out at the silent street. The locked gates of her dream job were just visible far to her left. She was still there, seated by the cracked window, when dawn rose in the placid sky.

Three hours later, she managed to shake off her blues as they left for the airport. There was little room for past woes here, standing in front of a tired city taverna. Carey was surrounded by a mob of people who had claimed her as their own. The rapid-fire chatter offered a verbal comfort, a sense that she was sheltered by people who had effectively taken her in. Logic played little role in this world. They had decided she was one of them, united by the dysfunctional economy. She had suffered the same injustice as their beloved Eleni. She was in need. They gave from the very best of who they were. Carey smiled at the tumult and the talk and the laughter, thinking that Nana Pat would love every one of them.

Which was why Carey felt so comfortable traveling to the Athens airport with her new BGFF. As in, best Greek friend forever.

Actually, it was more like BGFFAMOHEF—best Greek friend forever and most of her extended family.

Eleni's uncle, the taverna owner, drove a vintage Fiat van that smelled of goat cheese, vegetables, and herbs. Eleni's aunt occupied the front passenger seat. Carey and Eleni had the middle row, with Eleni's cousin and mother crammed into the narrow rear seat. Where Nick and his luggage would fit, Carey had no idea. Eleni's aunt noticed her vague smile, patted her knee, and launched into a musical outburst that Eleni translated as, "This is a wondrous moment. The man who broke your heart, he is drawn here. To Athens. Where you wait to greet him with open and empty arms."

Carey saw where this was going and pointed out, "Nick is coming because of work."

"Pfft. What work? All the night long we discuss. This is fate!"

"I don't need fate," Carey said. "I need a job."

"Who made you an old woman? Shall we dress you in black and give you a cane?"

"A paycheck will do me fine, thank you very much."

Eleni's aunt huffed. "Does your soul not long for romance?"

"Someday, yes. But right now I want work and a salary and a chance to stay here in Greece."

It was unlikely they even heard her, for the conversation had shifted abruptly, and now everyone was laughing—even Eleni's dour uncle.

Eleni went on, "When my mother and aunt were twelve, a distant cousin arrived from America. This was during the troubles, you have heard of it, yes? When the generals took over. Visitors were very rare from America then. And this family in Chicago, they had sent many packages and much money. My mother and aunt, they both wore dresses sent from America."

The chatter and laughter overwhelmed Eleni, who turned long enough to scold them to order before continuing on with her story. "So these two, they spent all night making signs welcoming the cousin. When they arrived at the airport, they handed them out to complete strangers. Then the cousin appears, and he is as handsome as his photograph. These two girls, they shriek out his name, and this is taken up by all the strangers holding the signs. This cousin, he thinks all these people are family, you understand? He has never been away from home before, and now he is being welcomed to Greece by dozens and dozens of people, everyone shouting his name and fighting for a chance to hug him. The number of people who greeted him at the airport grows with each telling, so that now it is half of Athens almost. This is one of my mother's favorite memories."

Eleni's uncle shifted the rearview mirror so he could see her, then asked something that Eleni translated as, "So what does your Nicholas look like?"

"First of all, he is not *my* anything." Though her heart fluttered at how they changed his name into a song. "I used to think he looked like Johnny Depp's twin."

The entire van went still. Eleni said, "You mean this?"

"When I was eleven I started collecting photographs of Johnny Depp. My grandmother thought I was obsessed. And I suppose I was. But not with the actor. Nick looked so much like him. The shaggy hair, the unkempt appearance, the round glasses, the smile."

Behind them, Eleni's mother planted both hands over her heart and sighed. Eleni explained, "My mother is in love with Johnny. Since many years."

The woman murmured some words of poetic heat. Eleni said, "It is a good thing my father is not here. He is very jealous of Johnny. And my mother, she is glad you do not care for this one. She would not want to have competition with her new adopted daughter."

When Nicholas's flight landed in Athens, he had good reason to be worried. Frightened, even. Instead, as he passed

53

through customs and collected his suitcase, his biggest concern was whether he would recognize Carey.

His clearest recollection of Carey Mathers was as a gangly tomboy who followed him everywhere. The eleven-year-old version had hair the color of a campfire that refused to be tamed. She had been tall for her age, and both strong and agile. She loved soccer and played on the boys' team, which they hated until she started winning games for them. Looking back, it seemed to Nick that Carey had always been around. She ate at his place a couple of times each week. His mother doted on her. Stevie, his younger brother, considered her the sister he'd never had. Since his departure for Paris, Nick's every phone call home was punctuated by the latest news about Carey Mathers.

And then six months back, just before his office shut down and he lost his job, Nick returned home for Stevie's wedding. Stevie was five years younger in age only. Nick had always looked up to him and nearly always followed his advice. Nowadays Stevie was the rising star in some Austin software company. He married the girl he'd been in love with since third grade, Carey's best friend, Amanda. It was only natural that Carey would be paired with Nick and serve as maid of honor while he served as best man. Nick had thought Carey looked stunning, despite wearing what he thought was possibly the ugliest dress ever made, a tent of taffeta the color of an overripe peach.

His mother had noticed the direction of his gaze and said, "Hasn't she turned out lovely?"

"Shame about the dress," Nick replied.

"Don't say a word about the dress. It was Amanda's mother's debutante dress. She considers it an honor to have Carey wear it. You can't imagine the fuss that's gone on backstage over the thing."

"Actually, I can." The pinkish-yellow color made Carey look washed out and wan, and she was neither. It was a frilly thing, a generation and more out of date. "She looks like somebody's bad idea of Halloween."

"Shush, Amanda's mother might hear. Besides, anybody with eyes can see Carey is a beautiful young lady."

The familiar message came through loud and clear. His mother had always considered Carey her almost-daughter. Having Nick marry her would only make it official. Nick's mother had been pushing them together for years, but Nick wasn't looking to marry anyone. His choice of career and the transient nature of his work made such a thing ludicrous.

Then Carey had walked over and offered him a cool, strong hand. "Nick Hennessy, as I live and breathe."

"Carey, is it really you in there?"

She lifted the hem with both hands. "My grandmother says a proper lady should exclaim over the honor I've been given."

"Is she in there with you?"

They stood in the back of the church nave, surrounded by the excited, chattering families. Carey pointed at the closed doors leading into the vestibule. "Soon as I take one step in there, I'll vanish. I couldn't be better disguised if I wore camouflage paint. The entire place is awash in peach-colored bunting and every yellow flower in the state of Texas."

"Probably what Amanda's mom had in mind all along," he replied. "Less competition for the bride."

"No, this dress is her mom's idea of revenge. Something we did when we were nine. I let Amanda say I was the one who planned it, which is a total lie, but Amanda had to live with the woman. Her mom has never forgiven me."

"What could possibly be so bad, the woman's carried a grudge for sixteen years?"

But the wedding planner had chosen that moment to rush over and herd them into position. The wedding had swept them up. He spent much of the celebration wondering at the different orbits his closest friends had taken. Later that evening, Nick and Carey had shared another brief orbit, spinning across the dance floor, though he hadn't thought of the unanswered question then, for her fragrance was as captivating and inviting as the feel of her arms.

Her enormous eyes were the same remarkable mixture of emerald and gray, her voice a honeyed combination of Texas and intelligence. "So, is Paris as French as they say?"

"More than ever."

"And the ladies?"

"I wish I knew. I'm too busy and too poor."

"Their loss, right?"

The music stopped, and he kissed her fragrant cheek, let his place be taken by another smiling young man. He carried the memory of Carey's arms back to the groom and bride's table. Stevie gave him a knowing grin as Nick seated himself. "The girl's done grown up, bro."

"Not you too," Nick said.

"Mom's been on you?"

"Since before we left DFW. All about this doctorate she's doing, how she's even teaching classes now. Mom asked one question about my work and that was it."

"She was the one who urged Carey to chase her dream." Stevie watched their childhood friend swirl across the floor. "That really is an awful dress."

"Mom told Carey to do a PhD?"

"Sort of. Carey came home all bent out of shape over her grandmother wanting her to stop with school. You know Nana Pat. She wants her brood within shouting distance.

Mom told Carey she had what it took, that she needed to go out there and live her own life."

"Archeology, right?"

Amanda leaned forward so she could talk around her new husband. "Carey is basically inventing a new field. She's designing methods to detect forgeries of ancient treasures."

"Forensic archeology," Stevie said. "I love the sound of that."

The man dancing with Carey stepped on her dress, almost pulling it off one shoulder. Carey threw her head back and laughed. The delightful sound took Nick straight back to nights around campfires, the way Carey could halt traffic by shouting her joy to the stars. Today her laugh drew smiles from all around the wedding feast.

As casual as he could manage, Nick said, "Maybe I should see her again before I take off."

"Maybe not, bro."

"She's taken?"

"She was, but last year the slimeball broke her heart." Stevie shook his head. "Mom wanted to go play headhunter."

"Your mother never liked him," Amanda added. "I didn't either."

"Why not?" Nick asked.

"Too slick," Amanda replied. "The undergrad version of a snake oil salesman."

"The guy never put much effort into anything," Stevie agreed. "But Carey was too much in love to listen beyond what he was telling her."

Nick was about to suggest that made for as good an opening as he was likely to need. Stevie saw the thought before he spoke it, and for the first time that day the groom lost his smile. "Word to the wise. Mom loves you more than anything, but if you mess around while that girl's still in recovery mode, you'll break our mother's heart. And I'll break your head."

"And I'll help him," Amanda promised.

"So go for it, bro," Stevie said. "But only if you're open to taking the same step we did today. Which I for one would love to see happen."

Because Nick knew it was true, he skipped the second dance and left Dallas without phoning her. Ever since then, however, there was a spice to his phone calls home, whenever his mom eagerly shared news about this girl who had grown into an intelligent and beautiful young woman.

Shame about his job.

In the arrivals hall, Nick found himself embraced by a group of strong, dark-haired women with flashing eyes. Carey wasn't able to get close enough yet for a hug, though he'd caught a glimpse of her over the crowd. An older lady offered him a coquettish smile and held on an instant longer than was proper, only to be slapped on the shoulder by the one called Eleni. Then he was swept away, connected now to this noisy clan.

They were herded outside the airport and into a dilapidated people mover. Nick was directed to a rear seat beside Carey, facing out the back window. His suitcase was stowed at the feet of the women in the middle seat. Carey smiled at his efforts to find a position that didn't jam his knees painfully against the rear door. "Shame Paris didn't shrink you down to size."

The conversations in the front of the van offered a semblance of privacy. Nick had several things he wanted to say, but what came to mind was, "What was it that riled Amanda's mom so badly that she made you wear that taffeta frock?"

Carey gave him a smile that carried him straight back to Dallas, as though the years and the miles had just vanished. "I know, right? What could two nine-year-olds possibly do that she'd carry a grudge for sixteen years?" Carey leaned in close enough for him to catch a hint of her fragrance, lemons and some oriental spice. "Amanda's mama caught us talking about boiling her Chihuahua. It was something the pastor said. Drop a frog in boiling water and it hops out. Put it in cold water and heat it, gradually raising the temperature, and the frog will just keep paddling around. We didn't want to hurt a perfectly innocent frog. But that dog . . ."

And just like that, they were reconnected. Like she had been thinking about the exact same unfinished conversation from six months ago. "That dog was nasty," Nick said.

"A vile little beast," Carey agreed. "I've still got scars."

"Amanda's mom loved that dog." Nick shifted one leg, then the other. "But making you wear that dress . . . I don't know."

Carey nodded with her entire body. "What about forgiveness, right?"

Nick took his time inspecting her. "Your smile hasn't changed. Not since you were a kid."

"I've been told I have too many teeth for one girl."

"It's not that. Your smile has always made me think of the best Texas has to offer. Big and easy and welcoming."

A flash of something came to her crystal gaze, there and gone in an instant. "Why, Nick, I never considered you the gallant type."

Truth be told, he found himself embarrassed by what he'd said. So they settled into a mutual inspection of the highway flowing out behind them. Carey could be like that, he recalled. As comfortable with silence as any person he'd ever known.

"I'm really sorry about your fellowship at the Institute falling through."

"It was hard," she said. "I don't ever want to get closer to being broken than I was on that rainy day. But God was there for me. And introduced me to a whole new family."

That was another thing he'd half forgotten about her. How Carey could make God feel like a member of the clan, a friend who was as close to her as her own skin. He felt the emotion he always did at such times, a little impatient with the whole Texas thing, God at my right hand, like that. So he changed the subject. "Can you trust these people?"

"Yes, Nick."

Something in her tone left him fairly certain she knew perfectly well what was going on inside his head. "This is important, Carey. Knowing them well enough to say that. Our lives could depend on getting this right."

7

Dimitri stood by the gunnel as Duncan McAllister crossed the gangway. McAllister had invited Dimitri to join him out on his yacht. But Dimitri had no interest in being isolated with this stranger and the three hired mercenaries taking up station on the quayside. Dimitri ushered the older man into the wheelhouse of his own boat. He then brewed two mugs of tea, serving them with condensed milk and sugar kept in a chocolate tin dating from his childhood. Duncan McAllister was no doubt accustomed to bone china, but he seemed more than happy to grip the tarnished spoon and chip away at the solidified sugar. "We're in need of local transport. Six months, seven tops. At least two days' work per week."

Dimitri pointed to the Hatteras moored out in Skala Bay. "But you have your own vessel."

"Of course we do, laddie. And believe you me, it's a beaut. But one boat isn't enough. Besides which we want to get along here. We're in this for the long haul. Supporting the local economy is part of the package."

The man's cocky smile didn't change the fact that Duncan McAllister was a brawler. The man might seem friendly, but only so long as it was in his best interest. Between him and Stavros, Dimitri couldn't say which of them would make for a worse enemy. Serving as first again, the man did offer the first hint of hope Dimitri had known in months.

He sincerely doubted, though, that this represented the miracle his grandmother was praying for.

He asked, "Why me, Mr. McAllister?"

"You have something that fits us like a hand in a tailor-made glove." He sipped from his chipped mug. "I'm told you know the Turkish coast."

"Parts of it, yes, sir."

"'Sir' is what they called my old man. We didn't get along. I go by Mac or Duncan."

Dimitri shrugged his acceptance. "Why is Turkey important?"

"That's the million-euro question, laddie. Which parts of the coast do you know?"

"When times were better, I did regular pickups at all the major ports. Izmir, Kusadasi, Bodrum. Now . . ."

"Pickups?"

"Tourists. I serve as guide to the islands."

"Ah. Of course." McAllister set his mug on the ledge and idly picked at a fleck of paint. "Do all the seagoing locals spend time in Turkey?"

"Very few, these days. But I was born in Izmir."

"So you have dual nationality."

"I've kept both passports up-to-date."

"And you speak the lingo?"

"Fairly well." Silently Dimitri thanked his father for insisting. Even when during his teenage years it had become fashionable to despise everything Turkish.

"See now, I knew you were the man we were after. Our cargo is bound for Turkish Cyprus."

"I see." And he did. Turkish Cyprus, or North Cyprus as the Greeks preferred, was the last remaining rogue state in the Mediterranean basin. The only countries that even recognized Turkish Cyprus as a legitimate nation were Turkey, North Korea, and Syria. Turkish Cyprus was officially still at war with both Greek Cyprus and Greece. Smugglers operating throughout the Middle East used it as their principal base.

That was what this was all about, Dimitri knew. Smuggling.

McAllister must have seen the awareness tighten Dimitri's gaze, for he demanded, "You have any trouble with that, laddie?"

"None at all," he replied. And to his surprise, it happened to be true.

Dimitri stopped by his grandmother's cottage, but she was away, probably at the afternoon market. So he left her a note asking her to stop by, then went home and fixed his father's dinner and served it on the front patio. They ate in silence, which was hardly unusual. But the pile of cash Dimitri set in the middle of the table certainly was. Adoni studied it, as he did his son's face, yet was content to wait and watch the swallows carve their script into the sunset.

When Chara arrived, Dimitri rose and kissed his grandmother's cheek, cleared the table, and made a pot of tea. Chara's arthritic hand rested within inches of the cash, but her questions remained compressed within the folds of her once-lovely face. Adoni and Chara watched him set out the fourth tulip glass, waiting.

Daylight had faded to russet tones when Sofia entered the patio. She offered Adoni and Chara a cheery greeting. "I had forgotten how long a climb it was up here!" She blew out a breath. "Serving as first mate on Dimitri's boat doesn't prepare me for such a trek."

"Which means you have been too long between visits," Chara said. "How is Manos?"

"Complaining over the cutbacks. He's just left for Lambi, and he hates driving the hill roads after dark." Sofia looked at the cash anchored by the sugar bowl. "What's this?"

"Sit," Dimitri said. "I will explain."

"Tell me you didn't sell your berth to Stavros," she pleaded.

"How did you know about that?"

"Everybody knows." She turned to Chara. "How could you let him do it?"

"For one thing, I did not know until this morning. For another, he did not sell."

"Then where did the money come from?"

"Sit," Dimitri said again. He served her tea and refreshed the other glasses. His motions carried a formal tone, as though he were taking part in a theater of the dusk. He described the meeting with Stavros, then Duncan McAllister's abrupt appearance. Their discussion. The offer.

Sofia cut him off with, "He wants you to smuggle."

"There is no other reason for regular trips to Turkish Cyprus," Dimitri agreed.

Sofia studied the cash a long moment. "How much is he offering?"

"He asked me what my normal weekly take was. I told him that in the winter it was almost nothing."

"He was no doubt shocked by your honesty," Chara said.

Dimitri recalled the moment, seated in the wheelhouse's

two swivel chairs. Duncan had a ready smile that barely creased his beard. The man's eyes were blue and empty as colored glass. Dimitri found no humor in Duncan McAllister's gaze, just a cold and cynical menace. "He told me it did not do to be weak on the subject of cash. Duncan McAllister is Scots/Irish, and he claimed both cultures were known to drain a body of blood before letting go of a bent penny."

Dimitri's grandmother shifted in her chair, but did not speak. Sofia returned her gaze to the cash. His father watched him with the same grave affection that had been there during so many of their quiet evenings.

"I pointed out that he was a businessman," Dimitri began. "And a businessman knows the island economy is terrible. Winter tourism has dropped to almost zero. There is no other work. Fishing has been depleted by the bottom trawlers."

Chara surprised him by commenting, "You are as smart as you are handsome. If you had not made these points, he would have used them against you."

"He offered me twice my high-summer weekly take. For two trips a week. Half again if we went to three. I told him I needed to think about it."

Sofia pointed at the sugar bowl. "And the money?"

"He said it was to help me think."

Chara rose and entered the house. She emerged a few moments later with the pine-scented candles they used to keep the night insects at bay. She lit three, setting one on the table and two more on the patio walls.

Dimitri had fretted all afternoon over what he should tell them. As he watched the tiny woman settle back into her chair, he knew he had been right to share it all. The questions were too great, the mysteries as big as the night. He couldn't face such matters alone.

His father spoke for the first time that evening. "I worked as a smuggler."

The words were as shocking as a slap to his face. Dimitri asked, "When was this?"

"After Izmir. Two years. Cigarettes and wine."

Chara settled her hand on Adoni's, then said for him, "The Turkish generals were trying to tax away the things they considered to be against Islamic law. The Greek economy was in recession. Smuggling kept your family alive."

Dimitri gaped at one face, then the other. "And you did not object?"

"How could I? The food on my family's table also came from your father's midnight voyages."

Adoni rasped, "Your grandfather smuggled as well."

"And my husband worked your grandfather's boat," Chara added. "The sixteen longest months of my life. I hardly slept. Your mother and her brother were so young then."

Sofia nodded. "This was after the Athens coup?"

"No, child, before," Chara replied with a sad smile. "You think our troubles began when our generals overthrew the government? Back in the late fifties, the communists and the conservatives went for each other's throats. It lasted over a decade. The Greek economy was a wreck. Islands like ours were little more than slums. Then there came a winter when the fish vanished."

"I remember my mother speaking of this," Sofia said, her tone somber. "She made it sound like a legend."

"A nightmare," Chara corrected. "We survived on goat cheese and mussels and seaweed stew. Patmos lost all but a handful of its young. They immigrated to America, to Canada, to Australia. Those of us who remained, we . . ."

"Smuggled," Dimitri finished. "Why am I only hearing about this now?"

"What good is there in speaking of such dark times? Would you have your own children know of this night?"

"Definitely not." Dimitri moved the sugar bowl to one side. He counted the money into two equal piles, then slid half over to Sofia. "For all the trips when I could not pay you. And now when I cannot ask you—"

"You are firing me?"

"Your husband is the island's police," Dimitri pointed out.

"Manos has lost half his salary, and what is left arrives weeks late. He will see this money, and he will know not to ask questions." She shoved the cash into her pocket. "I will continue as before."

8

It was early evening when the taverna's battered, crowded van halted in the street in front of the guesthouse. The dim western hues were almost lost in the yellow wash of city lights. Nick rose slowly from their backward-facing seat, eased the cramp in his knees, and stared at the distant hill. The Acropolis rose like an earthen tower at the city's heart, less than a mile from where he stood. Crowned by ruins of alabaster purity, it glowed in the brilliant spotlights.

Carey stood beside him. "Nick, I have to ask you something."

"Sure thing."

"What you told me on the phone. The research job and the pay and the chance. It's all real?"

Nick thought her face wasn't made for the strain of disappointment. "Yes, Carey. It is."

"Because I've got to tell you, I just don't know if I can handle another jolt right now."

"Why don't I go check in, and then we can sit down and I'll tell you just how real it all is."

68

The single-lane road fronting the guesthouse reeked of rotting produce. It was partly blocked by a delivery truck, there to unload crates of frozen meat through the back door of a nearby restaurant.

Eleni's uncle stayed with the van while the women all accompanied them down to the guesthouse. By the time they climbed the crumbling front steps, their voluble conversation had gone silent. Nick stepped inside and took a slow look around.

The lobby, an elongated parlor, held stained sofas and chairs sagging from years of hard use. The handful of men and two women who occupied the seats looked mired in grim reflection and destitution. Here before him was displayed the bleak reality of Greece in crisis. Nick had stayed in worse places, though not recently.

He turned back to Carey. "Go get your things. We're out of here."

She looked twisted up inside. "But I've paid for a week in advance."

Recollections flooded back, of his mother talking about how rough Carey's beginnings had been, the narrow lifestyle imposed by grandparents with little money to spare. How Carey had always made do, and what was more, how she'd been grateful for everything. He hadn't thought of these things in years. Yet facing her now, with the disappointment and uncertainty clear in her gaze, he felt an unreasoning anger for all the wrongs this good woman had endured.

Nick replied, "I'm not staying here, Carey. And I need you close at hand."

Eleni went upstairs to help her pack as the others walked with Nick back to the van. The aunt spoke to her husband in a low voice. His only response was to glance at Nick, then nod his agreement.

The aunt walked over, her hands knotted together at her waist. "Please to excuse my English, yes? We cannot make the invite ourselves. My daughter, she is back with us. Eleni lives again with her, what you say . . . ?"

"Parents. I understand."

"Is hard time. We know Carey is here in this place, but what can we do?"

"I need a good hotel, clean and safe. Nothing fancy."

"Yes, is why I speak. We have friend. Family hotel. Not far. Very nice."

"You think they'll have two rooms?"

Her smile was bleak. "I think is no problem."

"Could you call them, please?"

Eleni's aunt gestured to her husband, who pulled out his cellphone and tapped in a number. She turned back to Nick and touched his hand. "Carey is special one, yes?"

"Very."

"This reason you in Athens, the job, it is real?"

"It is."

She sighed. "All of us, we are glad you have come."

The hotel was simple and functional and clean and almost empty. The woman behind the front desk was dignified and clearly desperate. She showed them to their adjoining rooms with sliding glass doors that opened onto narrow balconies overlooking a busy street. She pointed to the partial view of the Parthenon, but the act was mostly habit. When Nick asked if he could pay in cash, the woman practically swooned in delight.

They returned to the van and drove six blocks to park in front of what in America would be an upscale city diner, the sort of place where locals came when they didn't feel like fixing food at home. As they entered the taverna, more of Eleni's clan came out to greet them and inspect him. After the introductions were made and they were seated in the corner booth and a meal decided upon, Eleni explained, "The taverna is my family's for five generations. Kyriaki is sister to my father, the man you see cooking. He is Habel. Galen is my uncle, the chef. The four, they are like family since childhood. Before this was one house with a big veranda. We lived in the back. Then the year I was born, a man with many buildings . . ."

"A property developer."

"Yes, he came and said, 'Give me this land, I give you a new restaurant and home.' My family said, 'No, no, this we cannot do.' Then the developer said, 'Okay, I give you *two* apartments.' So they agreed, and the developer built this building you see now. Sixteen stories. Two apartments on each of the floors. My family lives on the fourth level."

Nick was beginning to understand the unspoken rhythms of this woman's speech and thought he understood where she was going. "Kyriaki already explained how your own family doesn't have the room to take us in themselves."

The vibrant young woman's features folded into unexpected lines, and for an instant she and Carey looked like mismatched twins. "We are proud of our hospitality to friends, you understand? This is not normal. We feel . . ."

Carey reached across the table. "You can't begin to understand how grateful I am for everything you and your family are doing."

"It is natural," Eleni said. "It is Greek."

Nick realized there was no question of discussing the project alone with Carey yet. These were not casual friends, drawn together out of sympathy for Carey. These people

71

actually had taken Carey into their clan. As he feasted on slow-roasted lamb drenched in a sauce of wild sage and plums, Nick noticed how every few minutes one or another of the family paused briefly by the table. He figured this was the Greek way of chaperoning their newly adopted young lady. They were taking his measure, just as he did them and their taverna.

The furniture and walls were all carved from the same wood, probably taken from the old place and refitted to the new rooms. Most of the tables were filled, but few people actually ordered more than coffee or tea. Underlying the happy chatter was a faint murmur of tension, a slow-burning mix of worry and frustration that he could see in many of their faces. A trio of musicians took their place by the far wall and played traditional tunes for an hour or so, then walked around the tables with a hat.

A half hour after the musicians finished, Hestia and Kyriaki shooed out the remaining patrons, posted a sign, and locked the door. They bustled about, placing chairs on the other tables and cleaning the tiled floor and preparing for the night. The men emerged from the kitchen with a fresh pot of tea and another of coffee and a plate of sticky almond-and-honey sweets. There was a certain formality to the way they all gathered. They introduced the other waitress as Gaia, cousin in name only. They made a process of explaining how Gaia was daughter to distant relatives in Thessaloníki. Gaia had trained as a lab technician, come to Athens, started a new life, and then lost her job. She had wound up working here as a waitress and trying futilely to land another job in her field. Her fiancé emerged from the kitchen, an accountant turned dishwasher. They were careful to explain how Gaia's beau was son to a dear friend who had health issues and had first been taken on as a waiter, his job then given to Eleni, and now he washed dishes.

Nick gave them his solemn attention, because he could see how all this was important to them—the bonds they shared, the details of their story, and the way the current crisis had affected them all.

They were seated in a loose circle around the booth. When the family connections were fully explained, they sipped their teas and coffee. And they waited.

Nick said, "I need to be certain that what I'm going to say remains just among us."

Eleni's father, the notary, was a precise little man in a vest. The jacket of his three-piece suit hung on the back of his chair, as though his clothes were an important link to his position. He spoke English with meticulous care. "This work of yours is illegal?"

Nick shook his head. "Absolutely not. But it involves the illegalities of others. I am tracking criminals."

"Here in Greece?"

"This is where I have been instructed to begin the search."

Habel smoothed his mustache with the thumb and index finger of his right hand while his daughter translated in a soft voice so that the rest could understand. "Who told you criminals were operating here?" When Nick hesitated, Habel added, "We are Greeks. We have learned through centuries of occupation and misrule to hold secrets as close as our family."

"Her name is Phyllis Karras. She is the associate director—"

"With the United Nations, yes? We know of this woman. She served on the Olympic committee. For a time, her face was everywhere. We thought perhaps she would run for office."

Eleni added, "There was much corruption linked to the Olympic buildings. Karras forced several people out of office.

73

Many say it is because of her that the work was completed on time."

With a nod, Nick said, "Karras believes a highly organized group is using the country's crisis as an opportunity to steal national treasures."

"Not for an instant do I doubt this," Habel said. He leaned back and folded his hands on the table. "Two questions. First, why have we heard nothing before now?"

"Ms. Karras thinks they are selective, taking one item at a time. They steal to order. And . . ."

"Go on."

"They have insiders who help cover their tracks," Nick said. "So she hired me, an outsider, because she thinks they have infiltrated the top levels of her own organization."

9

The next morning, Dimitri walked to the center of Skala, feeling intensely conspicuous. It was the first time in over two years that he carried so much cash it bulged in his pocket. He entered the stone piazza by the harbor and seated himself in the café facing the municipal building. The Italian architect had combined Moorish and Mediterranean influences into a structure that some townsfolk loved and others loathed. Five minutes later, Sofia's husband emerged from the door leading to the police station.

Manos wore his best uniform, the trousers pressed and starched so the creases caught the morning light. Manos greeted the café's owner and slipped into the table's other chair. The proprietor himself served Manos a tulip glass of tea and then brought over plates of unleavened bread, goat cheese, and olives in brine. Dimitri had never much liked Sofia's husband. Manos was dour by nature, with a compact build and round face that hid his strength well. Dimitri had watched him subdue men twice his size in bar fights that ended with shocking swiftness. Dimitri had always wondered if behind the mustache and the hooded gaze lurked the heart of a bully. When Dimitri had asked Sofia to arrange this meeting, she'd warned him that Manos would never verbally grant his blessing to such an enterprise. But Dimitri wasn't after an official sanction; he simply wanted the island's chief of police to have a chance to speak his mind.

Manos sipped his tea and asked, "What did the Englishman say you would transport?"

"He is Scots/Irish," Dimitri corrected. "As for cargo, he didn't say."

"Because he did not need to."

Dimitri used a toothpick to spear an olive.

"It is not drugs," Manos mused aloud.

"Not if I am delivering into Turkish territory," Dimitri agreed. Opium was smuggled from the Caucasus into Turkey, refined into heroin, and shipped out to Western Europe. "Besides, he and his men did not have the look of drug dealers."

"What did they look like to you?"

Dimitri had pondered that all night. "It is a mystery. Very professional. Intelligent. Former military, I suspect."

Manos sighed. "It must be artifacts."

"I think that as well."

"Valuable ones, by the look of their vessel." He shook his head. "The choices I am forced to make."

Dimitri studied the man. Manos was three years younger and had been raised to the south, in Groikos. It was said that the southern villagers were a doleful lot, and Manos certainly lived up to that reputation. Dimitri could not recall ever seeing the man smile. What Sofia saw in him, Dimitri could not imagine.

The policeman's phone chimed. Manos pulled it from his

pocket, checked the screen, and sighed his way from the chair. He answered, told the caller to wait a moment, then turned back. His lips parted, but Manos stopped before the first word emerged. He stared down at Dimitri for a long moment before turning away.

Dimitri nodded his thanks to the policeman's back. He felt a genuine gratitude toward the man for not giving voice to his warning.

Dimitri rowed himself out to the yacht moored in the middle of the harbor. The hills surrounding Skala shone in the morning light. Perched on the highest ridge to the southeast stood the village of Hora, its ancient white houses gleaming like pearls. The peak behind Hora was crowned by the fortress monastery of Saint John the Apostle. In his youth, his mother and grandmother often made pilgrimages to the monastery and the cave of visions. His father accompanied the women whenever storms shut down the fishing. Adoni had always claimed such journeys to be a gift and a cleansing both, but Dimitri had never understood. They had tried to bring him along when he was ten, but he'd wailed and fought until finally they deposited him with friends. Dimitri stared up at the fortress and wondered at the strange directions his thoughts often took him.

The Scot and two of his silent minions were standing by the aft railing as Dimitri stowed his oars and stepped onto the stern transom. Duncan McAllister greeted him with "What's the need of all this sweat and bother? You had my number. Next time call and I'll send the boat."

Dimitri replied with the traditional "Permission to come aboard?"

"Aye." The man's false affability was in full flow. "Will you not join me for coffee?"

Dimitri lashed his line to a cleat and stepped onboard. "Coffee would be nice. Thank you for asking."

"So it's a formal meeting we're after." He made a grand gesture to the two padded stern chairs. "Sit yourself, laddie, and let these boyos earn their keep."

Duncan McAllister wore a rich man's idea of seagoing garb—silk T-shirt, pleated shorts, alligator belt, and boat shoes without socks. The man's legs were muscled, his skin the color of an old saddle. Though his ginger hair and beard were laced with silver, there wasn't an extra ounce to his frame. As they settled into the rear swivel chairs, he asked, "When did you get into the tourism business?"

"Right after my father retired." Dimitri nodded his thanks to the silent man, who set two porcelain mugs on the round table between them.

"You hated fishing? Smart lad."

Dimitri saw no need to correct the man, but he didn't dislike the trade so much as not have a gift for it. His father and grandfather had spent many evening hours on the front patio, staring out over the waters, predicting where they would find the next day's catch. Dimitri had found that to be a mysterious aspect of the trade, one he himself had never captured. "Actually, sir, I'm here to set things in motion."

Duncan unlocked his chair so he could swivel back and forth in time to his words. "When someone grows formal on me, I assume it means they're wanting to change the terms of our deal."

"There is no deal," Dimitri countered. "Not yet."

"But you're asking for more, is that it?"

"Your offer is a fair one, sir. But I need an upfront payment to cover my initial expenses."

He cocked his head. "Where did you learn your English?"

78

"I worked in Canada for eighteen months. My mother's cousins run a restaurant in Toronto."

"Harsh winters for an island lad."

Again Dimitri saw no need to correct McAllister. He'd loved the winters and had marveled at the snow, but during the second summer he'd come to realize that Patmos was in his blood.

The mate returned with a satellite phone in his hand. Duncan frowned, then rose from the chair. "Give me a second," he said.

Dimitri used the time to inspect the vessel. Despite the evident luxury, it was far more than a rich man's toy. He was seated in one of four fighting chairs, the chest straps tucked into pouches in the seat backs. Chrome holders for the fishing gear extended from both chair arms. The middle table was designed to be folded down snug to the deck. The teak deck merged with two side cabinets, no doubt for scuba gear, and a compressor for refilling tanks had been fastened beneath the exterior skipper's chair. Dimitri approached the controls, fingered the deerskin covering of the captain's chair as he inspected the dash. Along with the standard radio and radar equipment was a pair of flat-screen monitors.

"Sonar mapping," Duncan said, walking up behind him. "Latest generation."

Dimitri nodded. "I've heard of that."

"Nothing better for scouting the seafloor. We can develop a clear image down to ninety fathoms."

Which confirmed that the man and his team were hunting seabound treasures. Dimitri said, "For this to work, I need thirty thousand euros. Now. Today."

"That's a whopping great sum for a man who's not yet done a lick for me."

"Half of that will go into an account for my father should anything happen to me."

To his credit, Duncan McAllister made no attempt to gloss over the risks. All he said was, "I recall hearing about his illness."

"Emphysema," Dimitri said. "And I need another five in an account for my first mate."

"Whose husband is a copper, do I have that right? You might want to think about a different choice there, laddie."

Dimitri persisted, "A further five goes to paying off my fuel bill, overhauling my engine, and buying an ice machine."

"Ice? *Ice?*"

"That's right. To keep our catch fresh." Dimitri remained calm before the man's ire. "What other reason could there possibly be for a Greek vessel to enter the waters of Turkish Cyprus than to fish?"

Duncan hid behind his mug, then, "That leaves us with five thousand unaccounted for."

"That will be carried in cash onboard," Dimitri replied. "As an emergency fund."

"Say I agree to this, which I haven't yet, mind you. But say I do pay out this whopping sum of money, when can you start?"

Dimitri wondered if this was how pirates felt before setting off on another voyage. "Tonight."

10

Thanks to Eleni's father, Nick's explanation of his investigation resulted in very surprising outcomes. The next morning at eight, he found himself standing on a bustling Athens sidewalk, waiting in the rush-hour traffic, looking for a taxi.

Carey stood beside him, nervousness radiating from her. By contrast, Nick felt an intense calm, every sense on alert. He was aware of her in ways he hadn't felt since his brother's wedding. He remembered how it had been to dance with her. She smelled like she had then, a faint floral fragrance as if she were holding a bouquet. Her jeans accented long and shapely legs. Her hair was barely kept in control by a ribbon the color of her eyes.

"How did you sleep?" he asked.

"Fine. I slept . . ." She looked up at him. "Are you sure we can afford those rooms?"

Eleni stood three paces removed, attempting to hail a passing taxi. Only there weren't any. Which was a good thing, because in truth they didn't want a taxi at all. Yet that didn't stop Eleni from waving frantically whenever one passed. This time of day, the cabs had picked up their regular fares from the suburbs to the north and east and were now driving into the commercial districts south by west from where they stood. Every taxi was occupied.

The previous evening, when Nick had explained what he needed, Habel the notary had risen from his chair and entered the kitchen. Nick had watched him through the service window, walking back and forth, talking softly into his phone. Eleni explained that she had obtained her job at the Institute for Antiquities in the normal Greek way—through family connections. Her father had handled several land transactions for the woman who had become her boss. The woman Habel was now phoning.

Nick watched Carey check the time again. She had checked so often that Nick saw she wore a vintage Bulova, too large to be a woman's version. He assumed the watch had belonged to either her father or grandfather. He meant to ask her about it, but later.

Carey said, "Our contact is late."

"It's fine."

"How can you say that? You've never met the woman."

"I don't need to."

"Have you even been in Athens before?"

"Same answer. We're operating on Mediterranean time. Just like Paris. Ten or twenty minutes either way doesn't count for zip."

Eleni dropped her hand from yet another futile attempt to halt a cab. "Nick is correct."

"How can you be so calm?" Carey asked him.

"For one thing, I've done this before," Nick said. "A lot. But, really, this is how I get."

"What? Like when a contact tells you she's being followed and is afraid for her life?"

"No. When I get confirmation that the story I'm chasing is real."

Eleni called to them, "She is here."

A battered Renault pulled to the curb and stopped. The light in the triangular taxi shield on the roof switched to a different position, which Nick assumed signaled the cab was off duty. The driver's door opened, revealing a dent below the handle shaped like a football and framed in rust. A woman stepped out. To Nick's eye she appeared far too elegant to be a taxi driver. But she also had the drawn features of fatigue and hardship, and her movements suggested a body fighting off sleep.

The woman shut the car door and entered the pastry shop. Nick said to Eleni, "Go."

Eleni skipped through the traffic, moving against the light and waving her apology toward several vehicles with their horns blaring. She arrived at the opposite sidewalk just as the woman reappeared holding a paper bag. Eleni asked her something. The woman shook her head and started around the cab.

Eleni pleaded and pointed over to where Nick and Carey stood. The two visiting Americans, desperate for a ride. The woman glanced over, then shrugged wearily.

Eleni gestured frantically for them to join her.

As far as Nick was concerned, both Eleni and the driver deserved an Oscar for their performance.

"My husband bought the taxi and the license as a gift to his brother, who was born incompetent. The brother died, and my husband and I have both lost our positions and our pensions. The taxi now keeps us alive."

Nick sat in the front passenger seat. Carey and Eleni sat behind them. Nick's seat felt as though it had an individual lump for every one of the taxi's two hundred thousand kilometers. The suspension could only be described as nonexistent. The brakes squealed. The woman fought the wheel with practiced disregard. She spoke English with a precise British accent. Her voice was filed down to a raspy monotone. Or perhaps that was how she sounded at the end of a twelve-hour shift.

Nick asked, "You're being followed?"

"If I knew for certain, I would not be here. But my suspicions have been alerted. For a week now, I have been seeing three vehicles off and on. They come and go in rotation. They are there when night falls, and they are there at dawn."

"So your trackers are professional, and they are willing to spend a considerable amount of time and money to make sure you don't contact anyone who might be considered a threat."

Adriana Stephanopoulos had dark eyes that defied the red-rimmed weariness. "Shouldn't you be trying to assure me that our conversation won't endanger me?"

"I would if I thought you'd believe me," Nick replied. "Do you know who it is you're not supposed to be seeing?"

Dark humor flashed at him a second time. "I assume it is you, Mr. Hennessy."

Dr. Adriana Stephanopoulos was the former associate director of the now-closed Institute. She'd been educated at the Sorbonne and Cambridge and had held her position for eleven years. Her husband had served as the chief finance officer for a now-defunct steel company. Like many Greeks, they had lived well beyond their means, assuming the easy credit was theirs for the rest of their lives. Then they lost everything—the boat, the cars, the house in the suburbs, the vacation home on Chios. They rented an apartment where they lived with their daughter and son-in-law, who fought constantly. All this Nick had learned the previous evening from Eleni's father.

"Dr. Stephanopoulos, why did you agree to see me?"

"Agree? Agree? I have been waiting and hoping you would show up ever since all this started! Your arrival confirms that my suspicions are real!"

Nick pulled a notepad and pen from one pocket and a tape recorder from the other. He set the recorder on the brake lever between their seats so that the mike was aimed at her, with the device kept too low for any outsider to see. "What suspicions are these?"

"That the treasures of my country are being systematically looted. That is why you have come, yes?"

"It is. Dr. Karras shares your concerns."

"Phyllis Karras is a good woman by all accounts. We have never met. I have wanted to, but my director forbade it."

"Why would he do that?"

"Initially I thought it was because Chronos Boulos hogs the limelight. That is his trademark. He wants to be seen. He steals credit. Chronos Boulos insists that all articles written by Institute associates bear his name as primary author. He is ambitious."

"And greedy?"

"They go hand in hand, yes?"

"And corrupt?"

"It is said that all officials who rise so far within the Greek bureaucracy must learn how to give and to receive. Dr. Karras and I were rare exceptions." She flashed him a weary smile. "That is, if you are willing to accept that I am indeed being honest with you."

"She is," Eleni insisted from the back seat. "And you must."

Nick gave the woman a moment. "But you're talking about something much greater than the occasional bribe, aren't you?" When she remained silent, he switched gears. "What do you now think is the real reason your director kept you from meeting Dr. Karras?"

"For the same reason I was fired."

"The Institute closed," Nick said. "You lost your job. There's a substantial difference."

"Not," she replied, "if the Institute was closed in order to halt my division from performing its new role."

Nick tracked with the woman beside him. It was one of the things he most loved about his profession. Arriving at a point where he could see where they were headed, almost like reading an invisible script. Flowing into a tighter and tighter pattern, circling around the prey that assumed it remained well hidden. "You hired Carey Mathers as a part of a new task force. You had heard about the thefts."

"How could I not have heard? They were taking place all around us."

"And you suspected that anyone currently working inside the Greek bureaucracy was possibly part of the problem."

"People claimed items were being looted. Then they went silent. When I approached them about their original claims, the same people who had lodged the complaints were too frightened to speak with me. All around us, Greece was failing. The crisis was everywhere. People were terrified over losing their jobs."

"So you drew in Carey Mathers. Doing forensic archeology in Austin, Texas. Someone completely removed from the current situation. Just like Dr. Karras did with me."

Eleni put in, "Carey and Nick grew up together."

Adriana waited until the cab pulled up to a light to turn and inspect them. "This is true?"

"I've known Carey Mathers all my life," Nick said.

Carey added, "I'm sorry hiring me got you fired, Dr. Stephanopoulos."

"Call me Adriana, please. And it was not you. It was what you represented. A threat to a system that was making the wrong people rich."

"Phyllis is concerned that the corruption extends to her World Heritage Sites organization as well," Nick said. "Which is why I was hired as an outside investigator. My official task is to check about a theft of religious artifacts from the Halkidiki monasteries."

"A very good ploy," Adriana responded.

"You know these items?"

"Of course I know them. Three icons, each over a thousand years old, one dating back to the time of Constantine. Gold and jeweled frames. Painted on wood, as they all were in those days. Coated with a special wax made from paraffin and honeycomb. I know. I asked the questions myself."

"And?"

"I was told to leave the investigation to the proper authorities and get on with my job."

"You were ordered by your director to ignore the thefts?"

"Correct. What is my job, I asked him, if not to investigate such transgressions?"

"So you began assembling an investigative team."

"I did not get very far, I am afraid." She glanced at Carey in the rearview mirror. "I am most sorry, my dear. I should have communicated with you. But I was forbidden access to my files and my office. Eleni will confirm this."

"We all were," Eleni agreed. "One day we arrived to find the building shut. *Poof!* Finished."

Nick pressed gently, "Phyllis says I should use these incidents as my initial focus, because the priests have been making noise."

"It is hard to shut up an angry priest, no?" Adriana said. "What are you going to do, arrest him for telling the truth? You certainly can't fire him. And he has no pension for the bureaucrats to cut off. Perhaps that is the answer. We should all forget this and become monks."

"Should I visit the monastery?" Nick wondered.

"For what? To see the place where the treasures should sit? And talk to monks who don't know anything?"

"Then where—?"

"I learned a bit in those final days. Not much, but a bit. One of the icons passed through the hands of an art dealer in Bodrum. Selim is his name, and also the name of his business. Selim has been a target of inquiries in the past."

She pulled up in front of an American bank's Athens head-quarters. "I will leave you here. That will be twenty-three euros. I am sorry to ask for this money, but—"

"It's okay." Nick passed over the bills. "Can we be in touch?"

"Please buy disposable phones and minutes. Eleni should leave one for me at the taverna. I will stop by tomorrow for a coffee. If you need something, call me. But only at night, when I am driving, yes? That should be safe." She watched the two women slip from the car, and asked, "You will go to Bodrum?"

"Tomorrow," Nick said. "Today I want to meet your boss."

11

Carey followed Nick into the bank, where Eleni's former boss had dropped them off. Nick stepped to the central counter, a stand-up desk of chrome and glass that he used to make notes in his book. The cavernous lobby was busy enough for no one to pay the three of them much attention. Even so, Carey felt exposed and vulnerable. Nick worked in the notebook for about twenty minutes, long enough to satisfy any curious watchers. When finished he pointed them toward the door.

As they exited the bank, a taxi dropped off a woman with harried features and weary eyes, trademarks Carey was coming to recognize. Nick and Carey took the rear seat, and Eleni climbed in beside the driver. He could have been the twin of the grizzled and cranky old man who had formed Carey's introduction to Athens. Nick asked Eleni, "Do you know where the Institute's director lives?"

Eleni spoke to the driver, who ground the gears and hit

the gas, pulling away from the curb. Eleni asked, "Is this dangerous?"

Nick leaned forward and asked the driver, "Do you speak English, please?"

The man shrugged and spoke to Eleni, who said, "A few words."

Nick leaned back, satisfied. He said to Eleni, "A first meeting like this will be a shot across the bows. Nothing more."

Eleni's brow furrowed. "What does this mean, shot?"

"For now, we're just going to see who he is and how he lives. Get a feel for the guy."

"And if he won't see us?"

"We'll scope out his place and then take off. It's part of the job."

"Should I call ahead?"

"If you have his number, sure, why not?"

Carey watched her scroll through entries on her phone, select a number, and then launch into a cheerful Greek exchange. Seconds later, she shut her phone and announced, "He can give us five minutes only."

Carey spent the drive discreetly studying the man seated next to her. Nick was a mystery. She had known him all her life, but this side of his character was new. He appeared utterly calm, breathing easily, idly tapping the fingernails of his left hand on the windowsill. Now and then he uncapped his pen and made notes. His notebook was black and hardbound and had an elastic band to help keep it closed. She knew of these books. They were sold on campus as Hemingway tablets, suggesting anyone who paid five times the cost of a regular notebook would instantly be writing something worth the investment. Which, in Nick's case, was perhaps the case.

When she had caught her first sight of him at the Athens airport, Carey had instantly slipped back into the role she had adopted for years. She played the foil to his dry wit, bouncing back ripostes without pause, playfully handling whatever he tossed her way. Other than a few care lines in his face, he had appeared the same old Nick, handsome and scruffy with a nice hint of home.

Now she was not so sure.

Nick was leaner than he had been, but it was far more than just a few lost pounds. Despite the calm exterior, she had the impression that Nick Hennessy lived very close to the edge.

She watched as Nick leaned forward and asked Eleni, "Can someone at the taverna go ahead and get us four pay-as-you-go cellphones, so they'll be ready when we return?"

"My father will do this." Eleni drew out her phone. "You will pay, yes?"

"Of course."

Carey found being with Nick very exciting. Thrilling, in fact. And this disturbed her. The last thing she needed in her life at this point was to fall for a mystery man. Even so, Carey found Nick Hennessy to be incredibly magnetic. Part of her wanted to fling the door open and run for her life. Another part could not wait to see what happened next.

As they pulled onto the highway leading back toward the airport, Eleni said from the front seat, "The director lives in the area known as Penteli. It was once a very old village at the foot of the mountains closest to Athens. Before the crash it was the preferred spot for people with money. There are many developments, all of them with Penteli in their names. The director lives in the wealthiest of them all."

Nick nodded. "And you know this because . . . ?"

"He invited us out there. Several times."

91

"'Us' being the employees of the Institute he directed?"

"Correct. It is a habit among some Greeks who come into money. They keep their door open to associates. They do favors for friends. Chronos Boulos might steal credit and demand the limelight, but he will do favors for those who might one day help him in return."

They drove through a village that no doubt had once been both rustic and charming, but now looked like an upscale Hollywood film set. Every stone of every wall looked hand-polished, and the streets had been repaved with cobblestones. The glass windows along the main avenue were imprinted with all the luxury brands: Ferragamo, Cartier, Zegna, Valentino, Estée Lauder.

Eleni said, "There are still some people with money to burn."

The taxi halted in front of massive steel gates painted a matte gray. The stone wall was twelve feet high and topped by barbed wire. It went on and on in both directions. Eleni exited the car and pressed an intercom button set in a side pillar. A voice spoke, and she shifted over so the camera could capture her image.

Nick leaned toward Carey. "In case anyone asks," he said, "we're researching an article for *Archeological Digest*. They have a director who is allied to Phyllis Karras. If anybody calls the *Digest*, our creds are in place."

"I've coauthored a piece for the *Digest*."

"Even better."

"Are you actually working on an article for them?"

Nick shook his head. "No professional journal would hand over twenty-five thousand euros in expense money."

"The woman in Paris gave you twenty-five thousand euros?"

Nick patted the pack at his feet. "In cash."

Carey struggled to keep her tone conversational. "You're walking around with that much money?"

"Phyllis offered, and naturally I said yes. I didn't know what else to do with it." He watched as Eleni returned to the taxi. "Here we go."

The villa formed the centerpiece of a compound that must have covered five or six acres, and that was just what Carey could see from the front drive. She spied three smaller houses, shaped like stables and barns, but she suspected the only animals living there walked on two legs. The backyard came into view as the taxi scrunched down a gravel road. Carey spotted a sparkling pool and then the rear wall half hidden behind a row of cedars.

Eleni asked Nick, "Why are you smiling?"

"Because Carey is as nervous as a cat," he replied. "I like how she's holding it together, though."

The cab pulled up to the main house, and the driver said something to Eleni, who translated, "Do we want him to wait for us?"

"Absolutely," Nick said, reaching for his door. "We won't be long."

Carey rose from the taxi and said, "The director is corrupt, isn't he?"

Nick smiled at her across the car's roof. "This isn't corruption. This is the mother lode."

"Welcome! Welcome!" An overweight man stood on the top step, his arms open wide, his grin magnificent. "Eleni, what a delight to see you! And you brought friends from America! Another delight!"

Chronos Boulos was the Greek version of a true Texan, from his size sixteen loafers to his massive grin to his booming voice. And like a lot of such Texans, Chronos had eyes like the business end of a carbine.

Chronos ushered them inside a house as elegant and as soulless as a hotel lobby. He introduced them to his wife, a petite woman with dyed blond hair and a smile to match her husband's. Chronos said, "You will take coffee, yes? And some of my wife's special pastry, of course you will! You will love her cake. My wife is an excellent cook. The best! She has made me the man I am!"

He made a production of settling them into an ivory sofa set, lit by a crystal chandelier. Chronos exchanged a few pleasantries in Greek with Eleni, then turned to Nick. "What brings you to Athens?"

"We're here working on an article for the *Archeological Digest*."

"A fine journal. Very fine. I read it from cover to cover. Now that I have time for such interests, of course. You are both employed by the *Digest*?"

"Carey Mathers is my research assistant. She is on leave from the University of Austin where she's doing—"

"Mathers. Mathers." He clapped his hands as he turned to her. "Of course! We were to hire you at the Institute, yes?"

"Actually you did hire me," Carey said.

"And you came, and what did you find here to greet you?" He gave his head a mournful shake. "This crisis has caused such a terrible mess. Please, Ms. Mathers, accept my most sincere apology for all the hardship this must have caused. But now you are working for the *Digest*. How excellent." He turned back to Nick. "Who did you say was your editor?"

"Dr. Driscoll."

"Yes, I have heard of this gentleman." He paused while his wife handed around coffees, then asked, "How can I help?"

94

"We are investigating the theft of three treasures from the monasteries of Halkidiki."

"The loss," Chronos corrected. "That they were stolen has not yet been confirmed."

"We were informed that the police now treat this as a crime," Nick replied.

"So. I had not heard." He hid a frown behind a noisy sip. "Then it would be *three* crimes, yes?"

"They say one. By the same group. Exactly the same tactics used in each case."

Chronos replaced his cup in the saucer. "But you must understand, Mr. . . ."

"Hennessy."

"The police covering the Halkidiki monasteries are based in Thessaloníki. There are, shall we say, issues. Thessaloníki is very provincial. The police are not as capable as they might be elsewhere."

"Actually, this incident is being handled by Interpol."

This time, his surprise was not so well hidden. "How do you know this?"

"A good investigative journalist never reveals his sources, sir. Just as I will never divulge anything you can help me with to anyone else."

"Most commendable. But Interpol . . ." His fingers drummed on the white suede, and for the first time since she entered the home, Carey thought she was seeing a genuine response from the man. "Precious as these icons might be to these monasteries, why would Interpol become involved?"

Nick said softly, "I think you know."

"Eh, what did you say?"

Nick set down his cup with exaggerated care. Leaned back. Taking his time. In control. "You were director of an institute

95

charged with overseeing the legacy of your nation. Surely you must have seen. There is only one answer."

The lady appeared in the kitchen doorway, carrying a crystal plate piled high with glistening sweets. But something in her husband's voice caused her to freeze midway across the marbled expanse. Chronos demanded, "What exactly are you implying here?"

"The only possible explanation for why Interpol is now involved," Nick repeated. "The one solitary reason that could elevate thefts from three Greek monasteries to international status."

His wife asked something. Chronos ignored her. Quietly she retreated to the kitchen. Chronos said, "Go on."

"Two events must have happened," Nick said. If he was affected by the crackling tension, he gave no sign. "First, the crimes have been linked to thefts in other countries. A ring of criminals with a global reach . . ."

But Chronos showed a different response to the friction. He seemed to tighten, at a layer far below the padding that covered his frame. Carey had the sense that Nick was deftly peeling away the man's carefully fashioned mask. Revealing the hidden fury.

"And second," Nick said, his tone quietly cheerful, "the thieves are protected. They have bought a source. In each country. Very high up and very well paid. Someone to keep an eye on things. Let them know—"

"I do not like your tone," Chronos said, "whoever you are."

"Which brings us to the matter at hand," Nick continued smoothly. "What precisely were the reasons your institute was shut down?"

"Our visit has come to an end."

"Did it have anything to do with the new task force where Carey Mathers was to work? The one intended to hunt—"

"You must go. Now."

"Did you personally have anything to do with—?"

"*Get out!*"

Nick rose to his feet, his movements almost languid. "Thank you for your time."

12

Long after the gates slid open and their taxi trundled down the silent street, Carey was still working on drawing an easy breath. Nick went back to studying the view out his side window, idly tapping the glass with the fingernails of his left hand.

Eleni turned around from her place in the front seat, her face creased by the same tension Carey felt. "Why did he agree to see us at all?"

"He wanted to know how much we knew." Nick's tap on the glass had an almost delicate touch. "He wanted to know if we are a threat."

"Is Interpol truly involved?"

"I have no idea. They should be."

"You lied to him?"

"Phyllis has tried repeatedly to draw Interpol into this crisis. All they'll tell her is that they have made note of her concerns. She's hoping this is a ploy, that they cannot reveal a secret investigation even to her."

Eleni pondered that, then suggested, "Interpol does not trust her."

"It's possible," Nick agreed.

Eleni watched him a moment longer, then faced forward. The cab went silent again. Carey had a thousand things she wanted to ask, but her mind continued to scramble so frantically that she could shape none of them into a complete question.

The cab left the highway and entered central Athens, and gradually they were captured by a monumental traffic jam. They crested a hill and from this vantage point could see a dozen or so other roads. All of them had been turned into parking lots, which shimmered in the afternoon light. Through her open window, Carey could hear a cacophony of whistles and megaphones and drums.

The driver cut the engine. Carey asked, "What's going on?"

The driver didn't need for this question to be translated. He spoke, and Eleni replied, "Same crisis, different dancers. Today it is the students and the professors."

Nick opened his door. "Let's walk."

He paid the driver, accepted the receipt, and asked Eleni, "Where's your home?"

She pointed to the Acropolis, rising from the city like a stone beacon. "Three kilometers to the east."

"Okay. Hold to side streets as much as you can. Fast as we can make it."

They set off. The protest's din and the crowds soon swallowed them. The tide of people was pushing, surging, ramming from their left to their right. Crossing every intersection meant weaving their way through a tsunami of anger and whistle-blowers and sign-carriers. People shouting, waving fists, chanting—people pounding on drums. So much rage.

All three of them felt the change. The crowd had been angry, but just a crowd. Then something happened over to their right, a noisy, unified response. Carey felt as though the crowd had become a huge multi-legged beast. A ravenous animal that roared through a hundred thousand voices.

The surging tide attempted to lift them up and carry them along. Nick reached for both Carey and Eleni and pulled them against the flow. He shouted, but the words were shredded and lost. Carey saw his fear, knew they were caught up by something dangerous indeed.

Somewhere to her right, she heard a sharp *crack*. A smoking canister hammered a nearby shop window. Another whooshed overhead. Nick hauled them both forward so fast that Carey almost lost her footing. Someone slapped her face with a waving sign, but Carey was through and into the next alley before she could even identify the feeling on her forehead as pain. This time the narrow walls echoed his shout, "RUN!"

When they emerged from the alley, they were greeted with a slight drifting cloud, a tendril of something that floated smoothly about their legs. Then her eyes started burning, and suddenly her throat tightened until she had difficulty drawing breath.

Nick glanced around and then abruptly changed course. They flew down the sidewalk, thirty steps, fifty. He shoved past a uniformed guard and rammed her and Eleni into a revolving door of a large building.

Carey was coughing and retching so hard, she didn't at first see where they were. When she finally cleared her eyes, she realized they were standing inside a palatial hotel. The marbled foyer was home to Persian carpets and crystal chandeliers and antique furniture and elegant-looking people. She would have felt utterly out of place, but no one noticed them at all. Everyone in the lobby, customers and staff alike, stared in horror at the running street battle just beyond the enormous glass windows.

A gray-haired man rushed into the room and shouted something that jerked the staff into action. Giant steel shutters began grinding down over the windows and the main doors. The uniformed porter only just managed to slip inside before the hotel was sealed shut.

Nick ushered them into the hotel coffee shop, where they could sit out the riot in relative peace. The café occupied the corner position of the building, and repeatedly the steel shutters were hammered so hard they buckled inwards. Beyond the steel cocoon rose screams and gunfire and sirens and the grinding wheels of vehicles so heavy that they caused the hotel to shudder.

One at a time they went to the lavatories. Carey used an ironed linen napkin embroidered with the hotel's crest to wipe her tear-streaked face and dab at the cut on her forehead. When she returned, she found Nick had ordered tea and was pouring a small jar of honey into the pot. He said hoarsely, "It'll help soothe your throat."

Eleni managed to get a signal on her phone and called the taverna to let everyone know they were safe. They sat in stunned silence for a time, then Nick said, "Will you tell me what you think of all this?"

Carey doubted her friend was even aware that she continued to shed tears. Eleni sipped from her cup, her shaking hands spilling the tea. Finally she said, "Greece was the cradle of democracy. Everyone knows this. But modern Greece has never had a government that works." She winced as something pounded against the steel shutter nearest their table.

"Every election we have," she continued, "all the politicians, they tell the people, 'We know exactly what needs doing to make it all good. We can repair the damage, only us.' But then they come to power, and nothing changes. The corruption is still the same. The debt. The crisis. It all just grows worse."

Nick pulled a pad and pen from his backpack, though his rasping coughs made writing difficult. He scribbled quickly as Eleni went on, "The Greek Communists have been here since the Second World War. They grew stronger during the military dictatorship of the seventies, when the generals tried to wipe them out and instead turned them into heroes of the resistance. And then there are the far-right parties who supported the military takeover because they were tired of the chaos and disorder of Greece's postwar democracy. These people are back again, talking of the need for Greece to vote in a new leadership. These people openly call themselves Fascists, and their Golden Dawn party became the third largest political group in parliament, until their leaders were arrested for inciting violence."

Eleni paused and took a sip of her tea. "So we have the Communists on the far left, and the Fascists on the far right. And now, since this crisis began, they are echoing the same message. 'Tear down the entire Greek government structure. It is flawed, it is corrupt, and the only answer is to start over from scratch.'" Eleni shook her head. "This is an old message. The two extremist groups have been saying the same thing since they were founded. Only now there is a difference."

"People are listening," Nick said, writing furiously.

"People are *angry*. They feel *helpless*. They are willing to listen to anyone who promises that here is a way to retake control of our government and our lives."

"Even if it means tearing down the system. Creating chaos."

"There is *already* chaos. The government is *already* torn

apart. The news is filled with images of the people we elected, shouting and arguing with each other."

Nick finished writing, flipped pages back and forth, surveying his notes, occasionally adding something further. Gradually the din beyond the metal shutters had gone quiet. Nick said, "Okay, here's what's going to happen next. Tomorrow Carey and I are going to Bodrum, check out what we can discover about these middlemen." He looked at her. "That okay with you?"

Carey stammered, "I guess . . . sure."

"Great. Eleni, I want you to become our staffer here in Athens. But you need to stay on at the taverna. No one beyond this family can know you're doing this, you understand? How much do you want for your help?"

"You mean . . . you'll pay me?"

"Sure will."

"Nick, thank you, but this is not necessary."

"Yes, it is." He ended the discussion by reaching into the backpack and passing a manila envelope across the table to Carey. "I want you to take care of the finances. You're good with figures and you're better with records. I'm a mess with both. Phyllis needs receipts and documentation."

"Is this—?"

"The money Phyllis gave me. Right."

Eleni asked, "How much . . . ?"

Carey quickly made the packet disappear into her backpack. "Twenty-five thousand euros."

Eleni was aghast. "You walk around Athens in a riot with twenty-five thousand euros? Are you insane?"

"Absolutely. It helps." Somewhere along the way, Nick had recovered his buccaneer grin. "Are you in?"

13

As Dimitri exited Skala harbor, the sun was only an hour from fading into another starlit night. The big Hatteras yacht was gone—Dimitri had no idea where to, nor did he much care. His instructions were clear, his decision made.

Sofia entered the wheelhouse and asked, "Where do we pick up our cargo?"

He pointed over the bow. "One of the south islands."

She knew the shoals, and frowned over his words. "Is it safe?"

"I chose the place."

Between Patmos and the Turkish coast lay a number of rocky islets, only a few of which were inhabited. The larger islands of the Dodecanese were world-renowned—Kos, Samos, and Rhodes—while others contained fishing hamlets that hadn't changed much in a thousand years. Dimitri headed for the nearest of these, Apkoi, which was surrounded by numerous rocky atolls. Eons of wind and waves had carved strange designs into the porous rock. Caves were everywhere.

As a youth, Dimitri had dived many of them. His bedroom contained an array of items drawn from the sea.

Their destination was a narrow beach often used for moonlit trysts during the summer season. Now with a chill autumn breeze spicing the night, Dimitri knew they would remain far from prying eyes. The water was too shallow for fishermen, the seabed too picked over for the treasure hunters. Dimitri motored in slowly and anchored in waist-deep water. He dropped over the side, accepted the flashlight from Sofia, and pulled the inflatable dinghy to shore.

The goods were piled at the rear of a bowl-shaped cave fronting the beach. The contents of the seven tightly strapped bundles were hidden from view by layers of bubble wrap. Duncan McAllister had assured him one person would be able to lift them, yet two of the packets weighed well over sixty kilos each. By the time Dimitri loaded the last into his dinghy, he was puffing hard.

Sofia had the gaffs ready, and together they loaded the bundles on deck and slid them across the foredeck and into the open hold. Dimitri lowered them one by one into the scuppers, then covered them with the heavy canvas tarp used to shade the rear deck. When he returned topside, Sofia handed him a towel to wipe away the sweat. "Did they fit?"

"Barely."

"What happens when they have us transport something too big to hide?"

He'd been thinking the very same thing and had found no answer yet. "First we must survive this run."

Dimitri turned west and steered into the night. Sofia busied herself on the stern deck, feeding the hooks and running out the deep-water lines. They intended to play the part of fishermen. This meant at least trying to catch fish. Sofia had spent her youth working on her uncle's boat. Like Dimitri, she had loved the sea since before she could walk. Things changed slowly on the Aegean, and for years her uncle was chided by other islanders for employing a woman, even one of his own family. But her uncle was a cantankerous sort, who loved nothing more than pulling their noses, as the expression went. Sofia learned the trade and the sea both. Dimitri considered himself immensely fortunate to have Sofia onboard.

The distance from Skala to Turkish Cyprus was just over four hundred nautical miles. Dimitri motored south by west, passing between Kos and the hourglass island of Astypalaia. He steered well north of Syrna and Zafora, passed below Santorini, and entered the vaguely marked Sea of Crete.

Where the seabed dropped off, Sofia went aft and began preparing their deep-water lines. The baited hooks were larger than her fist. They were seeking tuna. For years their prey had remained very rare. But after years of battling the Brussels bureaucrats, Greece had finally managed to outlaw the hated bottom trawlers, the great refrigerator vessels from Korea and Japan and China and Brazil that plowed furrows along the seabed, pulling up all life and ruining the coral. Slowly the fish were coming back. The Mediterranean species tended to be far smaller than the North Atlantic tuna, but some claimed it was a sweeter fish. Over the past few years, several had been landed measuring up to three meters in length.

The lines Sofia fed off the stern could also possibly bring in mahi-mahi and blackfish, even perhaps a late-season amberjack. All in all, Dimitri decided, it was a lot of work simply to fashion a lie.

When the bottom sonar showed they had passed over the Aigaio Ledge, Dimitri slowed to a trolling speed, set the automatic pilot, and joined Sofia on the rear deck. They finished setting the lines, and then he sent her aloft and entered the galley where he made them tea and sandwiches. He returned to the wheelhouse just as a sliver of moon rose over the port bow. The sea was as still as glass, a normal part of many summer nights, though rare in the autumn storm season.

Sofia accepted her mug and said, "I've been thinking about your grandmother and her prayers for a miracle."

"I asked her about McAllister," he confessed. "She said the smuggling gig is most definitely not what she's been praying for. I pointed out that Duncan's arrival saved me from a beating at the hands of Stavros and his nephew. She merely shrugged and said God uses what is closest at hand, and that I should wait in prayerful expectancy—whatever that means."

"I like her very much." Sofia stood with one arm draped over the wheel, the customary position of an experienced hand, even when the autopilot was engaged. Her eyes constantly scouted the seas ahead and the radar and the sonar, as did his own. The sea was as clear and empty as the sky. "She always treated me well, even when most island women condemned me for working my uncle's boat. All they could see was how I took bread from the mouths of some man and his family. Your grandmother told me what I did was good for all the island women."

The engines rumbled a soft note, a deep bass chord that Dimitri found reassuring. They enjoyed the silence and each other's company, drifting across the dark sea. Dimitri tried to pierce the veil and see how they could survive the risks ahead, and failed. As he fought against his fluttering nerves, he noticed how Sofia's gaze tightened and realized she was attuned to the unspoken. He was about to say something when the deck shifted.

Sofia exclaimed, "What was *that*?"

A miracle was Dimitri's first thought, but all he said was, "Check the lines."

By dawn they had landed almost eight hundred pounds of tuna, plus another three hundred of mahi and amberjack.

Dimitri had never worked so hard in his entire life. Nor had he ever been so tired, not even after that frantic week spent converting his father's fishing boat into a cheerfully painted tourist vessel, complete with new lights, canopy, and bunting. He'd toiled day and night to complete the transformation in time for his first charter. Then afterward he motored through the steaming hot August day to Bodrum, his nostrils choked with the fumes of fresh paint, to meet a party of British tourists. Only there had been twice the number of tourists the hotel manager had promised, and they had already been drunk when they boarded. So drunk, in fact, that two of them had fallen overboard and would have been lost to the night had Dimitri not spent as much time leaning over the rear railing as he did steering the vessel.

While that experience had been exhausting, still it was nothing like this one.

Three times the next fish struck before the previous line was hauled in. They lost four because they couldn't move fast enough, two of which Dimitri suspected were the largest of all. One pulled the boat almost to a halt in a series of shuddering jerks. Sofia had paused in gaffing a furiously fighting amberjack and said, "Swordfish."

"Impossible." Dimitri hauled the forty-pound catch onboard. "Swordfish don't . . ."

He was silenced by a great silver behemoth rising from the placid waters, flashing in the moonlight, then hammering the inky sea and disappearing. With a jerk, the line was severed and the boat freed. Sofia wiped her face with a gloved hand, streaking her forehead with fish scales. "You were saying?"

The night at least was with them. They cruised across a starlit sea so calm the boat held steady as a table. The autopilot became their closest friend. It was a new design, connected directly to the radar and bottom sonar both. And expensive. Yet everyone Dimitri had spoken with in the tourist trade echoed the same warning: prepare yourself for emergencies. The equipment had served him well on any number of occasions.

Sofia was haggard and exhausted by dawn, but she could not stop grinning. As they pulled in the night rigs and stowed the gear, she said, "Maybe we should reconsider our trade."

They cleaned and dressed and iced the catch. Dimitri motored them well away from the feeding frenzy that the chum set off. He then joined Sofia in scrubbing and sluicing down the deck.

They were now within thirty miles of Crete's eastern point. Sofia directed him to a tiny island called Chrysi, which had an even smaller atoll off its eastern coast. They anchored in shallow water by a beach where Sofia's uncle had liked to moor. The placid water was so clear, he couldn't make out the depth. It felt as if they were afloat on nothing more than air. But the sonar assured him they had anchored in ten meters of water. They used the dinghy to carry their gear and dove into the crystal waters. The autumn chill bit deep, yet refreshed them enough for Dimitri to laugh for the first time in what felt like years.

The beach was forty paces across and framed by pink sandstone that glowed in the midday light. The silence was as intense as the sun. Sofia showed him an ancient stone cistern and foundations her uncle claimed had once been a Nazi-era barracks and gun emplacement. Dimitri used a plastic bucket from the boat and took a rainwater shower. While he set up the portable gas grill and cooked the tuna, Sofia collected wild sage and sorrel to flavor their steaks. They lazed about for a time, then returned to the boat and slept. Sofia took a bunk in the forward hold. Dimitri climbed into the wheelhouse and unrolled a futon he kept in the chart cabinet. They didn't post watches since no fisherman would bother. Dimitri dreamed of seven bundles wrapped in plastic burning like coals, the heat fierce enough to puncture the gunnels and send his boat to the bottom of the sea.

He was awakened by a subtle change to the world beyond his closed eyelids. Dimitri was enough of a natural seaman to be aware of such shifts, even when in a deep sleep. Before he opened his eyes, he heard the low rumble of powerful engines.

He scrambled to his feet and saw what he most dreaded. Off the port bow, a Greek naval vessel approached them.

14

A simple fisherman would hardly dash anywhere at the appearance of a Greek naval vessel. Dimitri raked a hand through his tousled hair and dry-scrubbed his face, aware that he was being observed all the while by two officers watching from the vessel's upper deck. He slid open the wheelhouse door and cinched his drawstring shorts tight before climbing down.

"Coastal patrol," a voice boomed through a megaphone. "Permission to come aboard."

Dimitri responded with the same sort of half shrug, half wave he had seen his father use on such occasions. The steel hull motored in close, and white fenders were set in place by a couple of midshipmen, who then tossed over lines. When Dimitri had secured the boats, a young officer dropped catlike onto the deck. He saluted and said, "Commander Stefanos Khouris. You are alone?"

"No. My mate is asleep."

"Your papers, please."

"One moment." Dimitri returned to the wheelhouse to get the boat documents, his ID, and the family's fishing permits. A moment later, he handed them over to the officer and then pounded on the aft portal. "Sofia!"

Dimitri suspected she was awake and watching. But she responded with the plaintive whine of an angry shipmate. He called, "Coast Guard. Bring your ID."

Many of the naval officers hailed from regional families, so Dimitri wasn't surprised when the commander asked, "Your father is Adoni Rubinos?"

"He is."

Sofia emerged and scowled at the afternoon and the officer. After handing over her ID, she said to Dimitri, "You woke me for this?"

The officer held up the plastic card so that he could check her against the photograph. "Your husband is Manos?"

"I suspect you're asking a question you already know the answer to," she snapped. "And I was up all night doing my job."

He handed back their papers, untouched by her ire. "Your catch?"

"A good one," Dimitri replied.

"I need to inspect."

He opened the stern hold, and the officer descended with practiced ease. Dimitri followed. The officer scanned the dressed fish, then pulled a metal baton from his belt pouch and snapped it open. He probed down through the ice to where he struck the floorboards to ensure they weren't hiding an out-of-season catch. "Late in the season for amberjack."

Dimitri didn't reply. A friendly fisherman would only heighten the officer's suspicions.

From above, Sofia groused, "Can I go back to sleep now?"

The officer climbed back into the sunlight. As Dimitri followed, the commander asked, "What was your business on the British vessel?"

The words struck like an unseen blow. Sofia hesitated in the process of descending into the bow hold, but only for a moment. Dimitri struggled to maintain his neutral tone. "What British vessel?"

"*Maiden Voyage*. Out of Portsmouth."

"That's the one Duncan McAllister sails?" Dimitri shrugged. "I forgot the name."

"But you were onboard, yes?"

"He asked, I came. It is a lovely ship. A Hatteras."

"What did the Englishman want?"

"He's Scots/Irish," Dimitri corrected. "But you know that as well, yes?"

"The purpose of your visit," the officer demanded.

"I was there twice. We also met once on the quayside. He looked me up. He wants me to transport people to and from Turkey."

The officer possessed a hard-edged expression for one so young. "People doing what exactly?"

"He did not say, and I did not ask. It is work through the winter. For good pay." Dimitri pointed to the hold. "One catch of this size will not see us through the down season."

The officer glanced back at his vessel, where a more senior officer observed from the control deck. "We have reason to believe the Englishman is engaged in illegal activities."

"Of what kind?"

In response, the commander strode back to the railing, gripped the stern line, and stepped onto the gunnel.

"Wait," Dimitri called. "Are you telling me not to take the job?"

"We do not have the evidence required to make such declarations." The commander waited until he had hoisted himself over the navy vessel's rail. "Naturally we would appreciate hearing of anything suspicious."

Dimitri released the two lines and stood watching as the vessel pulled away. When the massive diesels were a faint rumble on the horizon, Sofia called from the shadows, "Are they gone?"

"For the moment."

"What do we do now?"

Dimitri didn't respond.

15

The sun had set by the time the shutters finally rolled up and they were released from the hotel. When their taxi stopped in front of the taverna, they were given a weary and worried welcome, embraced by everyone. They were far from the first who arrived with personal accounts of the troubles. And this was far from the first riot the family had endured. They were fussed over, Carey's forehead was treated, and afterward they were shuttled back to the hotel. Carey took a long shower, scrubbing her hair twice. But when she finally lay down, she could still smell the acrid tear gas. Her exhaustion was a deep ache that followed her into sleep.

The next morning, Nick rang her room at nine. Carey's throat still felt raw from the gas, and Nick sounded like he had swallowed gravel. They walked down the road, entered the taverna, greeted the family, and slipped into the window booth that had become their own.

While they waited for breakfast, Nick sat in the corner by the window sipping another cup of honeyed tea. He called

Phyllis Karras and related the previous day's events. Carey listened to his tone more than the words. Nick remained calm, his voice almost a monotone. Carey also thought he remained unnaturally still, as though yesterday's events had left in their wake a steadying effect. One thing was certain. The man was cheerful. He seemed to glow with happiness.

Over breakfast, Nick asked, "What can you tell me about the stolen icons?"

"A lot more than you probably want to hear."

He rewarded her with another of those off-kilter grins. "Really?"

"It was the job I hoped they'd assign me. I researched them to death." Carey watched him reach into his pack for the notepad and pen. "The disappearance of the three icons is unquestionably a criminal matter. The treasures were well-documented. A lot of angry monks were only too happy to ignore the government's pleas for calm. The monks gained attention within the international arts market when they alleged the government's silence indicated a major fraud."

He started writing. "Okay. So I'm a complete beginner. What do I need to understand first?"

"The monasteries themselves. Halkidiki is made up of three peninsulas that extend from Greece's northern territories. The monasteries are clustered on Agio Oros, the easternmost of the three. There's a boundary wall at the northern end. Officially the road just stops there at a village. Outside visitors are required to walk, unless they receive special dispensation from the monasteries. Which is very, very rare."

"How many monasteries are there?"

"Officially, fifteen. But the peninsula is dotted with hermitages and cells carved from the rocks."

"You agree with Dr. Stephanopoulos that we shouldn't travel up there?"

"Absolutely," she answered. "It would be a total waste of time. The monastery where the most valuable icon was stolen is a full day's walk from the boundary. We might find a boat that could take us, which would save time. I imagine that's how the stolen treasures left the peninsula. But once we arrive, there's no guarantee the monks would even speak with us. They don't have phones."

He set down his pen. "You're kidding."

"Only a few of the buildings even have electricity."

"What do they do all day?"

"They farm. They weave. They illustrate manuscripts. They tend hives and herds. They make cheese. And they pray. Six times a day. Actually, three times during the day. Another just before bed, another just after midnight, and one more when they rise before dawn."

He mulled that over, his handsome features showing bafflement over the idea of people dedicating themselves to such a life. "And the icons?"

"They date from the early dark ages, which gets its name from how we know so little about the period. Most people didn't read or write, and nations had reduced in size to little more than city-states."

He wrote swiftly. "Which means the art we have from that period came from the church."

"Right. Icons were originally used as teaching tools. They depicted Bible passages and key figures, mostly Jesus and the apostles. Over time, some of them became associated with miracles. By the tenth century, the most famous were set in massive silver and gold frames decorated with gemstones."

117

"So they're basically stealing the frames that happen to hold icons?"

She felt a sudden surge of frustration. She knew she should do a better job of matching his calm, but failed. "Not at all. These icons are one of our few windows into this era. There's virtually no other artwork from this period. From around the year three hundred to nine hundred, these priceless icons hold a unique position in human history."

He set down his pen. "What's the matter, Carey?"

"How did you get this way? And don't pretend you can't understand what I mean. You've changed. I want to know why."

He cocked his head slightly, as though adjusting his vision so as to study her better. "Have I changed, really?"

"You know you have."

"Nothing's happened to me. I mean, nothing bad."

"So you just arrive in Paris, and one day you wake up and Shazam! A whole new Nick. Lean and cool and just loving the danger high." She shook her head. "I don't buy it."

Nick didn't say anything.

"Look at what happened to us yesterday. We meet up with the former Institute director, who plays charades because she's afraid for her life. We visit a guy who's corrupt as they come. He basically paints a bull's-eye on your forehead."

Nick sipped thoughtfully from his glass of tea. His gaze was dark, fathomless.

"And then we get caught in a *riot*. We almost have our heads handed to us on a platter spiced with tear gas." She knew her voice was rising, and she didn't care. "All last night I jerked awake from dreams that I was running and running and would never get away. How did *you* sleep, Nick?"

He leaned against the side window. "Fine. I slept great."

"So here you sit. Mr. Calm and Cool. Totally okay with it all. Just grooving on the scene. What *is* it with you?"

He nodded slowly. Like he was absorbing everything she *didn't* say. Like he understood more than she did herself. Which left her feeling very exposed. Uncomfortably so. But she was also glad she'd spoken.

"I'd been in Paris for five and a half weeks," Nick began. "Happy as I'd ever been in my life. I'd filed a few stories and played tagalong on some others. We were a small team of six. Three journalists, of which I was junior, a photographer, a researcher-interpreter, and one admin staffer. Our top guy was out covering the latest crisis in Damascus when he got hit by something, probably a slingshot. But he was struck hard enough to need an emergency evac to Paris.

"Reporter number two couldn't go take his place, because his wife was pregnant and about to pop. So they sent me. The new guy." He paused for another sip from his tulip glass of tea. "The night after I arrived in Syria, the rebels launched a major assault on our side of the city. The hotel used by the press corps was supposedly in the Damascus safe zone. We took a direct hit from an RPG. Thankfully it struck the other end from where I was sleeping. Even so, I was blasted out of my bed and slammed into the opposite wall. I raced down seven flights of stairs, helped the emergency teams work on the wounded, then at dawn I went to the embassy and filed my story. My first front-page article. Afterwards, as I was sitting in a different hotel lobby, waiting for a room, I realized I felt exactly like you describe. Not happy it all happened, but calm. The calmest I've ever felt. Because I knew this was what I intended to do for the rest of my life. Everything I've ever hoped for. Right here."

She spoke slowly, tasting the sound of the words. "Running toward danger."

Nick studied her. His unreadable gaze made her as uncomfortable as his words. Nick said softly, "If danger is part of the story I'm chasing, then yes. Absolutely. I will run straight for the target."

Carey opened her mouth, yet no sound came.

Nick seemed to know what she was thinking. He said, "Which makes me a terrible risk."

"What do you—?" Carey stopped because his phone rang. She decided this was a good thing, because as he answered she realized she didn't want to know exactly what Nick had meant.

He listened, asked a couple of questions, then thanked the caller and hung up. "That was Phyllis," he said. "There's been a change of plans."

16

The island of Cyprus was full of lies. Even the map failed to tell the truth.

Dimitri's destination was the eastern tip of North Cyprus. The island's southern half formed Greek Cyprus, a separate nation and a member of the EU. Greek Cyprus was officially at war with the north, although no shots had been fired in almost a decade. The dispute over land and invasion and language and race had been going on since the Ottomans, so wrapped up in tragedy and old rage that the stories told by either side might as well have belonged to two different points on the globe.

The Kleides Islands were a dusting of guano-encrusted rocks. They created a wretched punctuation mark at the northeast end of Cyprus. The closest city, Dipkarpaz, was two hours away on a truly awful road and had no port. North Cyprus patrol boats either set off from Famagusta or Girne, hours away by sea. Dimitri turned the wheelhouse wipers on high and hoped the weather would keep the Cypriot Navy snug in their harbors.

They stayed just outside the thirty-mile boundary, where Sofia set their lines. The water was oily, the night clad in a mist that tasted like cold soup. The last weather report said a storm was coming from the east, but so far the weather was with them. They trolled the waters, the lights set in standard position for line fishing, aimed down and surrounding the vessel with brilliant illumination. The mist was so thick, anyone tracking them would have caught them by radar long before they saw the lights.

Their ten o'clock rendezvous came and went. Dimitri searched the empty radar screens and struggled to hide his mounting concern. Sofia climbed into the wheelhouse and flicked back the cowl to her slicker. "Still nothing?"

"All quiet."

She accepted the towel he handed over and wiped the moisture from her face. "The radio is working?"

"Yes. I'm scanning all channels. We might as well be the only boat out here." He flicked on the wipers again, except there was nothing to see and so he cut them off once more. "I'm giving it another hour, then we'll load the dinghy, and I'll motor in and find a place to hide the packets."

"But what—?" Sofia stopped as the radio began crackling.

A man's voice said something, but interference ate all meaning. Dimitri unhooked the mike and spoke in English, "Say again."

This time the voice came through clearly. "Identify, please."

Dimitri responded as Duncan had instructed. "Sorry, I can't hear you."

The radio went quiet. Dimitri pointed the vessel north and slowed to an idling speed. "Let's get ready."

Dimitri doused the ship's lights and joined Sofia on deck. She brought in the lines while he slipped into the hold and began hauling out their cargo. Five minutes later, he felt the gentle nudge of a dinghy pushing against the gunnel. He heaved the two heaviest bundles onto the deck, then clambered out.

He started to chide Sofia for not helping him with the heavy items when he saw the direction of her gaze.

Two dinghies were lashed to the starboard rail, both of them oversized inflatables, capable of carrying six passengers each. But two passengers were all they could hold, since the dinghies were piled high with packages, each one about a foot square. Dimitri knew without question that the packages were meant for him. This was definitely not part of any deal he had made with Duncan McAllister.

One of the men stood in the bow of his dinghy and slowly twisted his body. From the way he swept back and forth across the empty sea, Dimitri assumed the man held a miniature radar gun. As the man turned, Dimitri saw the glint of a rifle hanging from his shoulder.

"Sorry we're late," another man called. "We've had company. It's been nip and tuck all night."

Dimitri could feel the tension radiating off Sofia and knew she was about to say something that might get them both killed. He touched her arm as the first package tumbled onto the deck. "I need you to go topside."

"What *are* those?" She jerked back as the men dumped another load onto the stern deck. "You said no drugs!"

Dimitri didn't know if the strangers spoke Greek. He didn't care if they heard. "It's not drugs."

"How can you possibly . . . ?"

Dimitri got tight in her face. "Go to the wheelhouse." He kept his voice even. "Keep a sharp watch on the radar. Sweep

123

in every direction. Far out as we can reach. Tell me you under-stand."

Fear congealed into bright flecks that shimmered at the edges of her eyes. "Manos will—"

"Manos is not here." Dimitri used the tone meant to draw passengers away from panic when one of the notorious Mediterranean storms blew out of nowhere and threatened to kill them all. Which was not far from what they faced tonight. "Pay attention. Do exactly what I say. And I will get you back to Manos."

She frowned as another load tumbled on deck, thoughtful now. Dimitri leaned back, satisfied that the message had gotten through. This wasn't about making peace with Manos. This was about survival.

"You want me to scan the horizon," she said.

"Set the radar for maximum range. The mist will create phantoms. So be careful. And start the engines. Soon as you're certain you've spotted something, you call down and you *go*."

She licked dry lips. "They're coming?"

"You heard what the smugglers said. They've been chased all night. So you get ready, and as soon as you're certain, you go in the exact opposite direction."

She glanced at the strangers and the rifles strapped to their shoulders. "But what if they're—?"

"I'll handle them. Your job is to aim in the opposite compass heading from the threat, and fly."

Dimitri waited until Sofia started up the wheelhouse steps, then turned in time to see one of the strangers hop over the gunnel onto the deck. Dimitri recognized him as the smallest of the silent killers who had accompanied Duncan McAllister on Patmos. Thankfully the stranger had left his rifle in the dinghy. The man gave a crooked smile, and Dimitri was certain he expected an attack, was probably even looking forward to it. Dimitri simply said, "Let's get this stowed."

He dropped into the stern hold and began accepting the plastic-wrapped packages. No way could he hide all this in the forward hold, and there was nothing to be gained from splitting the hoard. Each packet weighed about four kilos, ten pounds. Dimitri didn't bother trying to hide the new shipment under ice. If the authorities caught them now, a dark Athens prison would be the least of his worries.

The next package caught the hold's dim overhead light just so. Through the multiple layers of transparent packing he glimpsed exactly what he'd seen when the first load dropped on the deck by his feet. Despite being surrounded by ice, Dimitri became drenched in sweat.

They weren't hauling drugs. Their cargo was much, much worse.

17

The call Nick had received from Phyllis Karras directed them to the island of Kos, where they were to meet a possible new ally. But arranging travel proved more difficult than expected. The ferry's website was down, the phones constantly busy, so they took a taxi to the ferry office and joined a line that stretched out the door and down a block and a half. Eleni spoke with several people and learned nothing. There was a tension in many faces that Carey didn't understand. People jostled and kept uncomfortably tight together.

Eleni stepped away, pulled out her phone, and paced as she talked. Ten minutes later, she came back wearing the same frown as the others. She moved in close and asked Nick, "This money you spoke of, it is true?"

"Yes."

"You have it with you?"

"Some. The rest is in the hotel safe."

"This trip, it is important, yes?"

"Phyllis thought it might be."

"Then you must come with me now."

Eleni drew them away from the throng of customers. "I spoke with my friend in the police force, a cousin of a cousin. She says the Athens ports and stations are to be closed at dawn with a strike. Boats, planes, trains, buses, everything."

"So, what do we do?" Nick asked.

"She said if we want to travel, we must contact a man . . ." She searched the other side of the street, then pointed to a small park. "There."

They crossed against the traffic and entered the narrow strip of dusty green. Eleni motioned for them to wait, then walked over to a man standing by a tree and spoke with him briefly. He inspected them carefully before responding with a few words that left Eleni looking shocked. She hesitated, then walked back and said, "His wife, she works in the ferry office. He can get you a berth on the midnight ferry. But it will cost five times the normal fare."

Nick handed over the bills. "Can you trust him not to run away?"

"He receives the ticket cost in advance," Eleni explained. "The rest when he returns."

"Do it."

They returned to their Athens hotel to pack. Carey found exquisite pleasure in another dose of the clean bathroom and hot water and perfumed soaps. She dressed in fresh clothes and returned downstairs to find Nick kneeling in the hotel lobby, his suitcase open on the floor, his hair still wet from the shower. "It just occurred to me. We may need to . . ."

Carey heard the unspoken and felt her nerves jangle faintly. "Move fast."

He glanced up, looking grateful for not needing to say more than that while Eleni's father and aunt hovered nearby. "Maybe you should leave your case and just take the backpack."

"I can do that." Carey asked the manager, "Is it all right if we leave our things with you?"

"Sure, sure. Like I tell your gentleman, is no problem. We have a room for left baggage." She smiled wearily. "Many rooms, no guests."

Carey knelt beside Nick and did a quick reorganization. Skip the cosmetics. Ditto for skirts, matching shoes, business outfits. Down to basics—comfort and layers. Sandals. Sunscreen. She changed into hiking boots. Extra socks. Her computer tablet and new phone. She zipped her backpack shut and stood. "Done."

Nick rolled his case to the waiting manager and tipped her. "That was fast."

"For a girl, you mean?"

"For anybody. I've waited hours for a journalist to sort the papers in his briefcase."

Despite the late hour, Eleni and her family swiftly vetoed Nick's suggestion that they take a taxi. So they piled into the van with Eleni and her parents and aunt. Nick was directed into the front passenger seat. Eleni and Carey were jammed into the rear compartment, isolated from the chatter coming from the front two rows.

"What were you and Nick talking about back there in the restaurant?" Eleni asked.

"Oh, nothing."

"It did not look like nothing. It looked like a lot of something very serious."

So Carey told her. As she spoke, she wondered at this sudden openness. She was by nature a very private person, yet here she was telling people she'd known only a few days some of her deepest secrets.

Eleni's face had gone unnaturally still. In the passing headlights she looked ancient, timeless. "Is he worth it, this Nick?"

Carey wasn't sure how to respond.

"He is handsome, this American, but I feel no fire in him."

"He has fire for his job," Carey pointed out.

"Yes. So do other men who rise to the top. But for their lovers, their families?" Eleni shrugged. "I think perhaps here is one who will be happiest with the American blonde who is perfect in everything she shows to the outside world, and inside is . . ."

"An ice queen," Carey put in. "I can't imagine Nick being with someone like that."

"Perhaps I am wrong. Perhaps he will wake up in this time with you. Perhaps he will see that if he does not change, and act, he will lose the one he was always meant to love. Since before time. Yes, it can happen. But it is a risk, no?"

Carey disliked how the conversation drew out her confused mix of emotions. Regret and relief, hunger and fear, affection and a desire to turn away. While she still had time. "What happened to you, Eleni? Why aren't you with someone?"

The ancient gaze grew deeper still. "It is complicated."

"It usually is."

"The crisis started the year after I finished school. I wanted to go overseas. This is what happens with most young Greeks who are educated, ambitious. They leave. And who is left? The people who stay are the ones Greece does not need so much. So I too prepared to leave. But my father, he asked me to try and stay. For the family, you understand? He helped me find this job. And then I met an Englishman. He came to work at the Institute, and I thought we were in love. I thought there was fire. I thought . . ."

129

"I believe I've sung that very same song." Carey reached for her friend's hand. "I'm so sorry."

Eleni turned toward the busy street, the traffic seemingly unaffected by the midnight hour. "I keep thinking it is time to try again. But I am afraid. And the crisis makes for a perfect excuse to wait. So many of the young who remain here are waiting. For a job, a hope, a future."

Carey saw the sorrow crease her friend's features, and she did the only thing that came to mind, which was reach into her pack and pull out the manila envelope. She opened it and counted out five hundred euros in cash, about seven hundred dollars. "Here."

"What is this?"

"Payment for food and everything."

"For what? No, no, it is too much."

She liked how the pain had been so swiftly erased. Carey counted out another five hundred and added it to the pile. "And this is for you."

"Carey, no—"

"Will you *listen*? Work out what we owe the restaurant. Add something for the transport. Your father will object, so don't tell him. Just do it. Keep a careful record. I'll need receipts. The same goes for you. Work out a proper per-hour rate for your work. We'll settle up after."

Eleni stared at the bills. "So much."

Carey counted out another three thousand, stuffed those bills in her pocket, then put the rest back in the envelope and gave it to Eleni. "Can you keep this for us?"

"In the restaurant safe. Of course." Eleni stowed the packet in her purse. "What do I do to earn this?"

Carey had no idea, but that mattered less than the new light she saw in Eleni's gaze. "We'll think of something."

18

The diminutive stranger in midnight garb dropped into the hold beside Dimitri. Dimitri knew the man was there to monitor his activities, make sure he didn't try to hide away a package or two. But that was the least of his concerns. The hold was too tight with both of them below, so Dimitri clambered back up, leaving the stranger to stack the remaining bundles.

The other three men remained in the dinghies. Two of them tossed more packages up while the third aimed the handheld radar and swept the horizon. The deck lights reflected off the automatic rifles slung from their backs. Dimitri was busy passing more bundles to the stern hold when he heard Sofia fire the big diesels. The sound alarmed the strangers. Dimitri ignored their chatter and got on with the job, saying with his actions that everything was cool.

Sofia appeared at the wheelhouse's open portal and stared down at him. He called up in English, "Anything?"

"The screen is clear." She held to the same language. The

four men paused and listened as well. "There's a lot of flack. Looks like the storm is moving in."

"From which direction?"

"Straight east."

"But no boats?"

"None that I can see."

Dimitri turned to the trio in the dinghies and asked, "How much more?"

His matter-of-fact tone kept them subdued. "Almost done."

"Hurry."

The load continued to thunk onto the deck. Dimitri tossed them to the stranger, who was now stacking them almost to the hold's ceiling.

When the packets were all stowed, they turned to off-loading the cargo Dimitri had brought. The diminutive man pulled himself from the hold and helped lower the larger items over the gunnel. Together they maneuvered the flap back into place and locked the hold down. Dimitri straightened slowly. He had never felt so tired, so old, so burdened.

The stranger called to his mates, "How does it look?"

The man holding the radar gun replied, "Like the lady said, the incoming storm is making for a lot of noise, but there's no sign of our pursuers."

The man turned to Dimitri. "You know what you're carrying?"

Dimitri wanted to say, *My death warrant, if we're caught.* Instead, he answered, "You heard what he said. A storm is coming. You need to get ashore."

"You want to stay alive—"

"No threats," Dimitri snarled.

The man narrowed his eyes. "Still and all, mate, you need—"

Sofia's voice shrilled from above. "Dimitri! Alert!"

"Where?"

"Eleven o'clock, thirty miles, and closing fast!"

The stranger scurried to the lee gunnel and called down, "Anything?"

"My screen's still clear, but with all this flack—"

Dimitri didn't wait to hear the rest. He used the man's distraction as the best chance he was likely to have. He gripped the stranger by his belt and the collar of his navy sweater and tossed him high, up and over the rail.

The man yelled with genuine fury, his cry cut off by a splash into the inky water. The three others gaped up at Dimitri, uncertain how to respond.

Dimitri felt no such hesitation. He unsheathed the knife on his belt and sliced the line holding the first dinghy to the cleat. "*Go! Go!*"

The twin diesels roared with the fury of engines primed for just such a flight. The second dinghy's line went taut, and the two strangers were tossed off their feet, one joining his mate in the water. Dimitri cut through the second line, then turned away without a backward glance. He raced up the wheelhouse steps.

Sofia greeted him with the grin of a warrior queen. "That was a sweet move."

He stepped up beside her. "Where's the vessel?"

She pointed at the corner of the radar screen, which was empty now. "Just off the grid."

"But it was real, right?"

"Absolutely," Sofia replied. "Was that wise, tossing their man overboard?"

"Probably not, but I needed to slow them down."

Her grin remained in place. "Our direction means that, if the vessel's chasing us, they'll come upon the two dinghies."

Dimitri's only response was to push the throttles wide open.

19

When Carey and Nick arrived at the Athens ferry port, the place was heaving. Half past eleven at night and the traffic was completely jammed. Obviously word of the pending strike had gotten out. Drivers leaned on their horns and yelled out their windows. Others stood by their doors and pounded on the car roofs. Carey was ready when Nick turned and called back to her, "Habel thinks we should hoof it."

"Let's go."

The whole family piled out right there, in the middle of a six-lane highway. They offered farewell embraces and last-minute advice. Then Eleni, Carey, and Nick joined the flow of frantic pedestrians weaving their way through the traffic jam. The ferries were moored tail-in, a line of huge vessels angled against a long concrete wharf. Eleni hustled through the throng, reading the ships' names as they passed. She asked a steward checking tickets and IDs by one of the gangplanks and was pointed farther down the wharf.

The din was so fierce all Carey heard was one massive roar, like a tsunami wave of human voices. Then a boat's horn blared. Other vessels started honking. The passengers entered a new state of panic, pulling and shrieking and shoving.

Eleni waved from the next vessel's stern, pointing them to the gangplank. She hugged Nick first, then Carey, and shouted into her ear, "The trip should take ten hours, but it could be much longer. They will radio ahead and stop at islands where the ferries didn't dock before the strike. Don't eat or drink anything made on this boat, not even the tea!"

The ship's steward was flanked by a pair of burly guards. All three men looked unfazed by the surrounding havoc. The steward checked their tickets and IDs, then held up seven fingers. Carey assumed he meant their cabin was on the seventh deck. They hurried up the gangplank, wrestling their way through the mass of passengers yelling last-minute words to the quayside throng. Nick led the way up a narrow metal stairway that took them to a corridor. At the other end, a short man in stained navy whites checked their tickets, handed out a pair of keys, and then waited patiently for his tip.

After passing the man a bill, Nick unlocked his door and said, "I'm going to sack out."

Carey wished him a good-night, let herself into the next room, and dumped her pack on the bed. She stood there for a moment, until the ship's horn blared a second time and the engines rumbled beneath her. She returned to the corridor, locked her door, and raced for the stairs. She climbed as high as she could go before walking out into the chill night wind.

Their ship joined a line of ships pulling away from the wharf, heading for open waters. The smells of sea and diesel were pungent. Farther down the railing, a young woman wept while a man cradled her in his arms and murmured words musical with affection. The lights along the shore shifted ever so slowly, and the sounds of traffic gradually faded.

Carey remained where she was long after most of the other passengers had returned inside. She was cold, but she didn't care—not even when her entire body began to shiver as the wind picked up. Then she saw it. Far in the distance, the pearl luminescence of ancient ruins crowning a hill laced with legend and history.

It was really happening.

Nick sat at the cabin's fold-down table and stared at his notepad's empty page. His cabin had two bunks, one chair, a threadbare carpet, a porthole with heavily scratched glass, and a cramped but private bathroom. The towels were sealed in plastic wrap beside a thin bar of soap. The lower bunk's sheet was ripped in two places and poorly repaired. The cabin's air held a musty mix of people, age, hard miles, and hurried cleansings. Nick didn't mind. In fact, he noticed it only as he did everything else when he was framing a story. He was on the hunt. Or rather, he should have been. If only he could get his mind off all the things that would never happen. Like falling in love with the girl next door.

He knew he should be making plans. Projecting outcomes, identifying possible trails his story would require chasing. This overnight boat ride might be the last downtime either of them had for a while. If the story proved as big as Phyllis suspected, he could be moving at full speed for days, weeks even. He needed to prepare, and he needed to rest. But he could do neither.

Nick heard the door next to his click open and then shut again. There was a moment's silence, followed by a thump on the floor. Nick assumed Carey had shifted her backpack from the bed. Nick touched the wall shared with her room. The paint was flaking and the metal beneath slightly corroded. He felt trapped by so many things that just would not add up.

He recalled the way he had felt earlier that day, the two of them seated in the taverna's back booth. When she asked him those questions about himself, he had felt split in two. On the one hand, he remained the professional journalist, even when pressured by a beautiful young woman. On the other, he felt drawn out, utterly against his will, as though Carey were a magnet with the power to extract the most carefully guarded pieces of who he was.

Nick forced himself to rise from the desk. He switched off the light and stretched out on his bunk, fully clothed. He stared up at nothing, and reminded himself of all the reasons why he needed to keep this woman at arm's length. No matter how fantastic she might be, or attractive, or all the reasons his mother might offer for why they should be together. Because he was on the trail of the biggest story of his life. The chance he had dreamed of was finally in sight. There was no room for anything else.

She was his researcher. Nothing more.

20

Back when tourists had flooded the Dodecanese and the money came easy, Dimitri had replaced the boat's aging engines with two Cummins workhorses. Each was strong enough to power the heavy wooden vessel on its own. Together they could carry a full bevy of tourists through the strongest storm. Cummins were known for reliability, not speed. The heavy-beamed fishing boat cruised at twenty-two knots, which was less than half the speed of a naval vessel hunting smugglers.

Their only hope lay in stealth.

The storm closed in from the east, carried by lashing rain and heavy wind. Lightning flashed in every direction, a rarity for this time of year. Dimitri welcomed it, for it would distort the radar of those tracking him. And he was certain the hunters were out there. He could smell them.

They were less than two hundred miles from the Mediterranean's eastern shore, which meant there was little room for the incoming storm to kick up heavy waves. The breakers were no more than a meter in height, and they beat against the windward gunnel like the crash of cymbals. Dimitri knew his vessel would see them safely through the storm. The threat lay behind them. Lost in the ghosts that blanketed his radar screen. Hunting.

The question was, where to run and hide?

Straight north was the logical answer. But there were serious problems with that direction. The Turkish coast's eastern region, directly north of him, was heavily patrolled. The Syrian border was less than three hours away. Eastern Turkey was also home to the Kurdish rebels, who were fighting for self-rule.

The tiny islets that formed such a beautiful web of hidden alcoves up and down the Greek coast didn't begin for another two hundred miles. There was little chance they could make it that far. Whoever was hunting them would be expecting him to make a beeline for the islands of Megisti and Karpathos. They would set up sweeps, and with even an ounce of misfortune, Dimitri would never see another dawn.

Dimitri headed south.

Sofia watched the compass turn, saw the Cyprus headlands slip past on the radar's outer perimeter. But Sofia didn't object, which Dimitri took as a good sign. She would be justified in questioning his decision. South meant deeper waters. In fact, once they passed Larnaca Point, there was nothing but water for nine hundred miles—all the way to Africa. They had no experience down here, no working knowledge. Dimitri was taking a huge risk.

But all Sofia asked was, "Should I check the charts?"

"No need," he replied.

She didn't speak again for almost an hour. Eventually the lightning stopped, first reducing to occasional flickers that lit up distant clouds, then nothing. The wind settled down to around thirty knots, hard enough to shudder the boat but not so strong as to build up dangerous waves.

The air in the wheelhouse grew increasingly dense with rain-swept mist and their own breathing, so Dimitri turned on the air-conditioner. Clearing the front glass did not, however, grant them a better view. There was nothing to see. The rain remained strong enough to make even the waves invisible.

Sofia slipped out and was gone for a while. When she returned, she carried two steaming mugs and wore a grim expression. The wheelhouse was soon spiced with Sofia's own version of midnight tea: clove and ginseng with honey and condensed milk.

Dimitri set his mug down and said, "You went into the hold and cut open a brick, didn't you?"

The wheelhouse light had a soft yellow glow, intended to illuminate the room but not overpower the instruments. It cast Sofia's features in a ghostly pallor. "It was filled with fifty-euro notes," she said.

Dimitri nodded. "The one I saw held twenties."

"How much do you think we are carrying?"

He had been pondering the same question. "If there is an equal number of bricks holding hundreds, maybe four or five million."

"And if there are also packages of five-hundred-euro notes?"

"Then a great deal more."

Her hand was unsteady as she sipped her tea. "Since the crisis, currency smugglers are getting life in prison."

"With this much in our hold, prison is the least of our worries." Dimitri pointed at the empty radar. "We don't know if these hunters are navy, or if they are, whose navy. Worse still, we don't know if they are honest. Or if they are, if they would stay honest."

Sofia stared down at the mug in her hands. "With what we're carrying . . ."

"They could shoot us, sink our boat, and be set for life."

"What if . . . ?" She peered at the screen. "Vessel approaching from the east. A big one."

He studied the screen. "Making twenty knots, wouldn't you say?"

She glanced at him, then back at the screen. "Maybe twenty-five."

Dimitri sighed with a mixture of relief and fear. "Go lower our nets."

Sofia squinted at him. "Dimitri, we aren't carrying . . . Oh."

Dimitri saw she understood, but said it anyway. "Attach our heaviest weights to our longest lines and string them aft from the winch. Hook them together."

"Right. Like we're dragging full nets. Will it work?"

He pushed the engines to their max, taking aim for the approaching craft. "Hurry."

Seven minutes later by the wheelhouse clock, at precisely twelve minutes past one in the morning, a pair of spotlights pierced the gloom with such power that Dimitri felt it as a physical impact. The wheelhouse windows were turned into blinding shields. Every drop of rain was etched with excruciating intensity. A crisp American voice rattled the radio speaker. "Unidentified fishing craft, this is container vessel *Indiana*. You have entered the international shipping lanes."

Dimitri thickened his accent and responded, "So very sorry. We turn about, yes?"

"Make it snappy."

Dimitri spun the wheel, steering back the other way, then overcorrected the turn. His jerky alterations of course caused the boat to wallow in the storm. He released the wheel long enough to walk over, slide open the door, and yell down to where Sofia stood frozen in the spotlights. "Look busy!"

She sprang into action. Dimitri moved back to the wheel and kept at his erratic turning. His vessel rocked violently, just as it would if it had changed course while hauling heavy nets.

Dimitri picked up the mike. "There you are, sir. Have a good night, yes?"

"*Indiana* signing off."

The spotlight stayed on him as the other vessel rumbled through the storm, an immensely tall behemoth of black steel. Now and then he shielded his eyes and watched Sofia pretend at the manic dance of a mate grinding in a netful of fish. Over the rushing wind, Dimitri heard her lilting voice through the open portal. Dimitri realized she was singing.

For the first time since the dinghies had appeared in the gloom, he thought they just might survive.

Then the container vessel was past and the spotlights went off, a jarring shift from blinding light to darkness again. Dimitri waited for another endless minute before shouting through the door, "Hold fast!"

Then he doused the lights, spun the wheel, and opened the throttles. The engines responded with a hungry growl, as though sharing his desperate excitement.

Sofia pounded up the rear stairs as he slipped into the container vessel's rear shadow. The vessel's twin propellers were each two stories tall, and the turbulence rocked them worse than the storm's swells. But the powerful propellers also created what was known as radar wash, a small patch of instrument blindness.

The question was, would the ship's night watch notice that the little fishing boat had suddenly vanished?

Dimitri thought not. As close as he was to their vessel, it was highly likely that the radar didn't catch them at all. Especially if the night crew had their equipment set for maximum range.

Sofia stepped into the wheelhouse, no longer singing. Her breaths sounded as tight as his own chest felt. He kept his distance at four boat lengths and steered as best he could against the tumult. The vessel they followed was a massive dark wall, dead ahead.

The night remained black, the radio silent.

21

An hour later, Sofia went back downstairs to make sandwiches and fresh cups of tea. They ate standing side by side in the wheelhouse, staring out at the darkness and the container ship's stern. The storm finally subsided as the wind swung to the west. Occasionally the horizon was lit by lightning off to the south, with the cloud banks flickering like giants at war. Sofia took the empty plates and cups downstairs and then returned to pull out the futon from its cupboard berth. "Who takes first watch?"

"I will. You rest."

"Two hours, and we shift." When Dimitri didn't respond, she pressed, "We're not out of this yet. You need to stay alert."

"Two hours," he agreed.

When he glanced down a few minutes later, she was already asleep. He turned back to the night and the ship they followed like a beacon. The wind blew directly from their stern. The engines ran smooth. He checked the fuel gauges. The boat's tanks dated from the era when diesel cost pennies for an imperial gallon. He could cruise another day and a half easy. The ship remained dark, silent. In deep-water shipping lanes, in the middle of an empty night, the container vessel's radar would be set for maximum range. At dawn, the skipper would either walk the full three-quarter mile circumference of the upper deck or assign the duty to a trusted officer. But this wouldn't happen for several more hours. And Dimitri intended to be long gone before the first hint of light glimmered in the east.

Up to the north, the island of Cyprus slipped by unseen. He unfurled the chart and traced their way in the gloomy wheelhouse light. The southern port of Larnaca was already behind them. They would pass the Akrotiri Peninsula, then turn north after Pafos. He was calculating time and distance when Sofia sighed and rose from the pallet. "You didn't wake me."

"It isn't time yet."

She squinted at the brass-rimmed clock before wordlessly leaving the wheelhouse. Five minutes later she returned with a fresh mug. "I have the wheel."

"Two hours, remember. No more." He took her place on the pallet. The coverlet was still warm from her slumber. There was a singular intimacy to this moment. Dimitri stared up at the young woman, his trusted friend since childhood. "I'm glad you are here, Sofia."

She glanced back at him, her features vulnerable in the near darkness. "I have been thinking the same thing. There is no one with whom I would rather face danger. Other than Manos, of course." She returned her attention to the waters ahead. "My two strong, brave men."

The night and the shared threat made him able to voice the hidden question. "Why do you stay with a husband who makes you weep?"

She took her time, drinking almost half her mug before replying. "You have it all wrong, Dimitri."

"I have seen you—"

"I am the one who let us down."

"Impossible."

She gave him another of those looks. The ones only women could make, where age mattered little, and their gaze held the quality of ancient wisdom. "I have been told I cannot have children. Manos, he lives to be a father. Even so, he claims it does not matter. I begged him to divorce me. He has made me promise never to speak of this again."

Dimitri studied her, the taut frame and the strength and the courage. He saw her face reflected in the dark glass. Sofia's entire body was caught in the effort to hold back her tears. "I am so very sorry."

She needed several moments before she could release the sigh. "Sleep. Dawn comes," she said quietly.

When the first crimson hint of morning crept upward, they slowed and slipped quietly from the ship's wake. Dimitri left the ill-defined boundary of the international shipping lanes and pushed north at the top end of the diesels' cruising speed. They ran through the day, hour after hour, a tiny fleck in the endless blue. They saw other huge cargo ships and even one naval vessel, but it remained far enough away that Dimitri didn't bother to wake Sofia. They traded watches throughout the day, both of them sleeping in the wheelhouse, waking to fix sandwiches and mugs of Sofia's blended tea. In the late afternoon, Dimitri fired the grill and cooked two steaks he cut from one of the tuna, along with the last of their fresh vegetables. They ate in companionable silence, the windshield pulled open so that they could enjoy the breeze.

As daylight faded, they slipped through the narrow straits between Kasos and Crete and entered the Aegean. They passed the tiny islands Dimitri knew as lifelong friends. In the light of the rising moon they entered the home waters of the Dodecanese.

Though October was a fairly quiet month for tourist traffic, there were still ferries and private yachts and fishing vessels. Yet none of these moved in their direction. As the setting sun gleamed off railings and windows, the radio became filled with the chatter of fishing boats preparing for the night hours. Dimitri explained to Sofia what he planned to do as they journeyed on, making good time toward Patmos.

Their home island was shaped like a question mark viewed through a mirror. The top portion curved to the right, and down at its lower edge the island had two bays that sliced considerable portions from either side. Between them was a narrow strip of land with high ridges. The island's main road ended in this tight neck. Below that was a mostly un-inhabited peninsula, connected to the rest of Patmos by the narrowest of links.

Later that night, the moon's gleam formed a silhouette around Mount Prasovouno, a lone peak crowning the center of Patmos's southern peninsula. In the distant past it had been an active volcano, but now it stood in silent splendor, a beacon to a tomorrow Dimitri had feared might not be theirs.

Several small islands rose up from the southern coast of Patmos, carved by eons of storm and wind into shapes that yawned and beckoned in the moonlight. They arrived exactly when Dimitri intended, precisely one hour off low tide. He checked the radar in every direction, then called to Sofia through the wheelhouse window, "Fire up the light."

She shone the bow light where he had directed. The island

147

up close looked forbidding, with impenetrable shadows and eerie carvings and high rock cliffs. Seabirds screamed at being disturbed, then went silent. Sofia looked up at him, her face a pale wash of questions. Dimitri became caught up in memories as he slowly powered forward. For his twelfth birthday his father had given him a dinghy with a sail and a two-horse outboard. Dimitri had hunted and fished and dived and grown up exploring these waters. And one day when he had been out on his own, he'd discovered this place.

He hadn't been back here in years, but it was just as he remembered. Now at low tide, what from the outside appeared to be simply another narrow crevice opened into a fissure wide enough to accept his boat. There was no reason for any vessel to enter, for the walls rose in tight ocher shadows, and the passage ended a hundred feet in. The cliffs loomed on either side, like a fist ready to tighten with the tide and smash any intruder to bits. But on a series of calm days, Dimitri had dived and swam and explored here, and he found that the bottom was fifty feet down at low tide. What was more, a cave opened at the back, just high enough for them to do what they did now. Which was to pluck the packages of cash from the hold, run them forward, and toss them into the cave.

Dimitri heaved the cash out of the hold, and when it was emptied he started running along the opposite gunnel from Sofia, both of them puffing hard from the labor. The boat was lashed to rocky outposts on either side of the cave's mouth, where the spotlight illuminated a forbidding place of rock and water. The diesels warned them to hurry, for already the tide had shifted and the waters began to rise. Soon the mouth would close, and the rocks would seal them in.

22

As soon as they docked in the Skala harbor, Dimitri phoned Duncan McAllister. He felt the exhaustion fill him to the point that the phone weighed a hundred pounds. He didn't want to talk to McAllister. But he also didn't want the man to hear about their return from some other source.

Duncan McAllister answered on the first ring. "Are you safe?"

"No thanks to you."

"What's that racket I hear?"

"My mate and the market workers are off-loading our catch."

"Tell me you're not ringing me from some highly public place."

"I'm alone in the wheelhouse, and I'll phone you from where I please."

"That's some tone you're using, after leaving my boyos dangling in the storm like you did."

"We're talking about the same crew who dumped the

149

contraband currency on my vessel at gunpoint? A cargo we did not discuss and I did not agree to haul?"

"It was an unavoidable necessity." Duncan's tone grew clipped. "Will you at least tell me that it's safe?"

"Do you have a pen?"

"Fire away."

Dimitri described the island and the cave. "You'll see the opening from straight on. The cave is above the high-tide mark, but even using the inflatables you can enter only on a lowering tide."

"It's all there?"

"One of the bricks broke open. I have it stuffed in my pack. You'll need to pick it up."

"We'll go for the delivery tonight. Now, about payment for your troubles—"

Dimitri cut the connection and then turned off his phone. There was too much boiling up inside—exhaustion and rage and the closeness of his demise. He needed to set it aside and talk with his father before deciding what his next move should be.

As he descended to the main deck, a crowd of locals offered him and Sofia their congratulations. The sight of their catch being off-loaded and weighed had attracted both fishermen and idlers enjoying the morning sun. A group of old friends ushered Dimitri and Sofia to the local taverna frequented by fishermen. Everyone could see how exhausted the two of them were, which was hardly a surprise, as they had brought back one of the largest hauls of that autumn.

There was a ritual to such moments, as old as the village itself. Such traditions framed much of island life, so ingrained that they were scarcely given any thought. Everyone in the taverna knew of Dimitri's troubles: his father's illness, the drop in tourism, the debts, the crisis. They now celebrated with him, their boisterous laughter tinged with the hope that their own great haul would arrive someday soon.

When the island's largest fishmonger delivered the tally and the payment, friends berated him for being a chiseler. The merchant responded with the ease of a man who had endured many such public rebukes. He smacked his lips over a glass of the rough island wine before handing Dimitri the check and departing. Dimitri laughed when his friends suggested it was time to celebrate, go to Rhodes or Mykonos in search of lonely autumn tourists. He endured the ribald jokes about how he might make a second, more beautiful haul.

But all the while he felt more isolated than he ever had in his life. Cut off from their laughter. Bereft of the life he had assumed would always be his. He was alone in the midst of people he had known all his life.

Sofia stood, saying she needed to check in with her husband. Dimitri rose with her, claiming a need to pay his respects to the island's police officer. Saying it with just the right amount of sardonic humor for the crowd to send them both off. Dimitri followed her from the laughing throng, and didn't speak until they were on the road leading from the harbor to the municipal center and the office of the police.

"What I said back there was true enough," Dimitri said. "I need to speak with Manos."

"And he will want to speak with you. Come."

He followed her through the door and into the suite of offices that served as the island's police station. The walls were whitewashed, the two desks in the front area very neat. An older woman who had been a friend of his mother's rose and greeted them. She paid no mind to their bedraggled state, as islanders were used to boats returning from weeks on the open seas. Sofia's hair was so caked with salt and grime, it stood almost straight out from her head. Their skin was chafed raw from the work and the sun, their eyes red-rimmed from exhaustion. They both shuffled past her and entered the narrow corridor.

Three offices opened to Dimitri's left, two to his right. At the end of the hall was a steel door, and beyond that were the island's four cells. Sofia knocked on the first door to her right and entered her husband's office.

Manos had a round face, utterly without angles. It gave him a deceptively weak appearance. This was heightened by a neatly trimmed mustache that reminded Dimitri of a black toothbrush. He thought Manos had the eyes of a fawn, big and globular and mournful. Many claimed he could be as hard as iron when the job called for it, known to elicit rapid confessions from those suspected of a crime. But Sofia insisted this was never due to brute force. Instead, criminals looked into those doleful eyes and knew here was a man already so disappointed with the world that nothing they had done could ever surprise him. The courts and the people might condemn the criminal, but not Manos.

Manos leaped to his feet and ran around his desk, sweeping his wife into an embrace so tight that Dimitri heard the breath expelling from her body. Sofia melted into him, closed her eyes, and sighed again.

Manos held her long enough for Dimitri to feel guilty over all his misguided impressions about their relationship. Finally, Manos let her go, led her to a chair, and asked, "What do you need?"

"Sleep. Days and days. And hot food."

"Why did you not go home and call me?"

"Because we need to tell you what happened."

Then a curious thing occurred. Manos stepped back, and in that single pace he underwent a transformation from concerned husband to hard-eyed cop. He glanced from one to the other. "Are you sure?" he asked.

Dimitri hesitated long enough for Manos to point at the ceiling, then to his ears, and shake his head. "I agree with Manos. We have survived a hard voyage. That is enough for now."

Manos nodded once. "Did anyone . . . ?"

Dimitri replied, "No one was injured."

"Good. Very good."

"I just wanted to tell you that Sofia is the best first mate I have ever known, and I am grateful that she was there."

Manos looked down at his wife, touched her cheek. "Let me walk you out, Dimitri. No, Sofia, stay where you are. I will bring the car around and drive you home."

They didn't speak again until outside in the sunlight. Manos walked him to the municipal parking lot and beeped off the police car's alarm. Dimitri struggled to fit his knees in around the radio and the computer. Manos shut the door and said, "We have no concrete evidence that our offices have been bugged, but since the crisis began, everyone has become paranoid."

"No doubt for good reason."

"Perhaps."

"Are we safe?"

"That depends. I am still an officer of the law."

Dimitri pushed away his doubts. He had gone over and over this through the long night. It was the best way forward. The only way. "I have evidence of a crime. Perhaps."

Manos understood him instantly. "We are not required to reveal the identities of confidential sources."

"In that case, I need to show you something." Dimitri

153

unzipped his pack and withdrew two of the twenties. "These have come into my possession. I think they may be counterfeit."

Manos slowly reached over, took the notes and held them to the light. "What makes you think this?"

"The way they were given to me was . . . suspicious."

"Are there more notes?"

"There are."

"You are certain of this?"

"I am."

"Counterfeiting euro notes is a very serious crime."

"I understand. How long do you need to determine whether they are real?"

"The proper method is to send them to the Treasury in Athens. But in urgent cases . . ."

"It is vital I have them back in a matter of hours."

Manos continued his inspection of the notes as he talked. He wet his finger and rubbed the inscription in one of the corners. "If you had not come to me with your concerns, I would never have thought these to be counterfeit. Can we replace them with two new genuine notes?"

"Absolutely not."

Manos didn't argue. "In that case, I can speak with a friend at the bank. She has been trained by the experts in Athens to detect fraudulent notes."

"You can trust her to remain silent?"

"We will have to report this."

"But—"

"It must be done, Dimitri. These people with whom I will speak, they are also experts at keeping secrets. And no one will hear how the notes came to be in my possession."

Dimitri knew he had no choice in the matter. Despite the surge of new fear, he was committed. "Very well."

But as he started to open his door, Manos halted him with a hand on his shoulder. "Dimitri."

He settled back in his seat and readied himself for all the accusations he knew he deserved.

Instead, Manos said, "Thank you for bringing Sofia home safely."

"I meant what I said inside. I would not have survived without her help."

The policeman offered Dimitri his hand. "Nonetheless, I am in your debt."

23

The ferry from Athens arrived at Kos three and a half hours late. Nick and Carey waited by the upper-deck railing until the stampede had diminished. What people thought they might gain being a few minutes sooner off the boat, especially with all the shoving and yelling required, Nick didn't have a clue. Beyond the perimeter and the crowd waiting to embark, Kos town gleamed in the midday sun.

Nick found the taverna just where Phyllis said it would be, beneath the shadow of the looming fortress. They selected a table in the sun because the wind off the water was brisk. They ordered two plates of scrambled eggs and toast with grilled tomatoes. When they asked for coffee, the waiter explained that island coffee came in two forms. They could have it either Turkish-style or instant. They both went for instant.

Nick studied Carey as they ate. She wore her hair tied in what he had always considered a dancer's ponytail, clenched up high where it might bounce and weave with every movement. Carey's hair looked streaked with purest gold in the morning light. Her eyes changed color as well, shifting from gray to deep emerald green when the light struck them full on. That surprised him, how he could know this woman his entire life yet only now notice how her eyes changed color.

She ate with the same gusto and joy she applied to almost everything. She hummed over the grilled tomatoes, which were drizzled with olive oil and sprinkled with fresh basil leaves. A passing waiter grinned and said, "Your first time here on Kos?"

"My first time anywhere."

"Is very beautiful, this time of year. Unless it storms. The crowds, they are gone. The island is ours again."

"What do you do when it storms?"

He turned his metal tray into a pillow. "We sleep and sleep."

She shared a laugh. "This is the loveliest place I have ever seen. It's like a dream."

The middle-aged waiter wasn't flirting, Nick decided, just enjoying Carey's beauty. The man asked, "You will try our island's honey?"

"I'd love that."

He walked to the indoor bar and swiftly returned with a small clay pot. "The owner's wife, she collects. The bees, they feast on sage and sorrel and lavender."

Carey uncorked the pot, dipped in her knife, and declared, "It's like tasting a meadow."

The waiter smiled his approval. "I hope our island is kind to you."

As Carey watched him walk away, Nick realized her chin was quivering. She turned back, laughing with embarrassment at her emotion. "That is just the most beautiful welcome I've ever heard."

Growing up, Nick had felt awkward around girls. His

first date, which took place a few days before his sixteenth birthday, was disastrous. The empty banter that formed the majority of dialogue between the sexes had baffled him. He either wanted to talk substance or be silent. He'd always liked things quiet, though that tended to freak girls out. Gradually he developed a pattern where he listened closely and figured out what was important to them. He made it seem important to him as well. He never talked about himself, because he figured most of what interested him would bore them to tears. Long-distance running, what was there to talk about with a girl? Or journalism? Big yawns. So he hid behind this manufactured interest, and over time it became a habit, a polished tool. Women found him witty and engaging and handsome in a rough-around-the-edges manner.

Sitting there with Carey, warmed by the Mediterranean sun, watching her absorb the scene with every cell of her body, he added a new description of his own.

Distant.

Carey felt his gaze, and asked, "What's on your mind, sport?"

His normal type of response was already formed. How she was right, the people here had a natural quality of . . . yada, yada. But the words faded unspoken, replaced by the truth.

Nick replied, "I envy you."

She cocked her head, causing the ponytail to shimmer in the light. "Come again?"

"You're already so intensely involved in this place. It defines you. You dive straight in, heart open, senses alive. You *engage.*"

Carey went very still. Her eyes grew almost impossibly large, yet she didn't speak.

"I'm a professional at holding the world at arm's length. I look at the buildings, and I describe them in my head. Trying to work out what I want to say in a single paragraph, the biggest bang in the fewest number of words. I see, sure, but it's only because I need the stuff for my next article. I *analyze*. You *absorb*. I'll walk away from this place, and in a couple of days it will be just one more point I covered on the chase for this story. But you . . ."

Carey said slowly, "I will carry this place and these memories for the rest of my life."

"Right." Nick hated how he had laid himself bare. But he was glad he had spoken. The conflicting emotions left his chest feeling raw. "I wish . . ."

He stopped because the man staring at them from across the road carried the hint of unseen shadows.

"What is it?"

"Head's up," Nick said, straightening in his chair. "Here comes trouble."

Carey watched the stranger move catlike toward their table. He introduced himself as Stefanos Khouris, a commander in the Greek navy. He sat down, seemingly at ease, but Carey sensed he remained coiled and ready to spring. His face was darkly tanned, and he wore a starched, pale blue shirt with epaulets, dark blue trousers, and black shoes polished to a professional shine. The waiter treated him with deference. Stefanos said, "I apologize for the delay. But we have been followed here."

Nick asked, "Who is it?"

"We are not certain. We think . . ." He waved it aside. "That is for later."

Carey asked, "Are they gone?"

He studied them both carefully, as though trying to come to a decision. "Phyllis Karras says I should trust you."

"She said the same to me," Nick replied. "It's why we traveled here."

"You understand, the idea of divulging the details of an ongoing investigation to outsiders, particularly foreigners, is highly irregular."

Nick nodded slowly. His tone matched the officer's, steady and low, but very much on full alert. "Your English is excellent."

"I have spent a year in the United States, studying at your Coast Guard Academy."

"I would imagine that such an opportunity is only given to officers who are expected to rise very far."

"You are correct."

"What branch of the navy are you assigned to?"

"Intelligence."

"Is that common knowledge?"

"It is not."

Carey had the distinct impression that the two men had entered into some form of unspoken communication, one she wasn't following. She said, "You didn't answer my question. Are the people who were tracking you gone?"

Stefanos continued to meet Nick's gaze.

Nick said, "They're here."

"I don't get it." She looked from one man to the other. "Then why are we meeting out in the open?"

"Because," Nick replied for the other man, "Stefanos is using us as bait."

She gave the navy officer a chance to object. Instead, Stefanos said, "Where had you intended to go before Phyllis told you about this meeting?"

"Bodrum."

"Interesting." Stefanos paused as the waiter deposited his

tea glass. When he departed, Stefanos asked, "Will you tell me why?"

"Phyllis said I should trust you," Nick said again. "I'll tell you everything."

Carey felt excluded, an observer without importance. "I'd like some answers here."

Nick didn't look away from the officer. "Stefanos had to check with his allies before meeting with us."

"You mean because it might put us at risk?"

Nick shook his head. "Because they had to decide whether to tell us anything at all. Including that they were going to use us."

Stefanos showed Nick a tight flicker of a smile.

"That doesn't bother you the least teensy-weensy bit?" Carey asked.

"His job is to keep us safe," Nick said. "And I have the impression that Stefanos is very good at his job."

Stefanos added sugar to his glass and stirred. "So tell me what you have learned."

Nick said, "Can I ask you one question first?"

Stefanos hesitated a long moment, and his tight gun-barrel gaze shifted her way. "Ask."

"Do your superiors know what you are doing?"

"That is a very interesting question."

Nick waited.

"The answer is, some do."

"And others don't," Nick added. "Which means your investigation is off the books. Which is why Phyllis is involved. You trust her, and she trusts you, and neither of you fully trusts your superiors. Which means you need allies. Which is why we're meeting here. On an island as far from Athens as you can get and still be in Greece."

"There are other reasons for this location," Stefanos said. "But you are correct."

Carey felt her irritation fade. "You're asking what we know because your associates still haven't decided whether to include us."

"Precisely."

Nick launched in. He started with his preliminary meeting in Paris and continued straight through. The discussion with Eleni's family, Carey's discovery of the Institute closing, the confrontation with the director, their trip here. Stefanos finished his tea and sat toying with his spoon. When Nick was done, Stefanos stood, pulled out his phone, and said, "Please wait here."

After he walked away, Carey asked, "Why are you smiling?"

"Stefanos could have refused to work with us all by himself," Nick replied. "Calling this in means he wants to include us."

"You think this is important?"

Nick's gaze sparked with an almost feverish light. "I think it's solid gold."

24

But Stefanos didn't return for almost an hour, and when he did, it was to apologize. There were issues, he said. Nick noted the grim cast to the naval officer's features and thought it a good sign. He could see Carey was worried, but that would have to wait. When Stefanos asked if they could stay over in Kos, Nick instantly replied, "No problem."

Carey had the good sense to wait until Stefanos had departed before asking, "What happened to our rush?"

Nick, so accustomed to working unaccompanied, found it difficult to articulate his hunch. "Stefanos has people who don't want to let us in. But I'm pretty sure he has come down on our side."

"So whatever happens . . ."

"We have a new ally. Maybe."

"What do we do now?"

They found two rooms on the same floor in a harbor-front hotel and spent the day exploring. It was the first truly free time Nick had known in five months. Before, any idle hours had been spent desperately seeking work, chasing leads, making pitches, combing the local papers for some hint of a story he might pursue further. Nick felt guilty, the pleasure was so intense. He was on a Greek island with a beautiful woman, and nothing to do for an entire afternoon except to have themselves a nice time.

Which they did. Carey proved to be an ideal companion. She was excited about everything, chattering on in the disjointed manner of a child, alternating between explaining the region's history and exclaiming over flowers, birds, even clouds.

Kos was often twinned with neighboring Rhodes, with legends stretching back to Homer's *Iliad* and the Trojan War. There were reminders of ancient Greek civilization everywhere Nick looked. The most remarkable was the Fortress of the Knights of Saint John, which occupied its own small peninsula and dominated the harbor. They strolled the palm-lined avenue running along the massive outer wall, bought ices from a toothless vendor outside the main gates, then walked to the park where Hippocrates had lectured to his students in the fifth century BC. From there they explored the *agora*, ruins of the original market dating back twenty-five centuries. Then it was up a very steep road to the village of Platani and on to Asklepion, the oldest medical center in the world. By the time they returned to the harbor by taxi, Nick was exhausted.

Carey watched him slump into a chair at their hotel's café, and cried, "But we've hardly even gotten started!"

"Speak for yourself." Nick thought her dismay was genuinely charming. "Nobody's stopping you."

She protested, "It's not as much fun by myself."

"Do you know this much about every island?"

"Don't be silly. Only the important ones. You're really not coming?"

"Not a chance, unless it involves food." He glanced at his watch. "It's past five."

"Is it really?" She looked around her. "How could such a beautiful day leave me before I'm ready?"

Nick was about to tell her how cute that sounded and how lovely she looked, with the afternoon sun forming a glow about her, the boats rocking at their moorings, the gulls calling their discordant farewell, the waning day, the faint hint of lemon blossoms and jasmine on the wind. But something stopped him from framing the words, a tug against his heart, as though to speak what he felt would mean crossing some unseen line.

When he didn't respond, Carey sighed, as if defeated by the hour. "Actually, I'm kind of worn out myself. And starving."

"So let's go eat."

"Great. But first I have to clean up."

"Meet you back here in twenty minutes."

She was there before him, clean-scrubbed and dressed in a wraparound skirt and a blouse tied at her waist, exposing a hand's breadth of tanned skin. It was a retro look, especially with her cork-soled sandals, and suited Carey perfectly. She was strong and independent and remarkably confident, despite the recent setbacks. But she was also by nature a true Texan, holding fast to family and morals and church and everything timeless.

They meandered around the harbor, laughing over every little discovery, chatting with the fishermen as they laid out their nets. At a café owner's suggestion, they selected from the day's catch and sat at a candle-lit table while the fish was grilled. Nick found it the easiest thing in the world to confess, "You challenge me in a lot of unexpected ways."

"How do you mean?"

"One of the earliest lessons I learned as a journalist was never to take sides. An investigative journalist needs to be open to wherever the story takes him, even when it's not the expected direction. *Especially* then. To do this, I have to remain objective. Keep the world at arm's length. Never get so deeply involved that I lose the ability to . . ."

He stopped because Carey had returned to the wide-eyed solemnity that she'd shown him earlier. Nick asked, "What's the matter?"

"Nothing, Nick. Finish your thought."

But her response left him fumbling. "All I was going to say was, you're the exact opposite. You throw yourself into everything. It's incredible to watch how involved you get. You're excited, you're passionate, you *live*. That really impresses me."

"Thank you, Nick." Her voice was low, almost a whisper.

An old woman walked from table to table, offering long-stemmed roses to the diners. On a whim, Nick bought one. He was still fashioning what he wanted to say when Carey whispered, "Please don't."

"Excuse me?"

"I've spent two long years feeling like a part of myself will never be filled up again." Her gaze had gone as dark and deep as the night sky. "Please don't be so . . ."

Nick waited. When she didn't finish the thought, he said, "I thought we were friends."

"Yes, and that's all you want, isn't it?"

The night's spell continued to whisper to him on the fragrant breeze. "My mind says yes, absolutely. But my heart . . ."

"Isn't that just like a man."

The words, though spoken softly, pushed him back in his chair. "I'm trying to be honest."

"And that should allow you to play the romantic card when you never intend to follow through? Because that's what's happening here, isn't it? You're moving from friendship to romance."

"I feel drawn to you."

Her voice went flat. "But not enough to commit."

"We're only getting to know each other—"

"Stop. Just stop. Is it really about time? So we spend more days together, and then you'll be ready to . . . what? What will you do, Nick? After I've fallen in love, after I've forced myself to trust you. After I've convinced myself you won't break my heart. Will you commit? Love me back? Plan a life together? Dream together?"

Nick was silent.

"My life isn't great. I'm all hollow where I should have a heart. But it *is* a life and I *am* healing. One thing I do know for certain, though."

He forced himself to ask, "What is that, Carey?"

"It would be very easy to love you. So don't go there. Okay?"

Nick found himself unable to respond.

"Be strong for us both. That's very important. We'll work together, and then you'll go back to Paris. And we will always be . . ."

He knew she expected him to finish the thought for them both. So he made himself say it, though it felt like he was sentencing himself for a crime he had almost committed. "Friends."

"Right. Exactly." She glanced over his shoulder. "And here comes our food."

They dined in silence. When they finished and started back, the rose was still there on the table.

25

As soon as he arrived home, Dimitri greeted his father, then went inside. His father had been at sea often enough to know that now wasn't the time for questions. As he showered, Dimitri recalled when his father had climbed the road after days and nights fishing and taking the next step seemed to hurt. Adoni had moved with an old man's slow smoothness, every joint aching. He'd winced as his wife embraced him and welcomed him home, sighed into the chair in the sunlight, and often fallen asleep in the middle of a sentence. Dimitri hadn't thought of those early days in years.

He ate a cold meal standing by the kitchen window. His father assured him he was fine and that Chara had come by several times each day and seen to his needs. Dimitri slipped into bed and felt the aches rise up in a tidal rush, so intense he feared he wouldn't be able to sleep.

The next thing he knew, his grandmother was shaking his shoulder. "I would not disturb you, but Manos says it is important."

Dimitri rose to a seated position and accepted the phone. But when he tried to speak, his voice refused to function. He coughed, then accepted the steaming glass of tea, sipped, and finally managed, "Yes, Manos."

"You will no doubt need to deposit your check for the fish this morning."

He sipped again, hearing the unspoken warning in the policeman's formal tone. "Indeed."

"There is a café across the street from your bank. I will meet you there in an hour."

Dimitri showered once more, feeling every abrasion beneath the stream of hot water. By the time he emerged, his grandmother had cooked up half a dozen eggs and served them with a loaf of fresh-baked bread. His father watched him from the chair by the window. Chara stood as she so often did in her own kitchen, leaning against the stove, her arms clasped about her middle. Both of them listened intently as Dimitri described the recent events, speaking between bites, finishing the eggs and wiping his plate with another slice of bread. Neither of them responded until he was done, and then his father said, "You are safe. That is what matters most."

Dimitri swallowed his rejoinder with the last gulp of tea. What he thought was that he might never be safe again. Still, there was nothing to be gained from such comments. He would let them digest the news, then ask their advice once he had spoken with Manos.

Dimitri descended the street from his home, still burdened by weariness. The strain and the exhaustion was not erased by one long sleep. He passed a crone who had been widowed since before he was born. He greeted her respectfully, and the woman responded as she had since his childhood, a soft murmur that carried the weight of empty years. Abruptly he saw himself and the risk of arriving at an end that was as lonely as hers.

The town of Skala was too small to support a true business district. Instead, a three-block area extended from the municipal building that contained the nicest shops, a private clinic for doctors and dentists, and two office buildings fronting a small plaza. Dimitri entered the café opposite the island's largest bank and a whitewashed church. He greeted the waiter, a young man with whom he had grown up. Unlike so many others of their generation, this one had remained in Skala because he had fallen in love with a woman who refused to depart. She worked behind the counter now, and called a good morning through the open doorway. Dimitri replied automatically and sat down at a patio table.

He sipped a coffee and closed his eyes to the sunlight. He tried to tell himself it was just a release of the strain that left him feeling so empty. But he knew there was more to it. He felt anew the wash of terror, the sensation of his life being utterly out of his control. The helplessness left him so weak he had to struggle to draw breath.

"Dimitri? Is that truly you?"

He jerked slightly. The woman was silhouetted by the sunlight, so that he couldn't see her face. Only that she stood holding the handle of a stroller. "Forgive me, I was—"

"I'm the one who should apologize. You look exhausted. Did I awaken you?"

"Not really. I was . . . I've been out fishing the deep waters."

She shifted in a way that the sun struck her lovely features full on. Her smile was genuine, her eyes full of concern. "I thought you gave that up."

"I did. The economy . . ." He recognized her now, yet her name escaped him.

"I understand. How could I not? We left because Henoch had the offer, you remember?"

"Of course. You moved to Chicago." He rubbed his face, trying to dredge up her name. Henoch had been one of his closest childhood friends. His family had often fished with his father and uncle. Dimitri had danced at their wedding. Still her name stubbornly refused to surface. He rose to his feet. "Please, won't you join me?"

"Well, perhaps for a moment." She paused long enough to embrace the café owner and his wife, then pulled the stroller over and seated herself with a smile. After a brief look inside the stroller, she said, "It's been a long time."

"Too long," he agreed. The slant of her eyes, the full lips, and the subtly feminine intelligence all came together in a sudden flash of recollection. They had a brief romance before she fell for his friend. And then her name arrived. "Gaia."

She had a lovely chuckle, warm and easy. "I thought you might have forgotten."

He considered the standard response. *Never. How could I possibly forget you?* But he didn't have the energy for a lie. "You look lovely. And happy."

"Life is good. Chicago is not an easy city. The winters are a trial. But Henoch loves his work, and we have our little one. Who is here to meet her grandparents for the very first time."

Dimitri watched her lift the infant from the stroller. The café owners came back out and took turns fussing over the baby, who smiled in delight at the attention. Dimitri knew they considered him part of the happy moment. He was one of them. But the hollowness at the core of his being grew so large that it threatened to consume him completely.

Here before him was the truth of his existence. The easy flaming passion, the tears at his departure. The next woman always waiting and beckoning for a night, a week, a month at the most. And then there was the boat and the friends and the songs and all the adventures a young life could hold.

Only he was not singing now.

The alternative was there in the laughter and the infant and the lives of his erstwhile friends. They had built for themselves a haven against such empty moments. They rested in a circle of love and permanence and hope and the strength of lifelong companions.

And he was exactly who he had always wanted to be. The prince of idle hours and available women.

"Sorry I'm late." Manos slipped into the chair the young woman had just vacated. "Was that Gaia I saw? I thought she and Henoch had moved—"

"To Chicago, yes. She's only visiting."

"She looks good." Manos eyed him with a cop's keen ability to peel away the exterior layers. "Any regrets over letting that one get away?"

Dimitri shrugged and changed the subject. "Do you have any word about what I gave you?"

"Not here." Manos sprang to his feet. "If you're done, let's walk."

They moved away from the café and headed toward the municipal building. Midway there, Manos paused by a fruit vendor and began inspecting apples. "Your notes are counterfeit."

Dimitri felt the sunlight take on an immense weight. "You're sure?"

"There is no question. The finest quality fakes anyone has seen. They need to know where the notes came from."

"It will not get back to me?"

"Why do you think we are having this conversation out here?"

"The pickup was made off the Karpas Peninsula."

Manos frowned. "I don't—"

"North Cyprus."

The island's police chief pointed to the pears, showed four fingers, and said, "Tell me exactly what happened."

Dimitri related how the dinghies had arrived late, the offloading, the guns. The unexpected demand for them to carry back the cash. As he recounted the event, the dread he had known uncoiled in his gut. "You have to believe me. We had no idea any of this was going to happen. I agreed to take a shipment to North Cyprus. Nothing more."

"I believe you. And Sofia's story meshes precisely with yours." He paid for the fruit. "Your idea of shadowing the container vessel probably saved your lives."

"What do I do now?"

"Here, take a pear." Manos handed over the two twenty-euro notes with the fruit. "I will pass on this information. We will wait to hear from Athens."

"They can't ever know—"

"I promise you, no names. Not unless you give me permission."

"That will not happen, I assure you. I am quite fond of life."

"Well, sometimes things change." Manos patted Dimitri's shoulder. "Get some rest."

Dimitri crossed the main avenue and entered the bank his family had used for over a century. So much of his life was like this, tied up in tradition and the past. As he waited in line for a teller, he found his mind flickering over items that defined his days. Such as the way the island elders clucked their tongues over his good looks and easy smile, shaking their heads over the hearts he broke. As though this was who he was, this was his nature, and it would always be that way.

The assistant manager rose from her desk and came over to greet him. It was something that had happened often enough in the past, but then had stopped as Dimitri began racking up debt all over the island. Now she chatted agreeably as he deposited the fishmonger's check, letting him know that the balance had been restored. If only.

The burden he carried grew far heavier when his home came into view, for standing on the patio was Duncan McAllister.

26

The next morning, Carey pretended to sleep in. She felt very uneasy about what she had said to Nick over dinner. She knew Nick and his caring eyes and his warm voice were only part of the problem. Seeing him there, listening to him speak words she had once dreamed of hearing, had brought back the hollow void. Carey had no idea if she would ever be able to love another man. Even so, she needed to apologize to Nick.

She greeted the waiter and settled into a chair at one of the outdoor tables. The rose was such a sweet gesture. She knew most of her friends would tell her to enjoy the moment. She was in Greece. She should have an island fling. But her heart told her that she longed for something today's culture did not value, like lifelong commitment and . . .

"Do you mind if I join you?"

Carey was startled from her reverie. "How long have you been standing there?"

"Not long." Nick pointed to the chair. "May I?"

"Nick, of course, you don't have to ask." She smiled as the waiter deposited her coffee and breakfast, or tried to. "Do you want anything?"

"I've already eaten." He looked subdued. "I spent a lot of last night thinking about what you said. You were right. Every bit of it. Feeling drawn to you is no excuse for telling us both lies."

Carey felt caught in a beam of condensed sunlight. It was hard for her to breathe.

"How good an investigative journalist can I be if I try to tell myself things I know aren't true?"

"This is different," she said.

"You don't know that."

"Oh, don't I? Nick, I look back now at my college romance and I wonder if I hadn't known all along that one day he would walk away and leave me brokenhearted."

"I could shoot that guy for what he did to you."

"Thank you, Nick. But he isn't worth the bullet. Truly. I can see now that he gave me hints our love was one-sided. Only I didn't *want* to see that. So, yes, I know all about being willfully blind."

His gaze was entwined with the morning sun and the previous night's shadows. "So we're friends?"

She wondered if her smile looked as lopsided as she felt. Because along with her relief over being back in harmony with Nick, there was also a very real regret. She tried to tell herself it was for the best, knowing now and not after futile months of loving another wrong man. But no matter how much she argued with herself, she couldn't help but wish that Nick would change, become the man she yearned for. The love for all her days.

"Carey?"

She nodded her head, casting aside the impossible yearnings. "Yes, Nick. We're friends. For always."

Dimitri's grandmother appeared from the kitchen bearing two glasses of tea. "The gentleman arrived ten minutes ago."

Dimitri made the introductions because his grandmother expected it. Chara showed Duncan McAllister the blank mask of an island woman, polite and stony at the same time. "Shall I serve a meal?"

"He will not be staying that long," Dimitri replied in Greek. He then addressed Duncan in English, "Please have a seat."

Duncan settled into the chair like a king taking his throne, smiling his approval at the sunlit hillside and the harbor below. "Isn't this a grand place for sitting and reflecting."

"Why are you here?"

"I thought it best to offer my apologies in person." Duncan sipped from the tulip glass. "Does your family understand English?"

"My father, a few words. My grandmother, none at all. Speak your mind."

"Things fell apart on my end. That's as simple as I know to put it. We had ourselves a right mess, and my lads didn't know what to do but foist their problem on you."

"At gunpoint," Dimitri added.

"Aye, well, they had grown a bit testy, having spent much of the night avoiding arrest." He stretched out his long legs. His ginger hair showed gray, but his limbs remained taut, and his voice carried both energy and determination. "If it wasn't for the storm that swept in after the transfer, they'd be locked up sure enough."

"So they made it back okay?"

"They did, yes, although one of them in particular would like to have words with you. He lost his gun when you tossed him over the side. Brought that back from Basra, he did."

Dimitri did not respond.

"I told him you did exactly what I would have done," Mc-Allister went on. "Using whatever was available to shield myself and my cargo. It took a while for him to come round to my way of seeing things. But peace has been restored."

Dimitri remained silent.

"Yes. Well. At least from my end. Which brings us to the matter at hand." He extracted a thick envelope from his pocket. "A bit more of the ready. For your troubles." When Dimitri didn't reach out, he added, "These funds are both legit and untraceable."

Dimitri finally took the envelope and slipped it into his pocket. "You didn't come up here to apologize."

"I did, as it happens. But you're right, lad, there's more besides. Two things. First, we need that missing packet."

"Of twenties. I told you it broke open. I gathered the bills in my backpack."

"All of them?"

Dimitri shrugged. "As many as I could find. And the other thing?"

"I need you to head for—"

"No more runs. I'm being watched." Dimitri told him about his boat being boarded by the naval officer and the questions about his visits to Duncan's boat.

McAllister frowned over the news. "Did you happen to get the officer's name?"

"Stefanos something or other. A commander."

"I'll see what I can find out. That brings us to the other matter." He leaned in closer. "Being observed comes with the territory. I need to know how much they know. And who's working against us."

"I just told you, there's no 'us.'"

"That's where you're wrong. You accept the piper's coin, you dance to his tune. There's a pair of Yanks asking questions. I need you to meet up with them, see what they're after. It'd help to learn whether or not they're working with this Stefanos fellow." He stood and drained his glass. "Now, go get the packet that broke open. And then ready your vessel. Your targets are on Kos—two Yanks, like I said. The lad's name is Nick Hennessy, a freelance journalist based in Paris. Don't have much on the lady yet, except that she sounds to be quite the looker. You need to be on your way."

27

Carey and Nick loitered around their harbor-front hotel until the naval officer contacted them at midmorning. But all Stefanos could tell them was that he needed another day. Carey joined Nick in assuring the commander it was all good, and they could wait, while mentally she was making plans for their day off.

They toured the Roman amphitheater and the Casa Romana, a restored Roman villa containing exquisite murals and mosaics over two thousand years old. Then Nick declared he wanted to go play. Carey resisted the urge to point out that the Kos Museum was full of ancient treasures, some dating back to Phoenician times. Instead, she watched as he rented a pair of bikes and went over directions twice with the store owner. They cycled north through Kos town, then took the bike path that skirted the seafront cliffs.

The wind off the sea was brisk, and Carey thought she could smell rain. But the sky remained clear, and the frothy sea was a brilliant, shimmering blue. An hour later, they arrived at Tingaki's Blue Flag Beach. They ate a meal of grilled sea bass and a salad of wild greens at a waterfront shack. They breathed the air and smiled a great deal and were comfortable with the silence of longtime friends. When clouds started gathering to the east, they cycled back and managed to arrive at their hotel before the storm struck. Carey pleaded fatigue and bid Nick an early good-night. Upstairs, she showered and tucked herself in bed with a book, warm and snug while outside the wind howled. She cut off the light and lay listening to the rain hammer her balcony doors, telling herself she was being foolish, indulging in childhood yearnings. After all, Nick had agreed to give her exactly what she had asked for. She had a job. She had a friend. She had every reason in the world to be happy.

The next morning she was downstairs at sunrise and had finished breakfast when Nick arrived. He ordered coffee from the passing waiter and slowly lowered himself into the chair opposite her. He blew out a breath before telling her, "Stefanos called. He's coming over."

"Great. What's the matter with you?"

"I haven't been on a bike in years."

She grinned. "You're moving like an old cowboy after a bad night."

"Which is exactly how I feel. How about you?"

"I'm just an overgrown college girl, remember? I cycle everywhere. Austin is made for bikes."

He thanked the waiter and used both hands to cradle his coffee. Sip and sigh. Sip and sigh. "Not to mention how you walked me off my feet the day before."

"You don't get much exercise in Paris?"

"I gave up my gym membership. Couldn't afford it. I jog.

Some. Obviously not enough." He set down his cup. "Here he comes."

The commander stepped up to their table, dressed in navy slacks and matching sweater. He was perhaps an inch shorter than Carey, maybe five-nine, slender and very fit. His face didn't appear tanned so much as permanently browned. Carey wondered if he ever smiled.

He spoke with the waiter in Greek, then said, "I apologize for the delay."

"Not a problem," Carey said.

"Nobody would call this a hardship post," Nick agreed.

"There are others involved. There has been much discussion. There would be more, but the situation has been taken out of our hands."

"There's trouble?" Nick asked.

"There is . . . confusion."

"I don't understand."

"No. And we feel the same. We have all been looking in one direction, and now . . ."

"How can we help?" Nick asked.

"Yes, that is the question. And finally I have been granted permission for us to see if you can indeed help us." Stefanos lifted his sweater and pulled an envelope from his shirt pocket. "First, I must explain to you something. We are not working on an official investigation."

Carey commented, "You suspect some of your superiors are involved in the cover-up."

He had the most intense gaze she had ever known. Two unblinking gun barrels, dark and fathomless. "No, Ms. Mathers. We *know* some are involved, just not which ones."

"So this is off the books," Nick said.

"We are a group of allies. We know and trust one another.

182

Phyllis Karras has urged us to include you in this group. Others are uncertain. You are unknown. You are not Greek. You are not this. You are not that." He balanced his hand over the table to show the uncertainty. "Many are afraid for their jobs, their families, their lives. The fear, it makes progress difficult. So for days we have argued."

"Tell us what we can do," Nick urged.

In response, Stefanos opened the envelope and pulled out two photographs. He set them on the table. "Have you seen either of these two men?"

Nick inspected them carefully, then passed them to Carey. "No. Should I have?"

"Probably not. The older gentleman is Duncan McAllister. He is part of an international security consortium. He was an investigator with Scotland Yard. Now he supervises teams doing work in this region."

"What kind of work?"

"Officially, protective services for the very rich."

"And unofficially?"

"We would very much like to know the answer to that question." He pointed to the second photograph, the one Carey continued to study. "This is Dimitri Rubinos. He skippers a vessel out of Patmos. His family has fished these waters for generations. Dimitri retooled the family boat and now does tourist charters. Or he did until the financial crisis dried up that business."

"And now?"

"Again, we very much want to know. Dimitri has been seen meeting with McAllister. Soon after, he had the cash to pay off his debts."

"In the middle of the worst economic crisis Greece has known since the Depression," Nick finished.

"Just so. We know they have met twice. Then Dimitri became a fisherman again and has just returned from a very successful voyage."

Nick waited. When Stefanos didn't continue, he pressed, "Where did Dimitri fish?"

"At first, he held to the deep waters south of the Dodecanese. Then he vanished."

"You were watching him?"

"I told you. This is not an official investigation. I boarded his vessel and performed a standard search. Supposedly I was looking for out-of-season fish. I saw nothing out of the ordinary."

Carey asked, "Could he have received an advance against his catch?"

Stefanos rocked back and forth as though approving of their comments. "Most certainly that is possible. Except for one thing. When Dimitri returned, he went straight to the police chief of Patmos. The chief's name is Manos. His wife, Sofia, is Dimitri's first mate."

Carey asked, "Why are you telling us this?"

"Because two hours later, the police chief of Patmos entered the island's main bank and showed the president two counterfeit twenty-euro notes. Their exceptional quality has raised alarms all the way to Brussels."

"You think Dimitri obtained these notes from Duncan McAllister," Nick said.

"We have not been able to ask him. Both because we are not officially part of any counterfeit investigation and because the police chief refuses to tell us where the notes came from. He says this was part of being trusted with them in the first place."

"So Dimitri goes to a trusted friend with what he assumes

is bogus money," Carey said. "Which means he's both suspicious and trying to protect someone."

The rocking continued. "You understand, if this is the case it would be critical for us to learn whether these are simply a pair of false notes from a small batch . . . or something much larger."

Carey asked, "The money Dimitri used to pay his debts, this was counterfeit also?"

Again Stefanos showed tight approval. "This has been discreetly checked, and the answer is no. The money Dimitri Rubinos distributed about the island to clear his debts was genuine."

"What do you need from us?" Nick asked.

"We need you to approach Dimitri."

"Gladly. How do we get to Patmos?"

"You don't. You need to walk down to the boat moored at the harbor's far end."

Carey's eyes went wide. "The guy is here?"

"He arrived this morning."

Nick started to turn around, then stopped himself. "Why is he here?"

"That," Stefanos replied, "is the first question we would like you to ask him."

28

The Kos harbor was a broad affair with a right-hand bend that joined the small peninsula holding the fortress. Farther down the ancient stone quayside, modern slips had been built to hold the yachts and sailing vessels of the rich. Newer condominiums had been erected a block or so off the water. Carey had the impression of eyes following their progress down the cobblestone street. But when she looked around, all she saw were blank windows and nondescript modern construction.

The boat they sought was moored stern-in beyond the yachts. Like most of the fishing vessels it had for neighbors, the vessel was old but made cheerful by a bright new paint job and a blue canvas shade drawn partway over her rear deck. The tentlike covering was anchored by metal stanchions, outlined with pastel triangles fluttering in the morning breeze. A sign was stationed by the gangplank, reading in Greek and German and English, *Boat for hire, guided tours of the Dodecanese Islands and Turkish coast.*

Carey's first impression of the skipper was, a tanned cat. He lounged in a salt-stained canvas deck chair, clad in a sleeveless sweatshirt and cutoffs and deck shoes. His face was turned to the sun, with his back to the quay. Even so, Carey was fairly certain he was aware of their approach. She thought this man was probably aware of everything around him.

He was also, she decided, even more handsome than his photograph.

Nick called, "Are you free for a hire?"

The man turned slowly. "Not only that, I am bored. Which means you can have me cheap."

Carey thought his accent could only be described as delightful.

The city of Bodrum was soon visible across the narrow Skandari straits. Carey stood to Dimitri's left in the wheelhouse, Nick at his right. Dimitri was in his late twenties or early thirties, and at around six feet was taller than most of the Greek men she'd seen. He was broad-shouldered and slim-waisted, with strong hands and a face that defined masculine beauty. But it was his eyes that captivated most of all. Dimitri Rubinos had eyes of smoke—slate gray laced with gold flecks. Combined with a cleft chin and high cheekbones, he wasn't merely handsome. He was arresting.

Twenty minutes after leaving Kos harbor, they passed the tall Turkish headlands and wound their way between two islands that Dimitri identified as Beldisi and Kara. Carey thought the man's manner was rather offhand, almost as if he were not there with them, his mind somewhere else. As they entered the Turkish harbor, Dimitri politely asked them to go down and be ready to tie up. As they descended the stairs, Carey whispered, "What do you make of him?"

"The guy seems disengaged," Nick replied.

"Like he couldn't care less," Carey agreed. "Maybe Stefanos has identified the wrong man."

Nick glanced back up at the wheelhouse. "It won't be the first time I've chased a false lead. But somehow I thought . . ."

He didn't finish the sentence. Dimitri reversed the engines, and the vessel nudged the harbor wall. He called through the open wheelhouse door, "Make us fast."

They did so, told their skipper they'd be back in an hour, and then walked in companionable silence into the bustling tourist village. Remnants of the sleepy fishing port were visible here and there, but Bodrum had grown up into a town full of glitz and glamour. Fashionable people filled posh-looking cafés and restaurants. The roads were jammed with expensive cars. Many high-rise condos and hotels had security personnel posted out front, wearing jackets and ties and earpieces. This was altogether a different place from the quiet island they had left behind.

Nick stopped twice to ask directions, but when they arrived at the antiques business that Carey's would-be boss, Adriana Stephanopoulos, had mentioned, they found it closed. Steel shutters concealed both show windows, and several bits of mail had been threaded through the bars covering the entrance. Nick pounded on the shutter, then cupped his hands and peered through the door's dirty glass. He stepped back. "We're all done here."

The stores on either side offered no useful information about the shop or its owner. They asked directions and were pointed to the police station, where a bored officer shrugged at Nick's questions, then replied in heavily accented English, "The store owner breaks no law taking a day off."

"He hasn't been there for a lot longer than that."

"Day, week, is same law." He flicked his fingers as if he were shooing away flies. "Go find different store. Are many in Bodrum."

Nick maintained a thoughtful silence as they threaded their way back to the port. Soon the boat came into view, and Nick asked, "Do you want to hang around here?"

"Not a minute longer than necessary," Carey replied.

"Great. Let's go."

But as they crossed the gangplank and Dimitri rose from his deck chair to greet them, Carey said, "Do you think we could make another stop?"

Nick replied, "Where did you have in mind?"

"Ephesus. I know it's probably too far, but—"

"It's four hours by boat," Dimitri put in. "We can do this, but you will be returning after dark."

"Is that all right?"

Dimitri smiled for the first time. "Can you pay?"

Nick looked at her and shrugged. "Sure thing."

"Then the beautiful lady gets whatever she wants." Dimitri clapped his hands. "Cast us off."

Dimitri continued to play the experienced guide throughout the voyage. But that was all. He gave no indication that he cared who they were or why they were in Greece. They were simply his guests, and his job was to ensure they had a good time. He pointed out the various islands as they passed, yet he did so with the flat tone of a man going through the motions.

Twice, Nick asked leading questions, but Dimitri deflected them with professional ease. Carey imagined it was a routine he used a lot, and mostly with women, for he was one of the most handsome men she had ever met. Whenever he glanced her way, Carey returned to the same thought. Her

189

grandmother would say that this man had been born with moonshine eyes.

Carey studied the brilliant blue waters and recalled the first time she'd heard that expression. For her fifteenth birthday the family had traveled to the annual Fort Worth rodeo. She and her grandmother had been strolling down the carnival's main drag when a cowhand in a black silk shirt with mother-of-pearl buttons and the silver buckle of a rodeo winner had sparked her night with a smile and an invitation to dance. But her grandmother had leaned in close. "That boy's got moonshine eyes, Carey. Tell him your answer is no."

So Carey had reluctantly declined, then asked what Nana Pat had meant.

"Moonshine eyes is when you look at a boy and all you can see is the promise of what you don't know," Nana Pat said, using a voice that Carey hadn't heard before. Like her grandmother had suddenly shed fifty years and was looking back around the bend of time to some recollection only she could see. "The crazy electricity sets your heart to racing. You think one kiss and you might just grow wings. Moonshine eyes are a blessing and a curse all rolled into one look."

But Carey was still smarting from not being out there on the dance floor, smelling the sawdust and flying to the music. "You sure know an awful lot about a man whose name you never heard."

Nana Pat had a sharp tongue when she thought Carey was sassing. That night, though, she merely smiled. "I was young once, child. I've known my own pair of moonshine eyes. Several of them, in fact."

Standing there beneath the carnival lights, Carey had the sudden sense of growing up. She studied the woman next to her, the grandmother who'd raised her and loved her and given her more than a lot of her supposedly more fortunate friends could ever know or understand. "So why did you call moonshine eyes a blessing?"

"Because the boy who has them gets pretty much all he wants." The old woman's smile was in her voice now, like she was flirting with the shadows and the flashing lights from a long-ago carnival. "It's the ladies he leaves in the dust who know the cost. Not him. Not till it's too late."

Carey knew the answer, but she didn't want to let go of the moment. "When is it too late, Nana?"

"When the poor boy stops his twirling dance, when the rodeo throws him on his back, when the lights go out and the music stops." The hand holding Carey's trembled softly, as though vibrating to a song never forgotten. "When the moonshine eyes don't spark, and the boy realizes the good times aren't there for the taking. He's never learned the lessons a man needs to grow into somebody worth keeping around. And the truth is, he'll always worry the woman who lands him, on account of how he's always hungering for that next sweet ride."

29

Two hours into their journey, Dimitri asked if they would mind taking turns at the wheel. Nick readily agreed. Dimitri stood there for a time, ensuring he could trust Nick with the vessel before disappearing below. A few moments later, he reappeared on the stern deck carrying a portable grill. Carey descended the stairs and followed Dimitri into the main cabin, which was divided into a galley, the head, a lounge, and a forward sleeping berth.

"Can I help?" she asked.

"If you like. I am sorry, but I did not expect to be making such a long journey or I would have brought a mate." He moved over and pointed to the cutting board. "Would you wash and trim the vegetables?"

"Sure."

"Only run the water when you need to." Dimitri stood by her for a second, watching intently. Carey wondered if he did this with all activities, making sure the stranger could be trusted, offering no advice when none was needed. She doubted he was even aware of the act, it was so ingrained. Then he gathered up utensils and departed. When he returned, he surveyed her work and declared, "Perfect."

"What's next?"

"The cupboard there has baskets of lemons and garlic. Quarter two lemons and six cloves, please."

He returned a third time, filled a pot with water and set it on the small gas cooker, then opened a lower door to reveal a small freezer. He pulled out three packets. "You like tuna?"

"Love it."

"And your husband?"

"He's not . . ." There was no reason the question should make her blush. "Nick is a friend and my employer."

Even his smile carried shadows. All he said was, "This is very fresh. I caught it only a few days ago."

Beyond the Didim straits they entered open waters. Dimitri grilled the steaks, then returned to the wheelhouse and set the autopilot. When they joined him on the main deck, he explained, "In the summer, these waters are alive with boats. Now there is the occasional fishing vessel, but not even many of those. My radar will sound an alarm if another ship comes within range."

They dined on tuna seasoned with coarse salt and lemon and sorrel, with a side of grilled eggplant and garlic and asparagus. The breeze laced the meal with a hint of wintry chill. The air was fresh, the sea gloriously empty. A lone island was visible in the hazy distance off the stern. Otherwise the sea and the day were entirely theirs.

Midway through the meal, Nick asked, "How do you manage to make a living from this?"

Dimitri smiled. "Charm?"

Carey caught the edge to Dimitri's tone and felt mildly

irritated with Nick. She was certain such interrogation would reveal nothing—if indeed the man had anything to hide.

Nick persisted, "But with the crisis, it must be tough."

"Islanders have lived through hard times before."

"Still, keeping up a vessel like this must be challenging. What about smuggling?"

Neither Dimitri's smile nor his voice wavered a fraction. "Smuggling is illegal."

Nick glanced her way, and must have seen Carey's displeasure, for he gave a little shrug and asked Carey, "So this is the city named in the Bible, right?"

"Ephesus was a major city in the Roman era. And yes, it is a book in the Bible and referenced in several places throughout the New Testament."

"You've researched this place too."

"Yes, Nick. That's what I do. I research. I study. I learn."

His only reaction to her clipped response was to grin and say, "Why don't you share a bit of your hard-earned wisdom."

Carey wanted to snap at him, which was silly. Nick had only been doing his job, asking questions of a man others suspected of being part of this ring of thieves. Even so, she found it necessary to rise from the deck chair and step to the railing. She breathed in the Mediterranean air and stared out over the vast sea. Somewhere out there was Turkey.

"Two thousand years ago," she began, "the land beyond the horizon was known as Asia Minor. Ephesus was a provincial capital, like Caesarea in Judea. It was a powerful city, very wealthy. And it was quite aware of the role it played in anchoring Rome's power in this vital region."

She heard a zipping sound behind her, knew Nick had opened his backpack and was reaching for his pad. "What does that mean exactly?"

She kept her back to the two men and gave herself over to the world of long ago. "It's easier to understand if you look at a specific point in time. Between the years when Paul and Luke and Barnabas were here, and when John landed on Patmos, the Roman world had gone through tremendous upheaval. To the east, the Jews rose up in rebellion and actually defeated two Roman legions. But in the end they were overcome, and Jerusalem was destroyed."

"When was that?" Nick asked, pen poised.

"About forty years after Jesus was crucified. The region's political situation was thrown into chaos about sixty years earlier when Julius Caesar was assassinated. He was stabbed to death in the Senate chamber. Rome then entered a period of political upheaval as three rivals fought to succeed him. The Ephesus leaders backed Mark Antony and Cleopatra. When they discovered they had sided with the losers, the ruling council of Ephesus desperately sought to placate the winner, Octavian. They funded extravagant temples, statues, and religious festivals to demonstrate their loyalty. The alternative was to have them, their families, and their cities turned to rubble and ruin."

The engines hummed softly for a time, and then Nick said, "You said 'religious festivals,' not political."

She swung around. "I like that about you, Nick," she said, her previous impatience gone. "You don't just hear what's said. You listen to the meaning. That's very rare. It's probably what makes you so good at your job."

For the moment, it was just the two of them. The air sparked with the brilliant light and the brisk, salty freshness, and the infinite blue. Dimitri was a silent component of the backdrop.

Nick gave his lopsided grin and said, "Religious festivals."

"Our distinction between religion and politics would not have made sense to the Ephesians. Revering the ruler wasn't about worshiping a human being; it was their way of showing respect for the gods who placed him in power. The leaders of Asia Minor didn't see their obedience to the Roman conquerors as defeat by another nation. The Roman gods had been proven stronger than theirs where it mattered most—in battle. They were submitting to the will of the gods."

Dimitri rose from his chair. "Please wait a moment. I want to hear this." He climbed the stairs in a fluid movement. Nick watched him go, his expression thoughtful. Soon enough, Dimitri returned and settled into the canvas seat. "All is well. Please continue."

When Nick met her gaze once more, there was a new gleam in his eyes. And because she knew him so well, she sensed it had nothing whatsoever to do with her story. Rather, for the first time since they'd set off on this journey, Dimitri was fully engaged.

Carey went on, "Our biblical travelers would have been disgusted by what they found in Ephesus. Between the time Paul visited Ephesus and when John arrived, the provincial leaders had erected three massive structures. One was in Pergamum, a day's walk from Ephesus. The temple was one of the largest buildings the world had ever seen, and it was dedicated to Zeus. Nearby was a second building only slightly smaller, this one dedicated to Augustus and the goddess Roma. A half day's walk farther on would have brought them to the city of Aphrodisias, where these same officials erected the Sebastion Temple, over a hundred and fifty feet high. Inside the grand colonnades were huge panels almost ninety feet to a side, some painted and adorned with glittering mosaics, others carved in bas-relief. They celebrated Roman victories in wicked detail. One showed an armed, godlike emperor dominating a female slave, a metaphor for the way Romans viewed the nations they conquered. Another showed the Emperor Nero forcing a naked female to the ground as he prepared to cut her throat."

"Sounds brutal," Nick said, writing furiously.

"It was meant to be so. By accepting their status as Rome saw them, the rulers intended to show their absolute devotion to their new leaders. Abject helplessness, dominated by human and divine powers."

Nick's pen scratched across the pad for a time. "And then John arrived."

"It had been a terrible couple of decades for the Christian believers. Peter and Paul had both been sentenced to death for their faith. John was exiled with others who had survived the destruction of Jerusalem. The holy temple had been razed, not a single stone left standing. The world as they knew it was gone, and in its place they saw this. The glory of Rome painted in gruesome detail on the walls of unholy temples. For John, this became the basis on which he interpreted his visions."

Carey expected Dimitri or Nick to come back with another question about Ephesus. But Nick was now focused on Dimitri. And when Dimitri spoke, it was to ask, "You are a researcher of these times?"

"In a way. My field is forensic archeology. I study the past so I can determine what is real and what is counterfeit."

Her words rocked him. How she knew this, she could not have explained. Because Dimitri's only external response was to nod slowly. But she was fairly sure her words had struck a deep chord.

"And this is why you are here, this research?" Dimitri pressed.

She glanced at Nick. He thought for a moment, then said, "Go ahead."

Carey replied, "Nick is writing an article about the theft of Greece's heritage. I am helping him."

Dimitri looked from one to the other, still nodding. "My home is on Patmos. You must come and let me show you the island."

30

Carey and Nick explored the ruins of Ephesus until sunset. They returned to the boat by the last faint light of dusk. Dimitri had the motors running before they boarded and immediately cast off. After clearing the port, he came down the steps and returned with bottles of water and a plate of flatbread and goat cheese with olives and spring onions. Carey was famished and bone weary. Her legs ached, her neck and nose and arms were sunburned, and her shirt was stiff with dried sweat. She stood between the skipper and Nick, munched on her impromptu meal, and watched the sun set upon the Aegean. She was blissfully happy.

When they entered open waters, Dimitri set the autopilot and restarted the portable grill. He laid out kebabs of lamb, along with tomato, onion, and eggplant he'd bought in the local market. He left Carey to tend the grill and Nick up top to keep watch on the dark sea while he prepared fresh salads and more flatbread, which he grilled alongside the kebabs. They ate in silence. The night was so huge and the sea so black they might as well have been traversing the heavens.

Dimitri waited until they'd finished eating before asking Carey, "Will you tell me more about this region's heritage?"

Carey thought it was time for a question of her own. "You were born on Patmos?"

"Actually, I was born in Izmir, farther along the Turkish coast. As you must know, for many centuries Greece did not exist as a separate country. The Romans ruled it as a series of provinces, with all the Dodecanese Islands controlled from Ephesus. Then the Ottomans conquered us and for five hundred years Greece was a myth from the distant past."

It was the most Dimitri had ever said about himself. Carey decided to venture further. "Does your family still live in Turkey?"

"My uncle and his family still run a restaurant in Izmir. At one time, most Turkish cities had a Greek quarter. Izmir also had an Armenian quarter and a Jewish quarter." He gestured to the night. "But that is for later, yes? Please, tell me about the past."

So Carey talked about the times in which John lived and the tragic events that brought him to Patmos. She described the Roman world, the role played by such fortress islands as Rhodes. Patmos had been too small to house a garrison, so the Romans had used it as a place of detention. John was far from the only malcontent sent to live and eventually die there. The Romans probably kept a small garrison at the port, but the prisoners were most likely permitted to live where they wished. Such banishments were common in the Roman world. There were few prisons outside the largest cities, and they mostly housed prisoners waiting trial and sentencing. The Roman authorities saw no need for long imprisonment,

Carey explained. Their punishments were brutal and swift and public. Which suggested that John had committed no crime other than to be identified as the leader of an outlaw sect calling themselves Christians.

All the while Carey spoke, Nick sat in silence, cutting a silhouette against the dim wheelhouse lights. Four times Dimitri rose, scaled the ladder and checked the vessel and the empty waters. While he was gone, Nick continued his quiet vigil. Then Dimitri returned and spoke the same two words, "Please continue."

Carey talked until her voice grew hoarse. Dimitri stood a fifth time and descended to the galley. When he returned, he bore a metal tray with three steaming mugs. "We should go topside now. The straits are not far off."

Entering the wheelhouse, Carey saw no difference to the starlit sea. She accepted a mug of tea sweetened with honey and condensed milk. "This is delicious."

"My first mate, Sofia, makes the finest onboard tea. You must meet her."

"I would like that."

He offered Nick the third mug. "You will join me in Patmos?"

Carey waited for Nick to say something, but he took up station by the open door and remained silent. So she said, "We'd like that very much."

"I will berth tonight in the Kos port. We can go tomorrow, yes? I would like my grandmother to meet you."

"I would be honored." She took a sip of her tea. "Tell me about yourself. Do you live with your family?"

"My father only. My mother passed away years ago."

"I'm so sorry."

"Thank you."

"And your grandmother?"

201

"She lives alone. I want her to move in with us. My father is not well. She cares for him. But at night she goes back to her cottage. Before, there were problems."

"Your father and his mother didn't get along?"

"Yiayia is my mother's mother. She was against them marrying."

"Your grandmother's name is Yiayia?"

"Yiayia is slang for granny. Her name is Chara. It means joy."

"That's beautiful."

"Yiayia knew my father would immigrate to Turkey. She did not want to lose her daughter." He shrugged. "But they are good friends now. It is a gift in these hard times, how close they have become."

Carey sensed he was waiting for them to turn the conversation. She thought about using this as an opportunity to ask about other things the hard times had brought, yet she sensed Dimitri wasn't ready. She resisted the urge to glance at Nick. Either he asked or he didn't.

The silence stretched out for a time, and then Dimitri asked, "What about your family?"

"My parents died when I was very young."

He studied her. "You were orphaned."

"No, Dimitri. I wasn't."

"But you said—"

Nick spoke for the first time in hours. "Carey has her own way of looking at things. Take the word *orphan*. She can't be one, since she's been loved and raised by half a dozen families. Including mine."

Dimitri kept a hand draped on the wheel as he looked from one to the other. "So you have known each other long?"

"All our lives," Carey replied.

"Carey is one of my oldest friends," Nick agreed. "My mother didn't adopt her because Carey's grandmother wouldn't let her. But she spent more time at our place than I did."

"Are you . . . ?"

"Yes?"

"Nothing. It is . . ." A pall drifted over the wheelhouse, as though Dimitri's unfinished question brought a darkness to their conversation. "Those are the lights of Kos up ahead," he said tersely.

They entered the Kos harbor a few minutes after midnight and moored in an open berth directly in front of their hotel. They bid Dimitri a quiet good-night. Upstairs, Carey thanked Nick for the best day ever and received a response she didn't really understand. She was so tired she wanted to fall into bed in all her clothes, but she forced herself into the shower and actually dozed under the warm flow. She slipped into an oversized T-shirt and groaned her way to bed.

It seemed as though she'd been asleep only a few moments before the phone jangled. Carey opened her eyes to bright sunlight and fumbled her hand back and forth before finding her cellphone. Only when she tried to connect did she realize the ringing came from the hotel phone. "Yes?"

A man said something in Greek, and afterward there was a series of clicks. A man impossibly calm and alert said, "This is Stefanos Khouris. You must come now."

"But we . . ." She heard a thump resonate from the room next door, followed by a fist hammering the wall beside her bed. "Coming."

"Hurry," she heard before the click.

She slipped into clothes from her pack, laced up her hiking boots, stuffed her belongings inside, zipped the pack shut and slung it over her shoulder. Nick emerged from his own door in time to ask, "Ready?"

"Yes. What's going on?"

"No idea." He took the stairs in a series of leaps. Carey remained tight on his heels.

They aimed for the lobby desk, but the commander cut them off with, "Your bill is already taken care of." Stefanos led them to the front door, then halted them with an upraised hand. The sound of shouting came from outside. All the waiters in the café stood completely still, staring across the street. But the canopy and the sunlight masked whatever was going on.

Stefanos spoke into his radio, waited through two tense breaths. Then the radio clicked and a voice responded. Stefanos said in English, "You will walk directly across the quay and you will get on the boat and you will keep your eyes straight ahead. Do not look at anyone. Do not speak. Ignore all provocations. Understood?"

Nick asked shakily, "What is happening?"

"Later. Do as I say. Now go."

The instant Stefanos slammed open the hotel door, they bolted. Carey walked so close to Nick she might as well have been locked to his shadow. They rushed through the canopied outdoor restaurant and entered the sunlight.

They were greeted by bedlam.

She had no idea how many men filled the cobblestone quay. Dozens, perhaps more. They all seemed impossibly large. Their voices were like fists, roaring masses of rage. They waved their arms at her appearance and yelled. These men were held back by a clutch of sailors with rifles across their chests, facing the men down and forming a narrow corridor through which Carey and Nick raced. She did as Stefanos had ordered and kept her gaze locked on the vessel ahead.

Dimitri stood in the stern, waving them forward, one hand outstretched to help them over the gangplank. Nick bounded across, then Carey. She realized the engines were running because she smelled the diesel and felt the vibration rise up through her boots. She couldn't hear anything else except the crowd's fury.

Dimitri shouted words she couldn't understand. She and Nick helped untie the boat and stow the gangplank while Dimitri rushed up the stairs and powered them away. A fish flew past Carey's face, then a stone. The sailors responded by using their rifles like batons against the rabble.

Finally they were away, the din subsiding behind them. The day was clear and bright, the view an idyllic myth.

Nick offered her a shaky grin. "I sure hope you didn't forget your toothbrush."

"What just *happened*?"

"Not a clue. Let's go ask."

Now that the danger had passed, her legs felt so weak she could scarcely stand, much less climb the steep stairs. She watched Nick as he ascended to the wheelhouse, dropped her pack to the deck, and waited for her strength to return. A few minutes later, they slipped past the peninsula and the fortress on their way to open waters. Behind her, the harbor was as lovely as a painting. Of the mob, there was no sign now.

When she finally entered the wheelhouse, Dimitri greeted her with his sincerest apologies. "Are you all right?"

Carey nodded. Nick turned to her and said, "I was waiting for you to come up before I asked about the crowd."

"For generations, sailors of the Dodecanese have worked by a set of unwritten rules," Dimitri explained. "You know this word *Dodecanese*? It means the twelve islands. The largest of these are Samos, Ikaria, Patmos, Kalymnos, Kos, Rhodes, and Karpathos. We share the waters and we share the ports and we share the tourists. But with the crisis, this has broken down. The big man shouting, you saw him?"

"They all looked big to me," Carey replied. "They were all shouting."

"The biggest, his name is Stavros. He has tried to do the same as me, switch from fishing to tourism. But Stavros is a bully. He loves to fight. He scares the ladies." Dimitri opened the throttles another notch. "Stavros has money. How he has this cash is a matter of much discussion. He wanted to buy my berth in Patmos, take over my business. I agreed. Then I changed my mind. Stavros was very angry. This morning he discovered I was here."

Nick said, "Someone from our hotel probably told him you were carrying tourists."

"Stealing *his* tourists from *his* island," Dimitri corrected.

"What changed your mind about selling your business?" Carey asked.

Dimitri nodded slowly. "Yes. That is the question, is it not?"

"Will you tell us?"

"Perhaps. Perhaps I will answer all your questions. But first I must speak with my family." His voice was grave, his features hollow. "They too must meet you. They must help me decide. Because the questions you wish to ask will endanger us all."

31

Dimitri settled the two Americans into the nicest of the Patmos harbor-front hotels, then climbed the steep road to his home. As he walked, he phoned Duncan McAllister.

The man answered on the first ring. "I've been expecting to hear from you long before now."

"I'm being watched."

"You're sure about this, are you? It's not just idle fancy brought upon by an overdose of newfound wealth?"

"I told you about the naval officer who boarded my vessel when we were outbound for Cyprus. He was there on Kos. And I saw him talking to the two Americans."

The casual jollity vanished, revealing the steel beneath the man's polished veneer. "The officer spoke to the man and woman? You're sure?"

"He sat with them at their table."

"And then what?"

"They came down to the dock and asked me to ferry them to Bodrum."

"Nice place, Bodrum."

"They went to a gallery."

"Did they mention which one?"

"Selim's. It was closed."

"Yes, it would be. Seeing as how the man has a nose for trouble and no gut for danger. None whatsoever." Duncan pondered for a moment. "Then what?"

"They returned to my boat and asked me to take them to Ephesus."

"What on earth did they expect to find in Ephesus?"

"It was the girl. Carey Mathers. She serves as the journalist's researcher. She wanted to see the ruins."

"So they claimed they wanted to play tourist. Then what?"

When Dimitri's home came into view, he stopped and turned back toward the harbor. "They toured the site until sunset. Then I took them back to Kos."

"Where I understand you had a touch of bother."

"Stavros."

"Lovely name, that. So where are they now, your Americans?"

"Here on Patmos. Booked into the largest hotel on the harbor."

"Why on earth did you bring them to Patmos, lad?"

"I was doing as you said. Watch them. I can't watch them on Kos. I can't go *back* to Kos."

"No. There is that." Duncan went silent once more. "All right then. The journalist's young researcher . . . is she as fetching as they say?"

"What does that—?"

"I'm hoping you can lay your significant charms on her, is all. Don't get your feathers in a ruffle. Wait a sec." He cupped the phone, then returned and said, "You know the café where we first met with your friend Stavros."

"Of course."

"Drop by there this evening. There'll be a packet waiting for you at the bar. In it will be a new phone and a number where you'll be able to reach me. Don't use your old phone again, and don't call this number."

Duncan McAllister cut the connection. Only then did Dimitri unlock the tension in his chest. He used a shaky hand to swipe at the perspiration on his face. He started back up the hill—toward home.

Thankfully his grandmother was there when Dimitri arrived. She took one look at him and ordered him into the bath. Five minutes later, he eased into the nearly scalding water and used his father's pumice brush on his skin. Normally he hated the abrasive feel, but today it added to the sense of cleaning beneath the surface. As though it might truly be possible to scrub away the stain of everything that surrounded him.

When he emerged, Chara had a meal ready. The hour did not matter. She had married into a clan who lived from the sea, and the tides set their own calendar. Dimitri ate three helpings of her grilled lamb and salad enhanced with mint from her own garden, then settled back into the patio chair, drinking the sun like he did the glass of tea.

He caught them up on all that had happened. He knew his story was disjointed, but there was no helping that. He related the discussion with Duncan McAllister and the trip to Kos and the two Americans. His grandmother and father exchanged glances over his description of the journalist and the researcher, but they did not speak.

When he was done, Chara asked, "So the two Americans are where?"

"I left them in the harbor hotel. They were exhausted. I suppose they are still there."

Chara said, "You must ask them up. We must meet them."

His father nodded and spoke quietly, "Do this now."

But when Dimitri started to rise, his grandmother said, "No, wait. There is this other matter."

He sank back. "I know. What should I do about Duncan?"

"No, no, the smuggler can wait. We are talking about the money. How much do you have?"

"After Sofia receives her share, with the second payment, I'm up almost seventy thousand euros."

"You have it in your room?"

"I can't take it to the bank."

"Give it to me."

"But Yaiyai—"

"I am selling my cottage. I am moving in here." Her eyes sparked. "That is, unless you object."

"You know I've been urging you to do this. But why now?"

"Your father asked. How can I say no to my two dear men?" Her hands were curled by age and hard years. The fingers scarcely moved as she gestured. "Give me the money. I will declare the one price, you understand?"

"For the tax man. Of course."

"Who knows how much the cottage really brought? I will deposit your money with the payment for my home. In your name."

He gaped at her. "It is happening immediately?"

"Tomorrow. Why wait? You know the Castellanos family. Their daughter is marrying. My cottage will be the dowry for the wedding. They have discussed this with me for some time."

"But the money—"

"Is for you. And your future."

"Yaiyai, I don't know what to say."

"The way you care for your father, the way you honor us both with this trust you give so freely, what is the value of more words?"

His father reached forward and gripped his son's hand. "I am content."

Chara's eyes sparked again. "Now go and bring us this pair of Americans. And we will see if they are worth the risk their presence brings."

32

Carey followed the two men up the steep incline, glancing around in delight. She was captivated by Patmos and the town of Skala. Other than the fortress monastery atop the highest peak, Patmos contained no great edifices, no vast ruins, no museum, and very little tourist wealth. But Carey decided this was part of its timeless charm.

Two people waited for them on the flagstone patio. The man was seated in a chair covered in cushions and a quilt, as if every bone was so frail that even his forearms needed soft support. He was dressed in clean trousers and a pressed shirt. An oxygen tank was partly hidden beneath the chair. Clear plastic tubes ran up and into his nostrils. He smiled and made a welcoming gesture when they appeared. Carey approached the chair and accepted the proffered hand with both of hers. She stood there, willing to wait for as long as he wanted. Dimitri's father took his time inspecting her before turning and rasping a few words to his son.

Dimitri said, "Carey Mathers, Papa." When his father

spoke again, Dimitri translated, "My father says that you are welcome in our home."

Carey smiled. "Now I see where you got your amazing eyes."

His father wheezed a chuckle at Dimitri's translation of her words. The old woman spoke for some time, and Dimitri translated, "The islanders say we are descended from the mercenaries who fought with Alexander. The rest of the world sees him as a hero, but to us he was just another Macedonian conqueror. Soldiers of fortune flocked to his banner." Dimitri shrugged. "Legends have a long life in Greece."

Carey turned to the grandmother. She saw a tiny figure, less than five feet tall, yet the woman carried herself with remarkable poise. And her smile was a thing of beauty. "My grandmother says you honor us by coming," Dimitri continued.

"Please tell her I am grateful for her invitation."

Carey took a seat and watched as they welcomed Nick. It seemed to her that their attention on him was short-lived, as though Nick wasn't really the reason for this gathering. Which surprised her greatly. She had to assume Dimitri had spoken about them. Carey watched Dimitri hurry about, helping the grandmother lay out a series of small dishes and serve tea. He explained this was the traditional Greek form of hospitality, dishes called *mezze* that could be dined upon for hours. The patio table was soon jammed with plates of seasoned lamb, stuffed grape leaves, hummus, cheese, a salad of tomatoes and wild onions, and another of some chopped leaf that smelled of mint. On and on the dishes came. The grandmother watched approvingly as Carey ate. Nick spoke several times, thanking them for the meal and complimenting them on the food. Each time they acknowledged him politely, but then their attention returned to Carey. She didn't find their inspection the least bit uncomfortable, only curious.

When she set her plate aside, Chara spoke and Dimitri translated, "I told my grandmother about what you said of Ephesus. She asks if you know the heritage of this island too."

"Some. A little."

"My grandmother says perhaps more than a little."

There was something about the woman that reminded Carey of Nana Pat. On the surface, the two women couldn't have been more different. This lady of the island, her face etched by hard winters and strong sun, dressed all in black, had little in keeping with the woman who had raised Carey. But somewhere in that gaze sparked the same timeless wisdom, the same rich vein of humor.

"I only know Patmos from books," Carey said. "I do not really know the island at all."

Chara liked that enough to smile. Dimitri translated, "She asks if you will repeat some of what you spoke of yesterday. She has never been to Ephesus."

"But it's so close. And you're a boatman."

"Many women of my grandmother's generation did not leave their island home. I think this is one reason she feels so close to Sofia, my shipmate. Sofia was born restless. My grandmother likes how Sofia defies tradition and makes her own way."

Carey glanced a question at Nick, but he had reverted to the same silent watchfulness as during their voyage. He showed no impatience, nor any interest in asking his questions. He merely watched.

So Carey repeated what she had said, pausing between sentences for Dimitri to translate, until the passion caught her up once more. Then the chair became constrictive, and the day too beautiful, and so she rose and paced and spun and weaved the story with her hands as well as her voice.

Carey explained how much of what she said was educated conjecture. She described how the academic world had become filled with so-called experts who liked to claim that the John of Patmos wasn't the same as the apostle of Jesus Christ, how he might not have existed at all. And she countered these with arguments of her own. She described what the apostle would have heard from visitors to his island prison. How Rome was descending into decadence and chaos. How Nero soaked Christians in oil and burned them from stakes planted along the route leading to his palace. The Roman arenas held events pitting chained believers against lions and mercenaries skilled in the art of death. That a new name for Christians gradually became prevalent around the empire, the name Martyr. How despite the scorn and the opposition from so many different quarters, the numbers of Christians continued to swell.

And then John had his vision, she told them, and wrote down his Revelation. Within just a few years, copies of his letter had reached to every point in the Roman world and beyond. This was why Carey remained convinced that it was indeed the apostle of Jesus Christ who had been sent to Patmos.

She described how John wrote in an era when travel from Ephesus to the Roman province of Africa could take months, and such letters were often passed from hand to trusted hand. She mentioned several other revelations and prophetic announcements that arose during this same period. And yet within the space of a few short years, the entire world knew of John's prophecy. Not one shred of evidence from that era suggested any of the recipients ever thought the Revelation might have been recorded by anyone *other* than the apostle.

Of course the visions had been given to an apostle. And there she stopped.

She realized she had adopted her pose from the classroom, standing on her toes with her arms outstretched. Only now she had a steep descent and a lovely view stretching out behind her. She slipped back into her chair and said sheepishly, "Sorry. I get carried away."

Dimitri watched Carey return to her seat and try to hide behind her cup of tea. There was a moment given to sunlight and birdsong and a gentle breeze off the harbor. Then Chara told her grandson, "This one's passion is very beautiful."

His father murmured, "Not just her passion."

Dimitri translated, then watched Carey blush at the compliments. Chara rose from her chair and said, "Dimitri, come help me, please."

Dimitri had become accustomed to doing everything around the house. It came with being an only son and loving an invalid father. Since childhood, his father had been his best friend. It was the reason he had put up with fishing for as long as he had. The hours he spent on the sea with his father had been the happiest of his life. Such things were hard to explain, to share with others, but as he drifted back and forth between the kitchen and the patio, he found himself describing his life for this American woman. Nick Hennessy, the investigative journalist, sat silent and watchful in the corner. He studied everything, but did so without intruding. It was possible to ignore him entirely.

Once fresh tea had been prepared and the glasses rinsed and refilled, once the meal had been taken away and a platter of desserts brought out, once the small plates had been washed and replaced, once he had checked on his father,

Dimitri dropped into his chair and continued where he had left off.

"When my mother died, I started going out every day with my father on the boat."

"How old were you?"

"Eleven."

"What about school?"

"Papa had a word with my teachers. They gave me the autumn off." He glanced at his father, and confessed, "I hated fishing. No, not hate. That is the wrong word."

"You were not born with fishing in your blood."

He looked up, surprised at her words. "Yes, that is it exactly. My father assured me it would come with time, since I loved the sea. But it did not. I learned the lessons and I did everything that was required."

"But you never had a feel for the craft," Carey offered. "It was like wearing someone else's clothes. Or living someone else's life."

He stopped. "How is it you know this?"

"This is about you telling your story, Dimitri. It's like you told me on the boat. I'll answer all your questions, just not now." She tasted one of the multilayered sweets, a home-made concoction of pastry, honey, and crushed almonds, and hummed her pleasure to Chara. Then she asked, "Was your father right to take you from school?"

"Oh, yes. Papa said the sea would heal me from the loss of my mother. He was right."

She nodded at the silent, watchful man in the padded chair. "Your father sounds like a remarkable man."

"I wish you could have seen him then. The strongest man in the world. And the wisest."

"You were the best of friends," she said. "And he was very proud of you."

He started to ask how she could say such words when she reached up and swiftly wiped at her eyes. The gesture of a young woman determined to hide her emotions. And her secrets.

His grandmother asked, "What are you saying to this lovely child to make her sad?"

"I do not know, Yiayia." He swiftly translated what they had been discussing.

When he was done, his grandmother said, "Tell this one she carries her burdens with God's grace."

The words caused Carey's features to crimp down tightly. "Your grandmother reminds me of the woman who raised me."

Dimitri expected Chara to ask about her family, but instead his grandmother observed, "Beauty can be a remarkable mask, for sometimes that is all the world wants to see."

Carey studied the old woman as Dimitri translated, then he added, "My grandmother was considered the most beautiful woman in all the Dodecanese."

"You still are," Carey replied. "Where it matters."

After Dimitri translated that, Chara astonished him by saying, "Tomorrow is the Sabbath. Ask this lovely young lady if she would care to come with me to mass at the monastery."

For some reason this caused Carey to struggle anew for control. "I would be deeply, deeply honored."

Chara rose slowly from her chair. "Dimitri, join me in the kitchen, please."

As they left the patio, Carey called after them, "Can Nick come too?"

Once Dimitri had translated, his grandmother turned and

studied the young man intently, then asked, "Is this one a believer?"

Carey glanced over, clearly hoping Nick would reply. But the journalist remained silent. Watchful. She turned back and said reluctantly, "In his own way, I suppose . . ."

Chara had a wise woman's ability to dismiss with the softest intake of breath. "Perhaps it would be best for us to do this alone."

Dimitri followed his grandmother back into the house and took a moment to adjust to the shadows. His grandmother moved to the kitchen window and looked out on Carey Mathers and his father. Chara said, "You can trust this one with your life."

"You have an hour in her company and you are this certain?"

"Mark my words." She moved to the stove and set a fresh pot of water on it to heat. "This one has the power to change your world forever."

Dimitri took his grandmother's place by the window. The shadows were deep enough for him to observe the patio and remain unseen. Carey spoke softly to Nick, who seemed reluctant to respond with more than a shrug or gesture. The journalist was a strange one. Most American men that Dimitri had known were both brash and loud. Handsome ones like Nick often became uncomfortable when not the center of attention. This one, however, seemed very familiar with losing himself in shadows.

He shifted his attention to Carey. His grandmother's words were astonishing. Chara had met a number of his women. Foreign ladies loved being invited into the home of a local. His grandmother had made dozens of such meals. Chara always showed his guests island hospitality because it was her nature. Never once had she offered any comment other than the woman was nice or attractive. And not once had his grandmother asked what happened once the young woman had departed his life. Chara had always known they were only trysts.

He asked, "You truly think this is the one for me?"

Chara wheeled about, showing genuine astonishment. "Who said anything about romance?"

"You said—"

"She can change your world. That is what I said, and that is what this one will do. If you let her."

"Yaiyai . . . I don't understand."

"No. On that we most certainly agree. There is too much you have allowed to sweep past you on the tide of pleasure and easy living." She stumped over and pointed a finger directly at his face. "This one is special. This one is a *gift*. You will treat her with the care she deserves. You will *listen*. And you will *learn*."

33

Dimitri made arrangements to meet Carey at the hotel before daybreak. As she and Nick were getting ready to leave, Carey surprised them all by asking, "Would it be polite to kiss your grandmother good-bye?"

All of them, Chara and his father and Dimitri himself, found the question a nice reason to smile. "It would be charming."

After the guests departed, Dimitri helped clear up the patio, washed the dishes, walked his grandmother down to her cottage, and then helped his father get ready for bed. There was a thoughtful feel to the sunset, a sense of expectancy. Dimitri sat for hours on the patio, wondering at what his grandmother had said—a woman from a distant land who would change his life, if he let her. He felt as though his grandmother's words had been scripted upon the night sky.

Dimitri's alarm went off at four. His father made no complaint about getting dressed and being served breakfast in the dark. He was a fisherman by nature as well as by trade.

The family vehicle was a ratty Citroën van of uncertain vintage. Dimitri didn't know how old it was. The original color was a mystery. Years back, his father had spray-painted the exterior a modest tan that no longer hid the rust. The interior's fabric was frayed, and a faded cushion on the driver's seat covered an exposed spring. The vehicle smelled of oil and age and fish.

Dimitri stopped to pick up his grandmother and then drove to the harbor. As soon as he pulled up in front of the hotel, Carey came bounding down the front steps. His grandmother said, "Like a beautiful and excited child, this one."

Carey slipped into the back seat behind his grandmother. "Thank you again for this amazing opportunity."

His grandmother was dressed in her Sunday best, which meant a freshly washed and ironed black dress and a matching mantilla of hand-knitted lace. She passed over a folded kerchief and said, "Ask Carey if she would wear this for me."

Dimitri watched in astonishment as Carey folded the silk scarf in her lap into a triangle, then slipped it over her hair and knotted it beneath her chin. He asked Chara, "You have given her my mother's favorite scarf?"

"What is this, *give*? I loan her a covering." She pointed out the front window. "Your job is to drive."

Dimitri ground the gears and pressed down on the gas. They didn't speak again until they'd left Skala behind. As they climbed through the dark into the central hills, Carey asked, "Mass is this early?"

"Yiayia likes these days to follow a certain routine. She goes to say morning prayers at the cave. She watches the sun rise. Then we go to Hora. She likes to arrive early, because too much walking is hard for her, and on Sundays the parking areas become very full."

In the flash of passing headlights, he saw in the rearview mirror that Carey's eyes had gone very round. "You are taking me to the Cave of the Apocalypse?"

"Yes. I said that."

"No. You said we were attending mass at the monastery."

"Is this a problem?"

Her voice was very low, solemn. "No, Dimitri. Everything is fine."

The lone road through the central highlands was narrow, the curves sharp, and the incline steep. Dimitri preferred driving it in the dark. The sheer drop-offs and the absence of guardrails caused some passengers to swoon, and he was warned of oncoming traffic by their headlights. The people who lived in the island's interior were known to be the worst drivers in all of Greece. The trip took them about twenty minutes. Dimitri parked in the convent's forecourt and started to help his grandmother up the stairs.

This time, however, Chara reached out her free hand for Carey. The young woman slipped in close to Chara's other side. Chara gripped her elbow and started forward. "Ask her if she knows of Patmaida."

When Carey replied that she'd never heard the name before, he explained, "Below us at sunrise you will see a cypress grove. The buildings there are used as a theological seminary, over four hundred years old. It was founded when the Muslims still ruled us, and it was kept a secret for a hundred and fifty years. Still today it is a symbol of our island. We are the land that kept the flame of Christianity alive in a world that wanted to bury us forever."

Carey's voice remained low and unsteady. "Thank you for sharing with me the heart of your homeland."

Dimitri translated her words for his grandmother. Chara's response was to stop and say, "Give me a coin, please."

The convent was officially closed until midday. But the gatekeeper arrived early on Sabbath dawns, there to welcome the locals and accept their token payment. "Don't you want my help . . . ?" Dimitri stopped speaking, because his grandmother had already started up the path, arm in arm with their visitor.

For some reason, the sight of them entering the convent's small portal left him feeling bereft. Every other time he had come up here, Dimitri had escaped to the road as soon as he settled his grandmother into place. This morning, however, he felt as if there was nothing for him to do but follow.

34

Carey entered the compound feeling as though this was a gift she had waited a lifetime to receive. She had studied this place for years. The Cave of the Apocalypse and the Monastery of Saint John had formed major components of her thesis. The treasures now held in the monastery's museum had been almost lost several times over their long and difficult history.

The Apostle John had most likely been exiled to Patmos from Ephesus in AD 95. That year had been a particularly awful one for the early church. The Emperor Domitian was dying, and the empire had entered a period of brutal repression. Christians were classified as atheists, for they refused to worship the emperor as a deity and therefore didn't believe in anything as far as the Roman government was concerned. Laws were passed that granted regional governments the power to persecute and execute Christians.

So the disciple whom Jesus had called "beloved" was sent here, perhaps as banishment, perhaps by the Ephesus church in order to keep him safe. John would have been in his late seventies or early eighties at the time, and this cave would have served as an ideal refuge for an exile too old to build a home for himself. For the common people, such caves were viewed as places where the poorest and the outcast could find shelter. John would certainly have seen himself as one of these. He came to this place, high in the hills, most likely seeking a quiet haven where he could give up his earthly body and finally return to the company of his beloved Lord.

Only God was not yet ready to call him home.

John's experience and his subsequent writings became a timeless gift of hope, both to the seven churches of Asia and to the centuries of faithful who would follow. John's visions created a remarkable promise that the persecutors of God's chosen would be destroyed, that all such experiences would be turned to eternal good. The word applied to John's letter by its earliest readers was *apocalypse*, which translated as *holy unveiling*.

Carey and Chara fell into step with a number of other early arrivals, forming a silent procession through the small outer portal. Most pressed a small coin into the gatekeeper's hand. Carey set a pace that was comfortable for Dimitri's grandmother as they entered the first courtyard. She had studied the layout for so long that she could name each of the surrounding structures, even though all she could see were silhouettes carved from the night sky. The wall surrounding the entrance was adorned by a lunette, a mosaic symbolizing the moment of holy illumination. The courtyard was interspersed with a series of miniature doors, marking the cells used by women who sought to spend time in solitude and prayer. Carey knew there were almost a hundred of these women, drawn from all over the globe. Some came for a few days, others for the rest of their lives.

Straight ahead was the oldest part of the complex, a church whose foundations were set in place in the decades following John's passage to heaven. A larger structure had been erected in the twelfth century. Carey and Chara passed through the chapel of Saint Anne, lit by hundreds of flickering candles, moving slowly past icons and crosses dating back fifteen centuries. Carey could have named almost all of them.

A soft murmur rippled along the procession, one voice whispering to the next, like the rustle of cedars being touched by a fresh wind. Chara smiled and spoke to the woman ahead of them, who turned to Carey and said, "Your friend wishes you to know that today we have special treat."

"What is it?"

The procession moved even slower now. A step, a pause, another step. The woman replied in a reverent tone, "The bishop of Patmos is here. He will offer a benediction, and then together we will say the Lord's Prayer."

They were the last ones to find space within the cave itself. The cramped area was filled with penitents, many of them old women. But there were some young people too, including a child with fresh flowers woven into her dark tresses instead of a scarf. Each managed to find a place to either kneel or sit.

The bishop was a dark-robed figure seated at the very front. Carey noted that he was sitting on the ledge where John had slept. The man was in his late sixties or early seventies and had a gray beard that spilled over his chest. His eyes were closed, his seamed features calm. A younger woman slipped from the ledge where John's feet would have rested so that Chara could sit down.

Carey knelt on the stone by Chara's feet. A long moment

ensued, so silent she could hear the candles hiss and sputter. A man coughed from behind her, and the sound echoed through the cave and the chapel. Carey took a slow look around. The wall over the ledge was adorned by a brilliant iconostasis, painted over six hundred years ago by a Cretan artist depicting John receiving the Revelation. Beside that were fragments of a much earlier painting that had once covered the entire wall and depicted John relating God's message to his scribe. The design was partly obscured by written prayers, some dating back to the third or fourth century. Two silver frames marked the niche where John laid his head. To her right was the ledge where John's amanuensis, or scribe, whose name was Prochoros, rested the parchment on which he wrote down John's words.

The bishop began chanting. Carey bowed her head and allowed the words to wash over her. The man's deep voice carried a powerful sense of prayerful reverence. The group responded with a soft amen, took a long breath, and began the recitation in response. Carey joined in, perhaps the only one there who didn't speak the Lord's Prayer in Greek.

As she said the words she'd repeated all her life long, she felt joined not merely to the gathering but to twenty centuries of believers. Abruptly she had a sense of rising beyond herself. It wasn't a bodily experience, but rather a brief glimpse of her life as a flowing river with power and purpose. She recalled the tearful hours she had spent on her knees after breaking up with the one she thought she loved. The decision to throw herself into her graduate studies. The grim determination to shape her own course, to create a new direction in art studies: forensic archeology. The arguments with the faculty and deans, the research, the quest, anything to fill those forlorn hours with purpose and hope for a better tomorrow. All of it coming together with divine intent, a higher calling she could see only now. On her knees, in the Cave of Revelation.

Her long pilgrimage had come to an end.

Carey started sobbing so hard she could scarcely draw breath, much less rise when the prayer ended and the people began departing. At last she lifted her head and wiped her eyes. Only then did she realize Chara and the bishop were watching her, and smiling.

Dimitri's bench was situated between the long line of hermit cells and the main church, shaded by the wall and a pair of lemon trees. The morning had just begun to strengthen as the congregants poured out, their voices a soft punctuation to the new day. His time alone here had been excruciating. He felt pressed down from all sides, as though the prayers of those unseen hermits, all locked away in their tight little cells, actually carried the force to compress him physically. Only there was nothing inside him to be released.

Before the economic crisis struck Greece, if anyone had asked Dimitri to describe his life, he would have responded instantly with, "No regrets." It was a trademark response from the young men called *pedarosi*. The good-time lads who took pride in never growing up. Their world was defined by *gamaki*, flirting with girls, endless coffees and cigarettes with their mates, nights filled with dancing and laughter and music, competing good-naturedly with one another for the next *gomenos*—the next beautiful woman to hunt and woo and leave behind.

He was wrong to come here. He had avoided these places all his life, with their guilt and their blankets of black cloth draped over any hint of a good time. He had scorned the priests and their silly robes . . . but silently, because they were

229

the trademark of Patmos, and the island was his home. But now, as he sat on the stone bench and breathed air perfumed by the lemon blossoms, he saw the other side of his world. The emptiness that he ran from so successfully, the tears he had caused, the absence of meaning or a future or any lasting purpose.

He watched in numb silence as Carey and Chara emerged from the chapel. They were accompanied by the Bishop Galatas, leader of the Patmos church. Chara spoke with the bishop in the casual manner of an old friend. Carey, on the other hand, looked as undone as Dimitri himself felt. Her face was puffy with tears, and it seemed as though his grandmother worked to support her down the stairs rather than the other way around.

He walked over and asked in English, "Are you all right?"

"It's nothing," Carey replied quietly. "I'm fine."

"Can I get you anything?"

Carey shook her head. "I just need a moment."

His grandmother said, "My son, the bishop is asking us to join him for tea. Would you tell our guest?"

For some reason the invitation caused another tear to course down Carey's face. "That would be lovely, thank you."

"The bishop will walk back along the *kalderimi*, the pilgrims' path that leads from here to the monastery." He paused. "Does that make you sad?"

"No. I just . . ." Her lips trembled, but a single hard breath brought her back under control. "While we were praying, I felt as though I was here on a pilgrimage, only I didn't know it until I was inside there on my knees."

Dimitri translated, then watched the bishop's smile grow until his eyes almost disappeared. The bishop nodded slowly to Chara and said, "You were right to contact me."

"She is special, this one," Chara replied.

"Indeed." He turned to Carey and said in roughhewn English, "Please to join me. We walk, yes?"

"I would like that very much."

Dimitri told Carey he would bring his grandmother in the van, and Chara took her grandson's arm. She watched the two disappear along the path, then leaned on him and started toward the van. When she was seated, Dimitri started the motor and asked, "How do you know the bishop?"

She glanced over, her gaze sparkling with mirth. "He was the one who got away."

Dimitri turned off the engine. "And what does that mean, Yiayia?"

She looked toward the empty road leading up to the monastery. "His family comes from Rhodes. They are distant relatives, third cousins or perhaps fourth—we have argued over this for years. We met at festivals and such. There was once a spark. We might have whispered promises or even shared . . ."

Dimitri smiled at his grandmother. "A dance? A kiss? An embrace?"

"It was all so long ago." She made her familiar gesture, waving it aside. "We have remained friends. I called him last night."

"He came because of Carey?"

"He came because he has problems of his own."

Dimitri struggled to fashion words in his confusion. "Does this have anything to do with Duncan McAllister?"

"Perhaps. But it is not certain." She turned her eyes to him, brilliant in the dim light, filled with an ageless power. "That is for him to decide. And for him to share. If he wishes. At the time of his choosing."

35

Dimitri parked the van near the monastery, then helped his grandmother up the rough path to where the bishop and Carey waited by the main gates. He kept a slow pace, a habit he had followed most of his adult life, being the only grandchild and respecting his grandmother's desire for a supporting arm. He knew she did not actually need the help. Chara was constantly on her feet, continually walking Skala's steep roads. But in public she liked Dimitri close by. His willingness to show respect to his father and grandmother was one reason the island's older generation looked upon him fondly. They nodded their greetings and smiled their toothless blessings because he followed the island ways. His dalliances were shrugged off as part of the package. Dimitri knew what they said behind their hands when they thought he wasn't watching. That here was a man born to break hearts.

Only this morning, as he and his grandmother followed

Carey and the bishop across the monastery's main courtyard, Dimitri felt it was his heart that was broken.

But he could not say either how or why. Other than the inescapable fact that he deserved it.

The monastery was gradually coming to life around them. Dimitri watched as the bishop signaled to a passing acolyte. The young man listened to the bishop's instructions, bowed, then hurried away. He swiftly returned bearing a large ring of keys that jangled as he ran. The bishop accepted them and led Carey toward the museum's side entrance. As he cranked open the massive lock, he asked Chara in Greek, "You are up to a climb?"

"I will be fine. I have my grandson's strong arm."

"You can wait here if you like. The stairs are quite steep."

"I would not miss this, old friend."

When they arrived at the smaller portal up top, his grandmother was breathing heavily. Carey was already waiting for them with a chair. The bishop said, "Perhaps I should not have suggested this."

"Nonsense. I have not been up here since I was a little girl." Chara waved aside the chair. "Help me to the wall."

The view from the museum's rooftop terrace was breathtaking. All the island stretched before them, the water beyond on sparkling display. When his grandmother was settled comfortably against the waist-high wall, the bishop asked Dimitri, "Would you be so kind as to translate? My English . . ."

"Of course."

"Please tell our guest that the village is named Hora, which is an ancient version of your grandmother's name. It is separated into three distinct sections. Alloteina there to the west was the first settlement, and it is precisely dated to the year that Constantinople fell to the Ottoman invaders. Let me

233

see, I have difficulty remembering the year, perhaps the young lady might . . ."

When Dimitri had translated, Carey responded in a dream-like voice, "The capital of the Eastern Empire fell to the Muslim invaders in 1453."

The bishop smiled his approval. "Just so. And Christian refugees fled here, to the most famous pilgrimage site between Rome and Jerusalem. Then in 1669 the island of Crete finally fell to the Muslim navy, and refugees settled the area to your left, naming it Kritika. And finally, when the shipbuilders of Patmos gained a reputation throughout the Mediterranean, they built summer houses where they could walk out on their terraces and see the Skala harbor below. This section is known as Aporthiana."

"I have this poster on my wall," Carey said. "I've dreamed of this for years."

When Dimitri translated her words, his grandmother offered, "The national tourist board came here, oh, thirty years ago. They took the picture that has become famous all over the world. The bishop of that era allowed them to use it only after they promised never to say where it came from."

"The August crowds were already growing," the bishop agreed. "We want this island to remain a place of peace and refuge."

As if to punctuate his words, the bells of Skala's main church began ringing. The sweet melody carried on the still morning air, rising up to where they stood. This was soon joined by bells farther to the south. Dimitri knew they belonged to the monastery of Panaghia Koumana. Then the bells of Hora's own Panaghia Diasouzoussa chimed in, followed by the seminary's chapel farther down the hill, then Skala's three smaller churches, and then the convent. More could be faintly heard from the churches and monasteries north of Skala. As a boy, Dimitri and his friends would climb one of the neighboring hills and listen to this Sabbath chorus, naming each of the bells as they started pealing. And finally, as always, the monastery's own bells began their solemn tolling. Three different towers, atop the main church and the chapels of Christodoulos and Theotokos, all with bells proclaiming the glory of another Sabbath dawn.

Carey pressed her hands to her cheeks, her eyes brimming with tears Dimitri suspected she did not even know she shed. She tried to look everywhere at once, desperate to take it all in, every shred of the morning and the sounds that he had taken for granted all his life. Chara and the bishop watched her in approval.

When the bells and their echoes subsided, Carey took a long, unsteady breath and whispered, "Now I know what heaven will sound like."

The bishop made a soft noise deep in his throat. "I must go prepare for Mass. Dimitri, you will ask the young lady to come again? And you will ask that she bring her journalist friend."

"The young man appears to hold little real faith," his grandmother pointed out.

"Such is the way of this world," the bishop replied. "It seems to me that Miss Mathers has more than enough for our mission's success."

Before Dimitri could ask what the bishop meant, he added, "And you, of course, we need your gift for English. I could ask one of our young monks to assist me, but the fewer people who know of this quest, the safer we will all remain."

"Dimitri is a good one with secrets," Chara offered.

The bishop smiled down at the woman from his past.

"Knowing his grandmother as I do, I am not the least surprised."

Dimitri stopped at the house long enough to drop off his grandmother and see to his father's needs. He then drove Carey down to the harbor-front hotel, only to discover a note from Nick saying he'd been taken away by their friend from Kos. When Dimitri asked who that was, Carey looked at him thoughtfully and said, "Maybe you should ask Nick."

"Of course."

"I don't want to hide secrets from you. And if you ask me again, I'll tell you. But Nick is responsible for our being here, and some things should probably come from him."

"I understand." And he did. "What will you do with the rest of your day?"

"Go for a walk. Try to digest everything you and your grandmother gave me. The wonderful food and the even more wonderful experiences." Her eyes were guileless, her face a lovely picture of youth and health and allure. "I can't thank you enough."

"Would you like to go for another ride on my boat?"

"Don't you need to work?"

"I have just declared this day a holiday." It was a line he had used a hundred times, and the fact made him very sad. Which was odd, because he had seldom wanted a woman to agree as much as he did Carey. "Will you come? Please?"

Dimitri had always prided himself on his ability to focus fully on the woman of the moment. As far as he was concerned, this talent was the reason why he succeeded as often as he did. Being able to make his temporary partner feel she was the center of his universe.

He was doing it now, with Carey. Applying the same force-ful intent to another appealing woman who was not yet his. And yet this time there was a difference.

This time all he felt was dust. The usual flames refused to ignite. The furnace at the core of his being was empty. He opened the wheelhouse's front window, took a deep breath of the clean sea air, and felt the breeze threaten to pass straight through the void where his heart should have been.

He had known this feeling before, of course. Many times, in fact. The morning after a night of pleasure often carried such emptiness. The tearful encounters and accusations, the pain on beautiful faces, the words intended to rake his callous heart—all these had brought such a sense of worthlessness. But never before had they come at this point. When the lovely woman lounged in the stern and smiled at the gulls and the light. While she waited for him to join her and make the hour perfect. The one sweet hour that was hers to claim. Never had he felt like such a deceiver.

Dimitri cleared the outer island, slowed to a trolling speed, and set the automatic pilot. He stopped at the door of the wheelhouse and stared down at Carey. She wore a tank top with cutoff jeans. Her legs were stretched out, longer than the lee bench. Earbuds were fitted in place, and she tapped her sandaled feet in time to a song playing on her iPad. Her copper hair was trapped in a bandana, the tendrils not cap-tured looking frosted by the sunlight.

Who was this woman, really? The thought unsettled him and brought with it confusion. He tried to remember if he had ever asked such a question before.

As he started down the wooden stairs, Carey opened her eyes and smiled. She freed her ears of the buds. "Mind if I stay here for a couple of years?"

"Stay as long as you like."

"This is what I dreamed life would be like in Greece." She swung her feet to the deck. "What I thought I would never have."

This was the moment when Dimitri should have offered the first whispered promise . . . the hours to come, and other dreams he could make real for her. He opened his mouth to speak the words, but they turned to ashes and clogged his throat.

"Dimitri? Is everything okay?"

"I'm . . . glad you are happy," he managed.

He climbed back into the wheelhouse and headed the boat into open waters. Over the engines' rumble he heard everything that he could be saying, the provocations that started like little jokes and gradually became more alluring, suggesting pleasures to come. But he knew he would not speak any of them. For the first time ever, he would remain silent.

When she joined him and talked about fishing with her grandfather, he rigged a pair of bottom lines and set them in place before going into the galley to fix a late lunch. They ate at the stern table, and he swiveled the fighting chair around and locked it into a special place for her. Which turned into a good thing, because a fish struck the port line with such force that it tilted the deck.

He guided her as she fought and finally landed one of the largest amberjacks he had ever seen. The two-hour battle left her thrilled and exhausted. He gutted and dressed the fish as they motored toward home, stopping along the way at one of the small uninhabited islands that had a lovely beach with a view of the sunset. He anchored in the shallows and rowed the dinghy to shore, then built a driftwood fire. A picnic basket was packed for just such an occasion, with glasses and a frying pan and spices, along with olives, flatbread, and olive oil. He cut steaks from her catch to grill, and they ate in silence because the words still wouldn't come.

Carey's face glowed from the day's heat and the sunset and the simple enjoyment he had offered her. She smiled at him a smile that was part wistful and part welcome. He knew then it was time to make his move.

But she shocked him to utter stillness by asking, "Have you ever had a girl as a friend?"

He did not know what to say.

"I don't mean a girlfriend." Her tone was as easy as the autumn breeze drifting over the hills behind them, flavored by sage and dust. "I mean a friend who happens to be of the female variety."

He flitted through all the possible answers that would steer them away from such uncomfortable topics. Yet he found himself replying, "Sofia, my first mate. Otherwise . . . No, not really."

She smiled, and to him it felt like a reward for being honest. And it was almost enough, even when he felt raw inside from the admission. Carey asked, "Would you like to be friends, Dimitri?"

"What if I want more?"

In reply, she turned and whispered to the sunset and the molten sea. "Moonshine eyes."

"What did you say?"

"Something my grandmother told me." She turned back. "You would be easy to fall for. But I can't. Actually, I could. But I don't dare."

He nodded, feeling disappointed yet in an unexpected way, as though the words had actually wounded him. In truth what he wanted to tell her was that she was very smart.

He breathed in the sunset air. "Can I ask you a question?"

239

"Anything at all."

"What you saw in the cave at the monastery. What you were feeling. It made me . . ." He felt as if he were fighting against the man he had always been in order to form the words, "Will you help me see what you did up there?"

Carey's response surprised him more than anything else that day. She wiped her eyes with an unsteady hand, smiled with a full heart, and said, "And now the day is truly complete."

36

The hour after sunrise the next morning, Nick sat in their hotel café and sipped a final cup of coffee. Carey had phoned earlier and said that Dimitri was ready to speak with him. Nick watched Dimitri's boat ease up to the stone harbor wall. Carey stood in the bow, moving easily with the boat's gentle rocking. Carey's laugh rang over the distance between the café and the boat. A trio of old men repairing nets lifted their heads and saw her leap lightly to the pier and tie the boat's line to a cleat. One of the men said something, and the other two chuckled. Nick could well imagine they spoke about how Dimitri had returned to port with another beautiful prize.

The previous evening, Nick had arrived back just before dark, eaten a solitary meal, and was up in his room when Carey entered the room next door. He'd listened to her sing to herself as she'd prepared for bed. Happy, carefree, full of the joy that had always drawn him to her. He hadn't slept at all well. There was no reason for him to be as miserable as he felt. It was ridiculous. He had gotten exactly what he wanted. Precisely what he asked for.

Now Carey came running up, her nose plastered with sunscreen and her shirt splattered with dried salt. "Come on, sport. We're going for a ride."

Nick wanted to argue. Not because he was tied to the spot, but because he was locked away from sharing her happiness. "Where to?"

"Dimitri has something he wants us to see. And we've got to hurry if we're going to make it in time."

He followed her across the quay. "Time for what?"

"No idea."

He stepped onto the ship's rail, waved to Dimitri, and watched as Carey untied the line and leaped onto the deck. Dimitri gunned the motors and pulled away from the harbor. Carey said, "Go topside. I'll be right there."

Instead, Nick followed her into the galley. He leaned against the side wall and watched as Carey filled a pot from the freshwater canister, lit the stove, and set it on to boil.

"Do you want to know what happened yesterday?" he asked.

"I got your note saying you had gone off with Stefanos. How was it?"

"Okay. I spent the day touring the local waters on his naval vessel. They can't find Duncan McAllister."

"That's Dimitri's contact, right?" She set tea bags in three mugs. "Maybe you should ask him."

"You trust the guy to tell us the truth?"

"Yes, Nick, I do."

The easy way she said that tightened his gut. All the dread images he had fought off during the previous night returned with a vengeance. "Care to tell me why?"

She gave him the sort of look that only a woman could

manage, full of cool understanding and distance. "Would it make any difference, Nick?"

The way she said his name was almost like a slap on the hand, as though she were correcting a fretful child. Telling him to grow up. It only made his heart hurt worse. "Of course it would."

She made a process of pouring the boiling water into each mug, then adding a dollop of honey and condensed milk. "Dimitri and I have been talking about faith."

"Excuse me?"

"You heard what I said." Carey took two of the mugs. "You can carry yours."

He followed her out of the hold and up the steep stairs. Dimitri greeted him with a nod, accepted the mug from Carey, and asked, "You have told him?"

"Not yet." Carey propped herself in the opposite corner. "Nick says McAllister has vanished."

"I doubt that," Dimitri replied. "I doubt that very much."

Nick resisted the urge to rebuke Carey for speaking so openly. Instead, he asked, "Where are we going?"

"Like I said on the phone," Carey replied, "Dimitri has decided to trust us."

Nick saw the new familiarity between them. He saw how Carey had made herself at home on this man's boat. And he felt sick to his stomach. "Great."

"Yes. It is. He wants us to talk it over with his father and grandmother. If they agree, then he will tell us everything."

"I'm glad," Nick said. But all he could hear were the other words that echoed back and forth through his brain. That he had lost her. His chance to forge a deeper relationship with Carey Mathers was gone.

It took them a little over an hour to travel the length of Patmos. Dimitri only spoke twice, to point out the island of

Chiliomodi to their left, and then to name the high peak of southern Patmos, a great stone beacon rising in empty splendor. Carey left at one point and returned with sandwiches and fresh mugs of tea. Dimitri checked his watch several times as they rounded the island's southern rim. "It is a bit early, but we should be okay."

Carey asked, "Early for what?"

"You'll see."

She smiled at Nick, as though it was a perfectly good response. They slowed and approached an island that appeared to be little more than a boulder dropped into the blue waters. There was no beach. High cliffs were flecked with bird droppings and fell straight into the sea. The timeworn rock was creased with deep shadows by the sun. Dimitri took aim for a shadow shaped like a giant's mouth.

Carey asked, "We're going in there?"

Dimitri reduced the engines to a low rumble. "I discovered this when I was a child. I thought then it was the perfect place to hide secrets. I was right."

Nick felt trapped by far more than the sheer rock walls that rose up around them. He had never seen a better place for an ambush. Dimitri could be delivering them to their death.

Carey's face was now pinched tight. "What are we doing here?"

"I just told you," Dimitri said. He pulled the throttles into reverse for just a moment, then slipped the engines into neutral. "Sharing secrets."

They were in a cavern floored by water. The walls rose like a stone pipe, up to where a distant fleck of blue gleamed directly overhead. Nick asked as calmly as he could manage, "Why is this important?"

"Because . . ." Dimitri pointed at the cave in front of them, opening perhaps twenty feet above the waterline. "That is where I left the packets."

Carey's face was still creased with fearful conclusions. But Nick understood. "The counterfeit money."

"Yes."

"How much did you carry?"

"I have no idea. Over a hundred packets, maybe four kilos each, all plastic-wrapped. We weren't supposed to do this."

Nick interpreted the comment. "So McAllister did not hire you to transport counterfeit euros?"

"I would never have agreed to such a thing. Duncan Mc-Allister asked me to smuggle parcels from the Aegean waters to North Cyprus. Those were also carefully wrapped, but I know at least one contained painted ceramics."

"So they were historical treasures, probably stolen locally."

"Or found by his divers. In Greece, recovering treasures from the seabed is treated as seriously as stealing from a home or museum." Dimitri lifted his sunglasses, so that Nick could see the shadows that rimmed his eyes. "You understand, by telling you this I am putting my life and the lives of my father and grandmother in your hands."

Carey answered, "Thank you for trusting us, Dimitri."

He turned and studied her for a long moment. Finally, Nick cleared his throat and asked, "Will you tell us about this?"

"It is why I brought you here," he replied. "So you will understand that I mean to tell you everything."

Dimitri emerged from the waterborne tomb, returned to the harbor, and led them up the street to his home. The entire journey, Carey had kept expecting Nick to start with the questions. Instead, he remained not just silent but withdrawn.

Every time he looked her way, Carey had the distinct impression that her oldest friend was in pain.

Dimitri helped his father walk to the padded chair on the patio, then entered the kitchen to prepare tea. When he returned, he was accompanied by a young woman whom he introduced as Sofia, his mate and longtime friend. The woman was around Carey's age, but carved from very different days. Her skin was darker than Dimitri's. She carried not one ounce of excess weight. She kissed the father's stubbled cheek, then settled into a chair somewhat removed from the table.

Dimitri did not so much seat himself as crouch in the chair between his father and grandmother. He directed his words to Carey and continually translated so his family would understand. Neither his father nor his grandmother spoke at all. When Dimitri finished the narrative, the group on the patio remained silent, almost breathless. The only sounds were a pair of kids shouting from somewhere down below and Nick's pen scratching across the page. He hunched over his pad, writing slowly, like he had become arthritic and every letter required great effort.

Now that Dimitri had finished, no one seemed in any particular hurry. Perhaps it was the island life that instilled such an ability to be surrounded by risk and pressured on all sides and yet remain calm. Out in the harbor, a lone boat carved a white furrow through the sunlit waters. Directly in front of her, two gulls danced and weaved across a sky of porcelain blue. The afternoon was so quiet she could hear Dimitri's father struggle to breathe.

Sofia slouched in her seat and frowned at the open sea, out beyond the sheltering cove. When she spoke, her words carried a grim finality. Carey saw Dimitri wince in response. But before he could translate, his grandmother said something that startled Sofia and Dimitri both. Chara spoke at some length, gesturing to the water and the horizon.

Afterward, Carey asked, "Please, will you tell us what you're saying?"

It was Sofia who answered. Her English was heavily accented, but clear enough. "I spoke of my worries. That Dimitri might lose his boat. That I will not be crew anymore. Chara says now is not the time for such worries. She is right."

Dimitri added, "My grandmother also said she is very proud of Sofia. There are not many island women who work the boats. My grandmother says Sofia showed great courage, fighting for the right to follow her dreams. She says Sofia reminds her of Bouboulina."

"I'm sorry, who?"

"A legend," Sofia replied almost crossly.

When Dimitri had translated that, Chara clicked her tongue in admonishment. "My grandmother says Bouboulina is most certainly no legend."

Chara began speaking softly, her voice holding to a steady cadence, like she was repeating a much-loved tale. Dimitri translated, "Bouboulina was born in 1771 inside an Istanbul prison. She was the daughter of Pinotsis, a famous sea captain who had fought to overthrow the hated Ottoman Turks. When Pinotsis was captured, his entire family was sent to jail. Bouboulina spent much of her childhood in prison, before her family was finally released and allowed to return to the Dodecanese.

"When she was forty years old, Bouboulina inherited the shipping and fishing boats of her late husband, and transformed them into a secret fighting force. She used her own money to hire sailors and soldiers. When the war of independence began in 1821, Bouboulina was named admiral of the Greek navy. She died penniless four years later, but lived long enough to see her beloved country become free."

The patio went silent. Sofia's face gradually converted to a stolid calm. Nick stopped writing, but kept his eyes on the page. Carey waited for him to speak. The next step was obvious to her. She knew precisely what needed to happen. There was a question they had to address while they were gathered here together. Still, Nick remained as he was, hunched over the notebook in his lap.

Carey decided she had to take this on herself. "Why Patmos?"

Slowly all faces turned her way. Nick's were the last set of eyes to meet hers. The pain was so clear, she wanted to walk over and hold him. But they were simply friends, and they were there to do a job.

Dimitri said, "I'm sorry, what?"

When Nick still didn't speak, Carey said, "Duncan McAllister could have gone anywhere with his operation. Why here?"

Sofia replied, "Patmos is special. It is the quietest of the major Dodecanese Islands, with a good harbor and many boats. He could come and go at will."

"But Stefanos seemed to be aware of McAllister as soon as he arrived here," Carey pointed out. "So there was no secrecy, not even at the beginning. It seems to me there had to be another reason."

Dimitri nodded. "I have wondered about this as well."

Sofia said to Dimitri, "So Duncan came looking for you."

Carey felt the same unsettled reaction she experienced when dealing with incomplete research or poorly prepared reports. There was something more at work. What, exactly, she could not say. Nor could she pinpoint how she was so certain. She asked, "How many boats are there like Dimitri's?"

"Not so many," Sofia said. "Dimitri's English is excellent. His engines are new. He has a Turkish passport as well as Greek. He is both fisherman and tourist guide. He can go anywhere. He knows the waters extremely well."

"Okay, you may be right. But I think there's something else," Carey said.

Nick stirred in his seat. Again she waited, and still he didn't say anything. Instead, he looked out over the harbor. "Nick, maybe you should be asking these questions," she said.

He continued to gaze out over the sunlit display. "You're doing fine."

Reluctantly she turned back to the others. "I think Duncan McAllister came here for a very specific reason."

"Smuggling," Sofia said. "Treasure out, euros in."

"No," Carey said. "Duncan McAllister came to steal something even more important."

Dimitri translated, then said, "My grandmother asks why you are so certain?"

"There's only one place on the island with anything truly worth his time." Carey pointed at the fortress monastery on the high peak behind them. "They've already stolen icons from the monasteries of Halkidiki."

Dimitri's father spoke in his hoarse whisper. His son translated, "Have they also hired local boats there?"

"Nick?"

He rose from his chair and pulled out his phone. "I'll ask Eleni to check."

Then Chara said something that caused both Dimitri and Sofia to jolt upright in surprise. Carey asked, "What is it?"

"Wait, please." Dimitri and his grandmother and Sofia spoke back and forth for a time. Then he translated, "There was an attempted break-in at the monastery museum."

"When?"

"Three nights before Duncan met me. My grandmother says that after the thefts on Halkidiki, Bishop Galatas organized the youngest monks and acolytes into regular patrols. Very secret. They did not even tell the police. That night they heard the scrape of a tool and saw a burglar cutting a hole in a museum window. They raised the alarm, but the burglar escaped."

An hour later, Dimitri left to arrange for a meeting with the bishop, Nick in tow. Carey said her good-byes and walked down the steep road leading to the harbor and the hotel. Wordlessly, Sofia fell into step beside her.

Carey couldn't get over how quiet the island was. She knew the tourist season had ended. She could feel a faint chill on the afternoon wind, as though the sea whispered a forbidding note of harsher days to come. The empty street was a throwback to an era most of the world had forgotten ever existed. A lone woman climbed up toward them, stout and strong and turned old before her years. She and Sofia exchanged greetings, and the street returned to its timeless calm.

Now that they were alone, Carey could feel the tension radiating off the young woman. "Sofia, are you concerned about something?"

Sofia snorted. "Dimitri says you are very intelligent. That is not an intelligent question."

"I mean, something between you and me?"

Sofia stopped walking. "You know who my husband is?"

"The chief of police here, right?"

"There is no *chief*. Manos is the *only* police. All the others have been let go."

The afternoon sun lanced between the buildings to her

left. Sofia stood halfway in the light, half in shadows. Carey had no idea what she had done or said to make this woman so angry.

Sofia demanded, "What did you say to Dimitri?"

"I don't . . . That was private."

Sofia sliced the air between them. "We work the boat together. For three years we are on the sea, night and day, on our own. We have no secrets, Dimitri and I. I know his women. I know his family. He knows mine."

"This was different."

"I see his face, the sadness. Dimitri is made for song and dancing and laughter. Of course it is different. I want to know *why*."

Carey felt herself relax. The woman was angry in the manner of a mama cat protecting her brood. Carey felt as if a door had opened and granted her a glimpse of what island life really meant—when people lived in each other's pockets, when knowledge of their neighbors went back not just years but generations, where nothing raised their ire more than a threat against one of them from the outside.

Carey said, "We talked about faith."

Sofia squinted. "This is a joke?"

Carey nodded, not at the question but the sudden realization. Dimitri couldn't ask anyone on the island. He needed an outsider to offer something that didn't meet with either their expectations or their assumptions. She said, "You must have known Dimitri was sad before I came."

"This was . . . different."

"What made him so sad?"

"This you must ask?" But the heat was lower now. "His father is dying. His business is destroyed. The tourists do not come. The crisis made him . . ."

"A smuggler," Carey finished. "It has filled his life with danger."

"Dimitri is much stronger than even he knows. He has never—"

"Never felt so weak," Carey said, nodding again. "Never needed help so much. Or answers."

"You take advantage of him," Sofia accused, but Carey could tell she was uncertain now, as though she had to reexamine her own perspective.

"You know that's not true," Carey replied. "He asked me about where I find strength for the hard times."

"Truly, he asked you about God?"

"Yes." The light over the harbor shimmered with a force only Carey could see. "And I answered as best I could."

Carey knew Sofia furtively studied her as they continued down the street. The island lady remained in lockstep, her worn boat shoes slapping softly against the stones. Finally they arrived at the quayside and turned toward the hotel. Carey found herself worrying over Nick. Nick hadn't said anything about her going off with Dimitri. Surely Nick knew she wouldn't allow herself to be seduced by a man she had only just met, no matter how handsome he might be, how romantic the setting. Actually, under no circumstances.

When Carey stopped, Sofia walked back up. "You have thought of something else I should know?"

"It's not about Dimitri." Carey peered down the sunlit harbor, trying to pierce the mystery. "Nick wasn't himself today."

"You are speaking about the journalist." She shrugged. "He listened. He wrote. That is his job, no?"

"Right."

Sofia was watching her closely now. "This Nick, he is your lover?"

"No. Never. My oldest friend."

"So, your friend, he is moody. That is the word, yes?" When Carey didn't respond, Sofia started to speak, then glanced beyond her. "Something is wrong."

"What is . . . ?"

Sofia halted her in the process of turning around. "Go. Leave." When Carey remained still, she hissed, "*Run.*"

But as Carey started to bolt, an overly calm male voice spoke from behind her, "Move and your friend here dies."

The man was small and compact and had a smile that reminded Carey of a wooden mask, tight-lipped and dead-eyed. He and three others moved into a loose semicircle around them. They had chosen their spot well, where two former gift shops were now shuttered and locked. Carey's hotel was a hundred meters farther down the quay. The man drew a little pistol partway from his pocket. "Make a sound and I use this."

Her mind was a frantic tangle of conflicting thoughts. She was searching for some way out when a grimy van swept down a nearby lane and came to a stop directly beside them. The small man gripped Carey's arm and shoved her toward the van's open side door. "The both of you, inside."

"Do you know who my husband is?" Sofia asked, glaring at him.

The men hauled both women inside. "I know he'll be a widower if you don't do exactly what we say."

37

The van's rear hold had no windows. The guards positioned Carey and Sofia on piles of canvas tarp, then settled onto two wooden benches that ran down both sides. They held their pistols with casual ease, like they used them so often the weapons had become linked to their bodies, connected by sinew and sweat. They were all dressed the same, an indifferent uniform of navy trousers and wool sweaters and lace-up combat boots. The smallest guard watched them with eyes that glittered with an offhand malice.

They rode like that for over an hour. Twice, Sofia dared to threaten them with what her husband was going to do. The small man observed her with eyes like brown glass. Carey remained silent. The van's ancient engine whined as it struggled around tight curves, going up and up, then taking a very steep road back down again. The men were bounced hard on their benches, though none seemed to notice.

Finally they slowed to a halt. "End of the line," the driver said.

The man in charge lifted his pistol and said, "Stay right where you are."

When the van door opened, all Carey could see was a blinding reflection of the sunlight off a white beach. She squinted as three of the men climbed out. A few minutes passed, then one of the men returned and said, "We're ready."

The man in charge told them, "Here's what's going to happen. You're going to walk straight out and across the beach and get in the dinghy. Do that and everybody goes away happy."

Sofia started, "My husband—"

"Is at the far end of the island." The gun barrel moved a fraction toward her. "We checked. But it doesn't matter anyway. And you," he said to Carey, "don't bother screaming. There's nobody around to hear you. All right, let's go."

The light was painful. The beach scrunched hard beneath her feet, like breaking through a crust of snow with each step. Carey realized she wasn't walking over sand, but salt. She would have fallen on the uneven surface twice were it not for the grip one of the men kept on her elbow. The men wore sunglasses and hustled her and Sofia at a pace just a notch below a full run. The salt pan continued all the way down to where two dinghies waited.

A pair of women dressed like the men kept the boats in knee-deep water. One asked, "Why did you bring them both?"

"Because they were together. Any trouble?"

"We haven't seen anything except a gopher."

He hefted Carey over the side and dumped her in the space between seats. When she started to rise, he snapped, "Stay exactly where you are." He slipped over the side and said, "Let's move."

Carey furtively studied the woman now driving their craft's

outboard motor. The woman had spoken with casual brutality, as if they were hauling two corpses. Carey hunched up on the floor of the boat so that no part of her touched any of them. She wrapped her arms around her legs and held on tight, clenching her body so they wouldn't see the tremors.

The bishop was out visiting a church and village in the island's north, so Dimitri left a message asking Galatas to contact him immediately. The drive back home was as silent as the one going up. Several times Dimitri had the impression Nick was about to speak. It was like sitting next to a pressure cooker on slow boil. But Dimitri had too many other worries to concern himself with a moody journalist.

As he entered the house, a phone rang from his bedroom, a sound he had never heard before. Then he realized the ring tone belonged to the cellphone Duncan McAllister had left for him at the harbor café. Dimitri entered his bedroom wishing his heart did not surge into overdrive every time he had to speak with the man. "Yes?"

Duncan said, "You've let me down in a major way, laddy boy. I'm thinking I should have stood back and watched Stavros take you apart that day. Then hired the big man in your stead. But it's too late for all that now. And we don't have the time nor the space for such regrets."

"I don't understand." Dimitri felt another cold wash, part adrenaline and part fear. He sensed that Duncan McAllister had put his mask aside. "I've done as you said. The journalist is outside—"

"We've moved beyond distractions such as American journalists. This is about life and death."

The easy way he spoke the words made the threat even more chilling. "I did what you asked."

"Oh, is that a fact? And did I ask you to discuss my business with the Greek navy?"

"I haven't—"

"You told the journalist, and the journalist told the commander. Not to mention how you've become the bishop's new best mate. I don't even want to think about what you've discussed with the likes of that one."

Dimitri opened his mouth, but his brain refused to offer up a response.

"That's what I thought. Now listen up. The fate of your two lovely ladies is in your hands."

Dimitri found himself standing in the patio's sunlight. He did not remember walking out there. His grandmother stood to his right. Nick had risen from his seat and was staring at him.

Dimitri asked weakly, "You've taken them?"

"That I have, lad."

"Manos will—"

"Manos is *your* problem. You make that island cop behave, else he'll never see his wife again. Are you reading me?"

"What do you want?"

"Now that's what I like to hear. Nothing like a proper stimulus to make for a willing pair of hands."

His grandmother and Nick both spoke in two different languages, asking what was going on. Dimitri wanted to raise his hand and tell them to be silent, but he could not manage even a simple motion. His entire being felt trapped in a sunlit terror. "Tell me Carey and Sofia are all right."

"You'll have a chance to hear that for yourself in a bit. Now here's what's going to happen. You'll get rid of the Yank. Then round up the cop and explain the score. I'll be ringing back in three hours. You be ready to move."

38

After Dimitri related the conversation with Duncan McAllister, Nick immediately said they should contact the naval commander. Dimitri winced, as if it caused him severe pain, and nodded his agreement.

The phone connection with Stefanos was fairly good, as the navy equipped all their vessels with a sat phone. The man's voice was void of emotion and turned metallic by the connection. Even so, Nick sensed Stefanos's cold rage.

Nick cut the connection just as a powerful car engine roared up the road on the home's other side. A slender man in a police uniform hurried around the corner of the house. Dimitri winced a second time at the policeman's sudden appearance, but remained standing where he was. He said dully, "This is Manos, the husband of Sofia."

The policeman went first to Dimitri's grandmother, who appeared in the doorway leading to the kitchen. The officer embraced the old woman and held her for a time. Chara's scarred hands patted his back as she murmured something.

Then the policeman released the woman, turned to Dimitri, and embraced him as well.

Dimitri stood with his hands at his sides, unable to move. This time, it was the cop who spoke softly. Dimitri tried to answer, but it proved impossible. The policeman said something else, then stepped back and pretended that he didn't see Dimitri wipe his eyes.

The cop shook Nick's hand and afterward leaned down to greet Dimitri's father. Manos seemed to cultivate a non-descript air. Nick had met people like this before. They found ways to hide in plain sight. The way they held themselves was intended to make other people glance over and then dismiss them as unimportant. Most of the people Nick had known like this were professional criminals. Nick found it very interesting that an island cop would adopt such a manner.

Dimitri's grandmother emerged with two glasses of tea. She set one on the table in front of her son-in-law. The other she brought over and handed to Nick. She examined his face, then reached out and patted his cheek. The hand felt rough to the touch. Even so, Nick found himself swallowing against a rising tide of emotions: sorrow, anger, helplessness, frustration. All his studied control was suddenly dissolved—because an old woman had touched his face.

He realized Manos was watching him. The cop's features remained calm and expressionless. But Nick had the impression he'd passed some sort of test, because the next thing he knew, Manos spoke to him directly for the first time, in fairly good English. "I want Dimitri to tell me everything that happened."

Dimitri emerged with two more steaming tulip glasses. One he handed to Manos, the other he set on the table before his father. "I already told you."

"This man, Duncan McAllister, he spoke to you in English, yes? So tell me everything he said. Word for word, as close as you can remember."

Dimitri frowned in concentration as he spoke. When he was done, Manos checked his watch. "How long ago did he call?"

"I didn't notice, but almost an hour, I think."

Manos turned to Nick. "Did you note the exact time?"

"When Dimitri came outside, he was still on the phone, but I don't know how long into the conversation that was."

Dimitri said, "Three, maybe four minutes."

Nick looked at his watch. "Then the call came through forty-six minutes ago." Nick studied the two men and couldn't keep back the confession. "Carey is here because she agreed to help me with this story. I'm the one who should have been nabbed, not her."

Manos seemed to like his admission. "You want to talk blame? I am the man who told his wife that she should go on a trip to smuggle goods to Cyprus. Me. The policeman of Patmos. You deserve more blame than me?"

Dimitri said, "I took McAllister's money. I accepted the job. I risked her life then. I did it again today. And Carey . . ."

"Enough with the blame," Manos said. "Our job is to get them back."

Dimitri asked, "Why is the precise time important?"

Manos nodded at Nick, as though using the question as a test. Nick replied, "Manos wants to see if there is time to set up a triangulation and track him."

"Is there?"

"No," Manos said.

"Actually, there is," Nick replied. "I spoke with Stefanos, the navy guy. He's waiting for your call."

"Give me his number," Manos said. As he dialed, he added, "I think maybe you are a very good investigative journalist."

Manos spoke softly for several minutes, then hung up and said in English, "It would be helpful if we knew now what this McAllister wants."

Nick said, "Dimitri's grandmother said there has been a break-in at the monastery."

Both men were watching him again, their gazes as intense as the sunlight. Nick went on, "Our involvement in this whole matter started with suspicions about the theft of icons from monasteries in Halkidiki. I . . ."

"Go on," Dimitri said.

"It's something Carey said this morning, about their having a reason to come to Patmos. More than just wanting to hire you."

Manos nodded. "Go ask your grandmother if she will speak with us."

They gathered at the dining table, where Chara heard them out in calm silence. She had an old woman's ability to hide her thoughts and emotions down deep. When they were done, she tapped her fingers softly on the table. Nick assumed it was arthritis that caused all her digits to move together.

Finally she said, "Much of this will need to come from the bishop."

Dimitri translated in such a smooth monotone, Nick almost felt like he was hearing her directly. Dimitri continued with the same process when Manos said in Greek, "Anything you can tell us now will be very helpful. We need to find a way to place them under stress. Do you understand what I mean?"

"Not really. Do I need to?"

"I want you to understand what we intend, so, yes. Right

now these criminals think they are in control. They have our women, they are hidden, we do what they say. We must find a way to turn this around."

"That sounds dangerous."

"If we do it wrong, yes. But we will be right. And when we do this thing, it will become dangerous for them. Do you see? Very dangerous."

Nick thought it was an odd way to comfort an old woman, but Chara looked out the door leading to the patio, to where her son-in-law sat watching them from his padded chair. He rasped a few words, which Dimitri choked over, but translated, "I trust them with my life."

Nick had reported on dozens of crime-related stories. He had interviewed hundreds of people involved—cops, federal officers, Interpol, CSI, coroners, victims, witnesses, criminals. But he'd never been inside an ongoing investigation. Nothing could have prepared him for the quiet intensity that filled the room. The air crackled with a sense of urgency. He needed to start writing this down.

"Excuse me," Nick said, waiting for the faces to turn his way. "Is it all right if I take notes?"

Manos regarded him solemnly. "You understand not to write what will hurt our ladies?"

"I won't publish anything, or even discuss it with anyone else, until you give me the green light."

"In that case, you may write whatever you want." Manos took a sip from his glass, then motioned to Dimitri. "Please ask your grandmother to continue."

Chara said, "The bishop and I meet occasionally for tea. He says it does him good to have an outsider as a confidant. I think I am the last connection he has to an old life that he still cherishes. That day, he spoke of a young acolyte who had left the order. Snuck away like a thief in the night. Galatas said he had failed the young man and his own order. He took this very personally."

Manos asked, "When was this conversation?"

"Two days after the attempted break-in at the monastery. The day before my Dimitri was contacted by the smuggler."

Manos glanced at Nick as Dimitri translated, then said in English, "I do not trust such coincidences."

Dimitri asked first in Greek and then in English, "How did the bishop think he failed?"

"Galatas said he should never have let the young man enter their ranks. He sensed the man had never truly turned from the ways of this world. He was in confusion and some inner pain, and he claimed that he wanted nothing more than a monk's life. He begged. Finally Galatas agreed."

"Where is this man now?"

"He has vanished. Galatas contacted his family. They have not heard from him."

Manos allowed the silence to build. Nick's gift of clarity was only heightened by the pause. He knew Manos was going to take aim long before the island policeman said, "And now the bishop is fearful that the young man might have fed information to the smugglers."

"He is. Yes. The young acolyte was assigned duty in the museum."

Manos sighed and checked his watch. "So in eight minutes we will receive a phone call from a smuggler and a thief. We must assume Duncan McAllister has been hired by someone to steal a specific item. But this is no longer about stealing from an unguarded monastery. The island police and the navy are involved. So he reaches out to Dimitri. And he will now tell our friend to do this for him."

The pressure had been building in Nick ever since Chara started talking. He knew it was time. Even though he didn't have all the pieces in place. "There's something else."

Manos glanced over. "Can it wait?"

"No."

"Make it fast. We are seven minutes out."

"We need to go over the sequence of events. Duncan McAllister comes down here for an item. He links Dimitri to his plans by smuggling a collection of items out of the country. When Dimitri arrives at the drop, he finds himself hauling counterfeit notes. This tells us that McAllister is a major operator. Nobody handling five or six million fake euros is small fry. So why did he bring in Dimitri?"

Nick waited. Dimitri completed his translation, but no one spoke. He found the energy too compressed to remain in his seat. He rose and began pacing between the table and the patio doorway.

He went on, "Carey was right. That is the weak element. Somebody as big as Duncan McAllister doesn't need a local guy to haul his load. He is surrounded by professionals. Why doesn't he hire a professional criminal to do his transport?"

Dimitri started, "I don't . . ."

Nick waited to ensure Dimitri wasn't going to continue, then declared, "Duncan McAllister was setting you up."

Manos huffed a tight breath.

"He knew about the investigation surrounding the thefts from the Halkidiki monastery," Nick said. "Or maybe he organized it himself. Not even his allies at the top of the Greek government could stop the monks from raising a fuss. So now Duncan has to find somebody else to take the heat. Someone who is seen publicly talking to a stranger, someone already under suspicion. We know McAllister was a suspect by how the naval commander was already on his trail. Then Dimitri accepts his money and is later seen spreading it all over the island."

"His plan was to steal the item," Manos said, "and have Dimitri be arrested for the crime."

Nick continued pacing. "But things go south. More and more attention is being paid to what's happening here on Patmos. I show up. And Carey. And Stefanos connects us with Dimitri. And we become friendly with the bishop. And suddenly McAllister's scheme doesn't work any longer. So he kidnaps the two women."

Manos finished, "And now he is calling to force Dimitri to do what he was going to be arrested for in the first place."

Chara spoke a soft question. Dimitri translated the previous exchange for his grandmother and father. When he was done, Manos said, "This is better than good. It is correct."

"Whatever it is they came for," Nick said, "it has to be bigger than big. This isn't about some icon. I don't care how much such a painting might be worth. No typical relic in some island museum is going to bring a major international criminal ring into play like this."

All eyes turned to Chara. After Dimitri's translation, she said, "For this you must speak with the bishop."

"Do you know what the item might be?" Manos asked.

"I know the legends," Chara replied. "Galatas has never spoken a word about it. But years ago I heard stories."

Manos started to press further, but then the phone rang. The room froze.

Dimitri checked the phone's readout, and nodded.

Manos said to Nick, "Tell Stefanos to start the trace."

39

The two dinghies glided across the still Aegean waters for a couple of hours, maybe longer. Carey could not be sure. Her phone and her watch were gone. Why they felt it was necessary to take her wristwatch, she had no idea. But she felt its absence like a wound.

Now and then a ripple of wind creased the smooth water, and the inflatable craft rattled with little staccato beats Carey felt in her spine. The sun descended to where it fell directly in her eyes. The small man watched her, but didn't speak. The sky and the sea melted together in a blue that might have been beautiful under other circumstances, but soon became a blur.

There was nothing to see, which was undoubtedly what they had planned. The second craft held to a steady position about thirty feet away. Sofia was positioned like Carey on the deck and faced away from her. Carey shut her eyes, feeling tired for no reason other than the adrenaline draining away. She wished she could sleep. Just drift away from the droning engine and the empty sea and the kidnappers in blue and the danger.

When the engine slowed, Carey opened her eyes and saw they were approaching a small island. It rose from the waters like a prehistoric mound, a single hill with two rocky points forming a narrow cove. Three walls of a ruined structure protruded from the hill like old teeth. The late afternoon sun painted the island in miserable shades of yellow dust. When the two craft cut their motors, the silence was monstrous.

Once the dinghies were beached, the man in charge said, "Get out."

Carey remained where she was. "I want my watch back."

"I won't tell you again."

"What difference does it make whether I keep my watch?" She could see he was going to refuse. Though she hated hearing the pleading in her voice, she had no choice. "The watch was my late father's. Please."

His men held the vessel's sides and watched the drama unfold. The small man demanded, "You'll do exactly what I say?"

"Yes," Carey said.

He slipped the watch from his pocket and handed it to her. "Go stand on the beach."

The beach was perhaps fifty feet wide and ten deep. The white sand was tilted so that it formed a quarter-moon mirror for the descending sun. Two men started unloading the dinghies, moving back and forth to the ruined structure on the hill.

Sofia crouched on a rock to Carey's left. She said softly, "I know where we are."

"Later," Carey whispered. Just then she could only register one thing—they were going to leave her and Sofia here. But they were unloading supplies. Which meant their kidnappers didn't intend to murder them. Carey's relief was so strong she wanted to fall to her knees and weep.

The small man crossed the beach toward her, raising his pistol as he approached. He worked the slide, feeding a bullet into the chamber. "You will do exactly what I say or I will shoot you dead."

"I already said I would."

"Just so you understand." He turned to his crew. "Who's got the hookup?"

The woman with the casual voice walked over and handed him a satellite phone. The small man flipped up its stubby antenna. "One of you lot put a bead on the cop's woman."

The woman smirked as she drew her weapon and took aim at Sofia. Carey shrilled, "*No!*"

The man's voice was as calm as the sea. "Yell again and my mate shoots your friend."

Carey's breath hitched in her chest.

"That's better." He turned to Sofia. "Not one peep."

Sofia continued to crouch on the rock, her gaze aimed at the empty waters. If she even heard the man, she gave no sign.

The small man used his gun as a pointer. "You come with me."

The structure atop the low hill had a wide central opening with empty windows to either side. Age and storms had turned it the milky yellow color of the rest of the island. Even the graffiti streaked over the front looked ancient. Carey thought the ruin held a shocked expression. She followed the lead guard up the rise and through the portal. The rear third of the slate roof was still intact.

The small man punched in a number, lifted the bulky handset, and said, "We're good to go at this end." He listened, then said, "Hold on."

His pistol swept over the supplies stacked in the shadows. He said to Carey, "Take a good look. Three plastic water canisters, a box of cereal bars, two sleeping bags. All the comforts of home. Now pay attention. My friend will place a call, then patch us in. When I give you the phone, you will say you haven't been hurt and you have supplies for three days. Say anything more and your friend dies. We only need one of you alive to make this work. That was the plan. Keeping her alive is of questionable benefit. Her life is in your hands."

"I'll do what you want."

"That's right. You will." He lifted the phone. "Make the call."

Nick punched in Stefanos's number with fingers that trembled so badly he twice had to redial. Dimitri shifted his own phone to the dining table and put it on speaker.

Nick heard Duncan McAllister's voice for the first time when the man asked, "Can the cop hear us?"

"Manos is here beside me," Dimitri replied.

Stefanos spoke into Nick's other ear, "Move in closer so I can hear."

Duncan's voice sounded tinny over the cellphone's speaker. "Make sure the cop understands his wife's life depends on his remaining silent and attentive."

Dimitri glanced over to where Manos stood beside his grandmother. "Manos understands."

"Hold on a sec. There's someone who wants to have a word." He heard a couple of clicks, and then McAllister said, "Put her on."

There was a faint rustling sound, then Carey said weakly, "Hello?"

Dimitri was panting, each punch of breath capable of holding only one word. "It's me. Are you—?"

"Shut your gob, lad. Let the lady speak."

"We haven't been hurt." Carey spoke in a robotic drone. "We have three days of supplies. I—"

"That's all you get," McAllister said. The rustling sound was louder this time.

"Carey!"

"All right, lad," Duncan's voice went on. "It's just you and me now. Here's the plan. The bishop has something I want. Tell him either he hands it over or these two die. You've got forty-eight hours. Tell me you understand."

"But I don't know what you want!"

"The bishop will, and that's all that matters. Forty-eight hours and not a minute longer." The phone went dead.

Nick said into his own phone, "McAllister is gone."

"Give us a few minutes to see whether we had enough time." The naval commander's voice remained impossibly calm. "Making a trace over open water is much easier than people realize. The real problem is obtaining permission from the courts. But we are circumventing this."

Nick watched as Manos stepped in close to Dimitri. Chara stood on the dining table's opposite side, her hands laced across her middle, her head bowed, her expression inscrutable. Manos and Dimitri were poised in the doorway leading to the patio. The sunlight cut them into a silhouette resembling Greek athletes, the energy filling the tight space between them—a frantic scramble of power and rage and intent.

Stefanos's calm formed an odd contrast to the room's tension. "With Duncan McAllister, we are not triangulating his signal. We do not need to fashion a net using radio towers.

At least I do not think we will. One moment more and we will be certain."

Nick tried to match the navy commander's unruffled voice, but the tremors pushing his gut with each breath defied his control. "You think McAllister used a sat phone?"

"Correct. Hold a moment." The phone went quiet, then Stefanos said, "It is definitely a sat phone. We have piggy-backed on the signal from the phone Manos is using. We integrate satellite transmission data with GSM tracking. We have almost seamless global positioning within the Mediterranean basin . . . Yes. We successfully inserted the required software into McAllister's phone. Ninety seconds."

But for Nick, every second took hours to pass. "You were saying about the courts . . ."

"Everybody is frozen in the amber of this crisis. We put in requests and they vanish into the void of fear and lost jobs."

"But you have friends."

"I told you. We have been forced to build alliances everywhere we can. People of honor. People who do not seek to enrich themselves above all else. People who . . ."

When the naval officer went silent, Nick reported, "Stefanos thinks he can track McAllister's location."

Dimitri and Manos turned to the room. Nick held up his free hand. Wait.

Stefanos returned to the phone. "Duncan McAllister placed the call from international waters south of Crete. It makes things more difficult. But my allies will arrange an official request. Which we will hold back until this is over, and then postdate it."

"You are going after him?"

"I have arranged for an ally in our air wing to take me up

271

for a flyover. But only to identify his location. For now. Call me with updates, yes? And good hunting."

Nick related what Stefanos had said. Dimitri shook his head. "That cannot be the location of our ladies."

Nick asked, "How can you be certain?"

"It is too far from Patmos. Even with his Hatteras, he could not collect them and arrive there by this time. The trip would take at least twelve hours."

Nick waited as Dimitri translated, then asked, "What exactly does McAllister want?"

Chara sighed, shook her head, and replied through her grandson, "This will break the bishop's heart."

Bishop Galatas's office was located in what once had been the monastery's bakery. A huge stone fireplace dominated the north wall, so large that all five of them could easily have fit inside. The windowless room was forty feet long and thirty across. The broad stone cell held a desk, a refectory table, with a dozen high-back chairs arranged around it. The walls were graced with three icons and a silver cross, which glowed in the electric lights.

The bishop was unlike anyone Nick had ever met. He was tall for a Greek, right at six feet, and large-boned in the manner of a construction worker. Big hands and shoulders, and a wide neck almost completely hidden behind his flowing white beard. He wore a simple black cassock with a silver cross on a chain. As he ushered them into chairs around the table, Galatas tucked the cross into his breast pocket. He emanated a strong sense of muted power, as though the authority had been accepted but not especially welcomed. His gaze was soft and piercing at the same time.

The bishop spoke with Chara first in Greek, his voice a

rolling thunder that required little volume. She responded with a few words, waving her hand at the others, clearly telling the bishop to proceed.

Dimitri and Manos took turns explaining the situation. Nick studied each man in turn. It was what he did, this careful examination, labeling one specific trait of each person, so that when the time came he could make the story live for his readers by swiftly describing the people involved. In the trade, this was referred to as giving characters three-dimensionality.

Manos was as tight as a coiled spring, a cop waiting for his chance to take down the bad guys, staying calm because he was all that stood between his wife and her demise. Dimitri, on the other hand, appeared completely wrung out. Nick knew exactly how he felt.

When the two men finished speaking, the bishop sat and stroked his beard for a time. Then he replied in Greek, and Dimitri translated, "I will not have the blood of these two innocent women on my hands."

Manos replied in the same language, with Dimitri resuming his duty as unobtrusive translator. "We are not to that stage yet. It may arrive, but it is not what we are dealing with now."

"You are certain of this? You will accept responsibility if . . ." The bishop sighed heavily. "I have dreaded such a moment. Ever since the acolyte vanished, I have wondered if this might be the reason."

"May I ask his name?"

"Brother Timothy."

"His island name?"

"Pirro Glavan. From Mykonos."

"He has been here how long?"

"A year, a bit longer."

"You have been in touch with his family?"

"Three times. They have not heard from him."

Manos looked at Nick. A silent communication that Nick needed a moment to understand. Manos asked, "You have a telephone number for this family?"

When the bishop gave it, Manos rose from his chair. He spoke in English, his eyes still fixed on Nick. Making sure he understood. "I will just be a moment."

Nick was fairly certain he understood what Manos had in mind. The policeman wanted Nick—the outsider, the man with no authority or connection to the island and the monastery—to be the one to ask the bishop the difficult question. Manos didn't want to bear down unless it was necessary. And one glance at Dimitri was enough to know the man wasn't up to the job. But Nick was. In fact, it was what he was best at. It was all he needed to still the tremors that gripped him.

"Can you tell us something about the treasure?" Nick began.

The only sign the bishop gave of his nervousness was how the hand that stroked his beard accelerated. "We have many treasures," he stated.

Nick didn't respond to this, but instead let the silence linger. Establishing his own rhythm. Behind him, Manos spoke in a soft murmur into his phone.

The bishop's hand swept down the long beard, then pulled the cross from his pocket. He fingered it a moment, realized what he was doing, and then put it away again. He spoke in Greek. Dimitri translated, "Our treasury and the museum hold over three dozen icons, the oldest dating back to the fifth century. There are documents granting the island special status under the Ottomans, and others from the Holy Roman Emperor. Many riches."

"That is the party line," Nick said quietly. "That is what

you tell anyone who asks. But it doesn't explain what we are facing now."

"I had nothing to do with it," the bishop replied through Dimitri.

The man's evasiveness excited Nick. He briefly thought this had to be how a hunting dog felt when it first caught the scent of its prey. "No one is suggesting you did. But you need to understand something. This is a vital truth. Your awareness of what I am about to tell you is very important. The lives of two women depend on it."

Nick waited while Dimitri caught up. The bishop said in English, "I am listening."

Nick said, "The secret you are holding has already come out."

The bishop stared at the empty fireplace, his gaze distant. Nick waited as Manos slipped back into his chair, then continued, "Let me share with you something I've learned about those involved in organized crime. They love the dark. They move in secret. They prefer to operate unseen. If they come out in the open, it means just one of two things. Either their territory is being threatened, or the score is so huge they decide it's worth the exposure."

The bishop remained silent.

Nick went on, "Duncan McAllister isn't doing this because he thinks he can steal another icon. He's after something very special. And he knows what he seeks is right here."

Manos cleared his throat. "The former acolyte has vanished. His family is extremely worried. He called to say he was coming, but he never arrived."

Nick knew they had to proceed very carefully. Whatever it was the bishop held in confidence, he had been doing it his entire life.

"The young man said he was bringing enough money to cover the family's debts," Manos added. "They own a tourist hotel. The crisis, you understand?"

The bishop's sigh was so great it tore at his throat, like a half-formed moan. "What is it you want to know?"

Nick started by offering an observation. It was a trick he'd learned during his first investigation in Paris. His boss had been a thirty-year veteran, who carried the weight of a thousand hard-won secrets like battle medals. The man had said that even when the source was ready to reveal, even when they wanted to set down the secret burden, still the person needed a little help, a bridge to cross, something that would take the holder of the secret partway. And the best such moments, his boss told Nick, always carried an element of surprise.

Nick said, "A theft this big would never see the light of day in the auction world. This would go into the collection of a super-rich person, someone who has learned to be discreet because his wealth is so great that flaunting it would mean risking kidnapping or worse. He's been in contact with the crime bosses responsible for these thefts. Not directly, of course. This is where government links are crucial. These people know the ones in power. So the criminal's allies in the power structure serve as go-betweens. This senior bureaucrat has met with the potential buyers. They describe what might be available. A price is agreed upon. And these events are set in motion. But for this to happen, they had to know the treasure is here."

Dimitri's translation snapped the bishop's gaze into sharp focus.

"Think about it," Nick said. "The thieves were fairly certain of their target. Somebody had to have fed them the preliminary information. Somebody powerful enough for the thieves to trust, an ally in the government. Or someone you've known for years in a museum. Or maybe from your own—"

"We have many visitors," the bishop said abruptly. "Since the crisis began, it seems every politician and senior government official wants to be seen praying here, asking God for help."

Nick felt a faint whisper of an idea, but he put it aside for later. The bishop was fully engaged now. He was waiting for the next question. And he was ready to answer. Nick nodded across the table to Manos, his job done. For now.

Manos asked in English, "Tell us what treasure has brought this down on our heads."

40

"I t is a letter," the bishop answered.

Manos didn't blink. He didn't even appear to breathe, except to say, "It must be very valuable."

"Priceless. Beyond value."

"You are certain it is still in your possession?"

"I am."

"I do not doubt this. The criminals will be certain of this as well. I question only because I must."

"I understand."

"Tell us about this letter."

The bishop shifted uncomfortably. His tone grew deeper, almost apologetic. "The secret is part of the responsibilities I accepted when I became head of this monastery."

"You heard what the journalist said. The secret is already known."

"I feared as much when the acolyte vanished." The bishop seemed to gather himself. Yet the breath and the words remained locked inside.

"Tell us how you are certain the letter is in your possession. You have seen it recently?"

"Not since the day after I took on this role. I was taken down by my predecessor."

"Down?"

"Into a cave hidden beneath the museum. That is why the monastery is positioned as it is. Why it was built in this place. Because the cave offers us a secret hold, one not even the Ottomans could find."

"So there is a letter," Manos said. His voice was gentle, his manner soothing. Nothing the bishop said would surprise him. No secret was so great that Manos could not help him carry its burden. "Hidden away in the cave beneath the museum. And only the head of the monastery is aware of its existence."

"Only the monastery's head has *seen* it," the bishop corrected.

Manos interpreted, "Some of the monks and acolytes know something of the mystery, or at least that a mystery exists."

"And so it has been," the bishop agreed, "for nineteen centuries."

Dimitri paused over translating the number. It was only the briefest of hesitations, but enough for the bishop's eyes to shift over to him. He then returned his attention to Manos, and waited.

"What does the letter say?" Manos asked.

"I do not know."

"You must have *some* idea."

"I do. Yes."

"Will you tell us?"

"It was written by Prochoros."

"The scribe who served John here on Patmos?"

"That is correct."

"The scribe wrote a secret letter. Who was it addressed to?"

"Mary, the mother of James, the bishop of Jerusalem."

Manos barely managed to keep his tone level. The tremors entered his voice, rocked his frame, then subsided. "The scribe of John wrote a letter to the mother of Jesus?"

"That is correct."

"Why was it not sent?"

"Because word came that Mary had passed on to the other world."

"So Mary died . . ."

"And Prochoros soon after."

"And you were left with an unopened letter."

"A scroll," the bishop confirmed, "with an unbroken seal."

"Were you told what the letter says?"

"John, the author of Revelation, had passed on. Prochoros was ill. He wanted to relate his experiences as scribe and servant. That is all I know."

Manos breathed, and with it he released a shudder. "That is enough."

41

Dimitri asked Manos for his keys, saying he wanted to check his sea charts. When Manos excused himself and began making phone calls, Nick followed the bishop from the office, turned and walked alone across the central courtyard. Nick had the glimmer of an idea, and he needed space. He passed through the cavelike narthex with the massive icon of John the Apostle, dating back to the monastery's foundation. He saw several monks and acolytes and thought they all carried themselves with the same somber worry as the bishop. He wondered what it would be like to live in such a community, bound so tightly through prayer and ritual that they understood the unspoken and shared what they didn't even comprehend.

Nick paced the piazza fronting the monastery's entrance. The longer he remained out there, the more he thought he might have something. He set it out in careful steps, the same way he would track any investigation. He could not give in to the worry or the guilt or the ache that filled his chest like the vacuum of outer space. He needed to *focus*.

When he was ready, he took out his phone and found the number he had put into its memory. A young woman answered, and he said, "Eleni, it's Nick."

"Nick! Shame on you! You said you'd call back hours ago!"

"I'm sorry. Things are—"

"Where are you? How is Carey?"

"I'm okay. Carey is . . . I'm still on Patmos."

"Wait, wait, my aunt . . ." The phone was lowered, but Nick could still hear the rush of Greek back and forth. The familiarity of the two voices and their natural warmth caused the void in his chest to burn more fiercely. He clamped down hard. There was no space for such emotions now. *Focus.*

Eleni came back on the line. "My aunt has many questions."

"Not now, Eleni. I need your help."

She must have heard his tension, for she said, "Something is wrong?"

He could still hear the other woman pouring a stream of Greek into Eleni's other ear, so he said, "Please, ask your aunt to give us a minute."

Eleni lowered the phone again. Eventually the noise abated. When she returned, Eleni's voice was low, grave. "Is it Carey?"

"I need you to do something, and I need it fast. This is very important. Are you ready?"

"Of course. Tell me what you need."

"Get in touch with Adriana Stephanopoulos. Ask her to contact her sources at the museums and private houses that have been burglarized. She needs to ask them one question. In the days leading up to the robbery, were they visited by Chronos Boulos?"

"Oh. That one."

"It might have been one of his close cohorts. But I'm thinking he might have done this himself."

"She will tell me that she has survived this long by not being noticed. I can place these calls myself—"

"No. You can't. You have to get back to me with this information within the next thirty minutes. Tell Adriana we don't need an exhaustive survey at this point, just confirmation that Boulos visited at least a couple of the places. That's all."

"Nick, I'm sorry, but she will need a very good reason to do this thing."

"Tell her . . ." Nick took a breath that raked his throat and chest. "Carey has been kidnapped."

"Oh, Nick." Eleni's voice turned to a whisper. "You are sure of this?"

"We've just heard from the kidnappers."

"Boulos did this?"

"Not directly. But I'm fairly certain he's our link. I need confirmation. I'm looking for a pattern."

"For this, Adriana will help."

"Remember, thirty minutes. Call me the instant you hear."

Nick cut the connection as the cop car ground up the hill and pulled to a halt in front of the monastery. Dimitri emerged with an armful of rolled maps and bounded up the steps. "I may have an idea."

Nick followed him back into the courtyard. "That makes two of us."

Entering the bishop's office, Nick stationed himself next to the impressively large fireplace. He watched Dimitri roll out the sea charts on the refectory table, explaining his idea for locating the two women. Dimitri was certain Carey and Sofia had been taken off-island. The kidnappers ran too great a risk of being discovered here on Patmos. No matter how remote a cottage they might use, there was always someone not far away. Manos agreed with him, saying that he'd been contacting his allies in the outlying villages, asking them to check all isolated structures, looking for strange men with two young women, one of whom was his wife. News that their only policeman's wife had been kidnapped by foreigners, Manos assured them, would be enough to ignite the entire island. The two men spoke in English, making sure Nick was included. But he didn't speak and didn't approach anyone.

The bishop returned as the two men bent over the maps, arguing over which of the uninhabited islands within reach would be remote enough to ensure the women couldn't escape. Apparently there were several dozen, perhaps more. Nick remained where he was, hoping the call he'd requested would come through. They all felt the pressure of the passing minutes. They needed to act, but carefully and with intent. Their unspoken objective formed a powerful bond between them. They were going to bring the two women home safely. And take down whoever was responsible.

After the bishop left the room for the second time, Manos asked, "Should we ask to see it? The letter?"

Nick spoke for the first time since reentering the monastery. "Best not." The two men looked at him. He went on, "We might weaken and give in too early. Let the bishop be the one between us and our last resort."

Manos asked Nick, "Why do you stand over there?"

"I have an idea. Maybe." He lifted his phone. "I'm waiting for the missing pieces to fall into place."

Thirty-five minutes after he walked into the office again, Nick's phone rang. He didn't recognize the number, but answered anyway. "I'm here."

"This is Adriana Stephanopoulos. I have what you are looking for."

42

Dusk was slipping into its final farewell when Dimitri declared he was heading for his boat. Manos argued with him to wait until dawn, but Dimitri refused to listen. He insisted that he knew the waters well enough to begin his search in the dark.

But as Dimitri rolled up his charts, Stefanos called using Nick's phone. Nick listened to the naval commander's initial report, then asked him to wait and called to Dimitri, "I may be able to help you do this faster and better."

"How is that," Dimitri countered, "since you have never been to Greece before?"

"Just listen to what Stefanos has to say." Nick set the phone on the refectory table and hit the speaker button. "Where are you?"

"Spotter plane, nine thousand feet over Crete, heading north," Stefanos replied. "We have identified the vessel. It was where we thought."

"You're sure it's him?"

"A Hatteras yacht leased by a security firm based in Paris. Such leasing companies are handing over several million dollars' worth of boat to people who intend to sail off into the unknown. An individual is required to sign and take personal responsibility. In this case it was Duncan McAllister himself."

Dimitri asked, "What is their location?"

"Forty-two miles south of Lithinio Point, the southern tip of Crete. Not in our jurisdiction, which makes things very difficult for us. I would have to go through official channels to apprehend him. This requires filing an affidavit. If I did that, McAllister's allies would alert him."

Manos said, "We think it is impossible for them to have transported the women in the Hatteras."

"I agree. That probably explains his position. He has removed himself."

"Can you come pick me up?" Nick asked.

The sat phone turned the officer's voice metallic, but even so, his surprise came through. "What, on Patmos?"

"I have an idea," Nick said. He then outlined his plan, seeing only the holes, forcing himself not to worry over how such a puny effort might risk the lives of the two women.

But when he finished speaking, Stefanos said, "It is a good idea. Excellent, in fact. Phyllis Karras was right to trust you."

"For this to work, we need a plane," Nick said.

"We have only the one we can use without alerting their contacts among the authorities. I must come for you."

"Then how can we keep an eye on McAllister?"

"Through the same software we have inserted in McAllister's phone. Every time he turns the phone on, every time he makes a call, it will ping us. But there is another problem. Patmos does not have an airport."

Manos leaned over the table. "What plane are you flying?"

"Beechcraft Twin Turbo. Who is this speaking?"

"Manos. There is a road to the south of Hora. We have used it for prisoner transfers."

"It is long enough for us to land?"

"The police use the same type plane. We have placed a radio beacon at the north end, a wind sock at the south. We also have embedded lights for night landings."

Stefanos muffled the phone, then returned and said, "Give me the coordinates. I will be there in ninety minutes."

It was after ten when the plane carrying Stefanos, Nick, and Dimitri arrived in Athens. Dimitri frowned and fretted over being taken further away from his intended goal. But Nick knew they had done the right thing. Stefanos had already ordered the pilot to be ready for takeoff an hour before dawn. The plane was theirs for the entire day, enough time for them to scour every one of the islands on Dimitri's charts. Nick climbed into the back seat of a waiting unmarked vehicle, and he and Stefanos set off.

The airport had an entire section fenced off and heavily patrolled, assigned to the Greek and European armed forces. Dimitri and Nick were both given bunks off the pilot's ready room. The airport was on the same side of Athens as the ritzy village where Chronos Boulos had his compound. The main shopping street was jammed despite the hour, the cafés and restaurants full to bursting. In silence, Stefanos observed the array of expensive shops and elegant people.

The naval commander had done his job well, better than Nick could have hoped. The former Institute director's compound was encircled by police cars and official vehicles. The high stucco wall had been turned into an electric rainbow by their flashing lights.

As they pulled up, Nick asked, "You're sure he's inside?"

"An officer checked before they shut him down." Stefanos pointed to a van blocking the front gates. "His telephone and internet no longer function, and all radio and cellphone traffic has been jammed."

Nick felt his face tighten in a mock grin. "He should be stewing nicely by now."

"The police say he has come out several times to inform them of his contacts in high places. The officers have listened politely and refused to let him or anyone else depart. Wait here, please." Stefanos exited the car and walked over to return salutes and shake several hands. When the formalities were completed, he waved to Nick and called, "It is time."

Nick rang the buzzer attached to the front gate and stepped back so he was well inside the range of the security camera. A voice said in English, "Yes?"

"Mr. Boulos, my name is Nick Hennessy. You might recall our recent conversation. I am wondering if I might come in and speak with you."

"Who is that with you?"

Nick motioned for the naval commander to move closer. At his request, Stefanos had stripped off his uniform jacket and tie, replacing it with his seagoing navy-blue sweater. "This is my friend, Stefanos Khouris. If you don't mind, I'd like him to come with me."

They waited through a full minute of silence. Nick assumed the man inside was utterly confused. Which was what Nick had intended. Chronos Boulos had spent all day trapped inside his elegant compound, waiting for something official. Something bad. Instead, the man at his doorstep was a reporter who spoke politely and requested nothing more than a few minutes of his time.

The gate buzzed and began to swing open. Stefanos followed Nick inside.

The palms and lemon trees lining the graveled drive were aglow with spotlights, as was the forecourt's central fountain. What Stefanos thought of the opulent surroundings, Nick had no idea. But he was very glad for the man's presence, especially when an armed security guard drifted into view from behind the main house. Nick muttered, "Company."

"I see them." Stefanos didn't seem perturbed. "A man like this is never alone."

Chronos Boulos opened the door as they started up the front steps. "What is it you want?"

"Thank you for seeing me, Mr. Boulos. May we come inside?"

"Why am I under siege in my own home? I have done nothing wrong!"

Nick smiled, as if he had been granted a formal invitation, and stepped past the man's bulk. "I'm very grateful, Mr. Boulos."

The man had no choice but to follow them into his own living room. "What is it you want?" he demanded once more. "And who is this man?"

"I already told you. His name is Stefanos Khouris. May we sit down?"

"This is utterly outrageous. I have friends who will—"

"Duncan McAllister sends his greetings."

The man grew pale, but held his ground. "I know no one by that name."

Nick found an odd comfort in how his rage remained carefully locked away, simmering down where it wouldn't be a threat. "Mr. Boulos, I am here as an outsider, because they want you to know you have a choice."

"Whoever is behind this will be crushed, do you hear me? I have allies at the highest levels of government!"

"Those police are here to arrest you and take you where you cannot be found by your friends. You will be held until either you cooperate or the matter is put to rest. But I asked them if I could come in first. I pleaded with them, Mr. Boulos. Do you know why?"

The man panted through several half-formed words, then waved his hand in what might have been permission for Nick to continue.

"I asked them to let me speak with you, I begged them, because no matter how bad things might be right now, in just a few hours things could be much, much worse. For you, for me, and for my friends. The people you are connected with have committed a very serious crime. I am here because Mr. McAllister has kidnapped two young ladies."

"I . . . No . . . What?"

"He abducted them from Patmos. One of them, Mr. Boulos, is the archeologist who accompanied me here, the woman hired by your institute before you shut it down." Nick held up his hand, stiff-arming the man's unspoken protest. "The other kidnapping victim is the wife of the island's police chief. Can you imagine what those police gathered outside your gates will do if this woman is harmed in any way?"

"I told you, I have nothing—"

"It doesn't matter who you know. They won't listen to reason. They will take you away, Mr. Boulos. And you will never be heard from again."

"Whatever this man has done, I am not involved!"

"Before you say anything more, Mr. Boulos, let me please

tell you one thing. There are coincidences. I know this because my allies have checked. I know you personally visited at least two of the museums and a further three private collections in the weeks before these places were burgled. Those police out there will not believe that such coincidences can occur without your direct involvement. This is why I assure you that no matter how powerful your contacts, if you're taken into custody, you will not return to your lovely home. Ever."

The man didn't seat himself so much as drop like a stone onto the couch. His complexion was paler than the ivory leather.

Nick continued, "So I'm here to offer you the only choice you will have. You can tell me what you know, and we will arrange for you to be officially arrested. Then your friends in high places will come and get you out. But if you decide to remain silent, I will leave, and others will come in. And you will be made to disappear."

The man's lips trembled, and he could scarcely shape the words, "What do you want to know?"

43

After the two dinghies departed, Sofia rose slowly from her crouched position. Carey thought she moved like an old woman, barely able to make it up the rise and into the ruined building. Carey followed her inside.

Sofia unscrewed the top of a water canister and flipped it over, pouring the cap full and using it as a cup. She drank deeply, filled it again, and offered the cup to Carey. She hadn't realized she was thirsty until that moment. "Thank you."

Sofia waited while she drank. "More?"

"Yes."

She refilled the cup. "I'm sorry about what I said to you on the road."

"We were just kidnapped and you're apologizing about how you talked to me eons ago?" Carey finished the second cup. "I'm glad for a reason to smile."

Sofia screwed the cap back into place. "I thought those men were going to kill us."

"So did I."

"Are you hungry?"

"No. But I will be, when my stomach stops quivering."

Sofia walked out the empty portal and over to the left-hand point overlooking the narrow beach. She started kicking at rocks. "On the ride out here, I kept thinking of all the things I have done that I regret."

"I was too scared to think." Carey knew her sense of overwhelming relief was unfounded. They could still die out here. "But if I could have, it would have taken a lot longer than that boat ride to work through all my mistakes."

Sofia grunted softly. She stepped to one side and kicked once more, creating a divot in the earth. "Manos will be so upset."

"He can find us, right?"

"There are dozens of these islands. And this one, it is not a place he would naturally look. We are inside Turkish waters. This building was used by Greek fishermen who lived in Izmir. Thirty years ago, the Turkish generals overthrew the government. Then there were troubles between the vigilantes and Greeks who had been living in Turkey for centuries. The Greek fishermen all left Turkey. The waters became fished out by trawlers, who bribed Turkish officials for licenses."

"So maybe the Turks could find us."

She waved that away, took another half step, and kicked again. "That was years ago. There are no fish. No one will come."

Carey went inside and brought back two cereal bars. They ate in silence as Sofia continued to kick at the earth. Carey asked, "What are you doing?"

"Wasting time, probably." Another small step, another dislodged rock. "When I was young, all the islands like this, the fishermen left supplies."

"They hid stashes?"

"For other fishermen. In case of storm or shipwreck." Another step. "Always in the southwest corner. Away from the storms, which come from the northeast. A gift of hope. Fishermen looking out for each other."

"That is the coolest thing I've ever heard," Carey said. "When was this?"

"Before I was born." Another step. "Before the boats had radios and cellphones."

"If we have food and water, what do we need with supplies from fifty years ago?"

Sofia didn't look up. "They always left flares."

Carey joined her, kicking rocks and scraping at the loose topsoil. After twenty minutes, she said, "I keep thinking about the Starbucks across the street from my university's main entrance. I have a fantasy drink for whenever I really need to indulge myself."

"Like now," Sofia offered.

"Every calorie in the universe. A super-size frap with an extra shot of espresso. So much whipped cream it oozes over the sides of the cup. Chocolate sprinkles and extra caramel drizzled on top."

"I have no idea what you are talking about, but I'm sure I want one." Sofia moved over a few paces and continued kicking furrows in the yellow earth. The westering sun bathed them in a final glow. "When I was little, my aunt made what she called a fisherman's cake. Ground pistachios from an orchard in the north of the island. Honey from hives she and my uncle kept in the hills, where the bees drink from wildflowers. She served it with clay pots of more honey and fresh yogurt—"

"Stop," Carey said, waving a hand. "Just stop."

"On the sea, you dip one bite in the yogurt, the next bite

294

in the honey. Sweet, then sour and sharp. You could run all day and never stop with my aunt's cake."

"Nana Pat used to say there was no hurt that couldn't be made better with banana cream pie."

"This is your grandmother, yes? Dimitri said you were an orphan."

"Sort of."

"How can you be sort of an orphan?"

"I'll tell you what it's like. My clearest memory of the days when they buried my parents were hugs." Carey stared out over the water, seeing another world. "Every time somebody let go of me, there was another person waiting to scoop me up. They never let me get enough air to be lonely. And it's been that way ever since. I get sad, sure. I miss them terribly. But I've got folks doing everything they can to let me know I am family."

Sofia kicked harder still. "My aunt and uncle, they cannot have children. My father, he wanted a son. They all wanted boys. Then I come, and I disappoint everyone."

Carey started to object, but then held back. The sunset and the empty sea formed a confessional. This was neither the time nor the place for platitudes.

"And now I have Manos. And I disappoint him also."

Carey reached over and took her hand. "Does he say that?"

"He does not need to."

The skin of Sofia's hand was rough and callused, her grip strong. Carey didn't speak because she didn't know what to say.

Sofia went on, "All I want from life is to be on the sea. I love this world. I worked my uncle's boat, and then when he became sick, Dimitri came and offered me a place. Dimitri . . ."

"He is your friend."

"And Manos." She wiped her face with her free hand. "Manos is my husband and my best friend."

Carey said slowly, "That must be really nice."

Sofia studied her. "What about your Nick?"

"Nick is not mine. Even if I wanted—"

"Do you?"

"It depends on the weather." Carey released her hand and walked down to the little beach. "Before, there was nothing I wanted more than for Nick to be my love. But this trip has left me feeling as though I've never actually seen Nick for who he is. Which means I've spent my entire life fashioning my own version of Nick inside my head."

Sofia's squint reformed to include a smile. "It is a terrible thing when your myths dissolve."

"Awful," Carey agreed.

"Is it true, in America a woman can do whatever she wants?"

"You mean, take any job?" Carey shrugged. "Theoretically."

"That," Sofia said, "is a very Greek answer."

"Nana Pat always said that I should find out what I want and go for it. That lasted until what I wanted was to leave Texas."

Sofia took another half step, kicked at the earth, and nodded. "Also very Greek."

"She wants me to do what I want and be who I want to be, but stay within shouting distance."

Another step, another kick. "Again. Greek."

They kept at it until the sun slipped into the sea and the stars came out. When they could no longer see the earth beneath their feet, they wearily climbed the stairs and entered the ruined structure. They swept the stone floor beneath the remaining roof and unrolled their sleeping bags.

Carey hadn't realized how tired she was until she lay down. She left the covering open, for the night was still relatively warm. "It will get cold, won't it?" she asked.

"With the clear sky, almost freezing." Sofia sighed her way into the bag. "I feel as though I have fished for two days without rest."

Carey had almost drifted off when Sofia said, "You will tell me what you and Dimitri talked about?"

Rather than answer the question, Carey felt joy flow through her, as soft as silk, carrying her away.

Carey was awakened by the pattering sound of rain all around her, water running off the roof in a steady stream. The air was so cold it bit into her ears and face and neck and the one hand that had slid out from the sleeping bag. Sofia had moved closer, wedging Carey between her and the rear wall. Carey could feel the other woman's warmth. She snuggled deeper into the bag and listened to the rain for a time, reassured that she wasn't facing this storm alone. Eventually she fell asleep again.

Long before dawn, Carey and Sofia were back to kicking rocks by moonlight.

The last remaining cloud departed with the first faint light of dawn. The sun rose in gentle stages, a pale wash over a windless sea. Carey's skin still burned from the previous day. She didn't mind, for the scratchy feeling made it all seem real. She hated the sense of helplessness. Kicking rocks made the exposure and the vulnerability and the worries all easier to bear.

Sofia popped up with a question. What did she think of Dimitri? Carey found her ability and her desire to hide melting away. Turning over rocks together in the predawn light made it a morning for divulging secrets.

Carey related what her grandmother had said about boys with moonshine eyes. Sofia liked that enough to laugh, race down to the beach, throw off her clothes, and dive in. She came back out, shivering like a dog shaking off rain, and laughing some more as she dressed. "Your grandmother is a very wise lady."

"Nana Pat usually knew what I was going to do before the thought even entered my head," Carey said. "It used to rile me to no end."

"What is this, *rile*?"

"Make me so furious, you could fry an egg on my forehead."

"Rile. A good word." Sofia rejoined her in the rock-kicking business. "I love Manos more than I love my own breath. But sometimes . . ."

"You want to take a stick to him." There was no reason why the notion should make her think of Nick, or cause her heart to ache as it did. "I know exactly what you mean."

"The first thing Manos does when he comes home is to lock his pistol in a gun safe. He says it is so I can't shoot him. On the days when he riles me, he is correct." Sofia kicked another rock. "You should go swim. You look riled."

"I was thinking of Nick."

"He is always so quiet, that one?"

"No. Something's bothering him, sure enough."

"He would not tell you?"

"He wouldn't even admit he was troubled."

"So the American men, they are no better than the Greeks." Sofia shook her head. "Why is this so, do you think?"

"That they can't talk about their emotions?" Carey sent a rock spinning off into the water. "They must *have* feelings before they can talk about them."

"He does not love you, this one?"

"He does not love me *enough*."

Sofia mouthed a silent *ah*. "And Dimitri?"

"Oh, he'd love me as well as he could, I imagine."

Sofia tried not to grin. "Which is rather well, from what I hear."

"Oh, sure. But for how long. A day? A week? A month?"

"Probably not a month."

"There you go." She kicked another rock harder still.

"Dimitri is Dimitri. Or so I always thought. And then you come, and you make him sad." Sofia bent over and probed the earth, then dusted off her hands. "No, not you. Like you say, he was sad before you came. But he is my friend, and I wanted someone to blame."

"You wanted to protect him, like a friend would."

"Dimitri is a good man, but in some ways he is also weak. He loves his father. He cares for him. He is good with tourists, and this is not easy because tourists are not always nice people. Dimitri makes them laugh; he gives them a taste of the islands. It is not just a boat trip for Dimitri."

"He makes them feel special." Carey kicked another rock. The island's southwestern tip was scored now with their marks. "I fell in love with a man who burned me very badly. It's taken until now for me to accept that it was partly my fault. He wanted a college fling. I wanted . . ."

"Everything," Sofia offered. "A life together, children . . . a home."

Carey caught the hesitation over that middle word: *children*. But Sofia didn't elaborate, and Carey decided not to press her. "Anyway, I don't do flings."

"It is good to know yourself."

"Maybe so. But still I can't help wishing . . ."

"That things were different. I know." Sofia kicked at another rock. "I know all too well."

Carey walked down to the water's edge. She could feel the cold radiating off the surface. If she dipped her toe in, she knew she wouldn't go at all. So she stripped and dove in before she changed her mind. The water's chill was electric. She felt it ripple across her skin with such force, she screamed underwater. Then the cold became a part of her, and she could enjoy the thrill.

The Aegean was so clear that she could look up and see the rising sun. She came up for a breath, then went back down again and swam over to where the silver bottom disappeared beyond a deep ledge. Carey felt the rush of even colder water drift up from the endless depths. All the unseen dangers flittered about her, everything she'd pushed away in the conversation with Sofia. It would be so easy for something to rise up out of that Aegean shadow and capture her and pull her away.

She rose to the surface and swam hard for the shore. She was gasping when she emerged on the beach. The morning's chill bit deep, causing her to tremble. Carey wondered if she would ever fully leave behind the sense of helpless fear she felt.

She then saw Sofia, on her knees and digging frantically, and suddenly the dawn was infused with hope.

44

Two hours before dawn, they returned to the plane parked on the military airfield. Nick climbed into the Beechcraft behind Dimitri, strapped himself in, and asked, "Did you sleep?"

"Maybe an hour or so. You?"

"The same."

Dimitri was seated in the copilot's position, charts already opened on his lap. They waited through the engine's revving, and then the pilot aimed for the runway. He glanced at them, nodded, and powered the twin engines to full. Nick loved how the plane bounded down the runway and leaped upward, as though it shared their impatience to begin the hunt.

They didn't speak again until the lights of Athens were behind them, with the Aegean one giant black mass below. They watched a pair of ships forging along, and soon the lights of some island appeared. Dimitri called out its name, but Nick didn't catch it, nor did he care. Their plan was to arrive in the waters surrounding Patmos just as daylight began to strengthen. They wanted to survey as many of the possible islands as they could before the kidnappers awakened. That, at least, was the plan.

Nick stared out at the dark horizon, the moon a silver globe to the southwest, and recalled something a retired admiral had said during an interview. How a good military plan was one that remained intact after the first bullet was fired.

The interview with Chronos Boulos had gone fairly well, to a degree. The former Institute director had confirmed that he was indeed point man for an international ring of thieves. But he had insisted he didn't know a Duncan McAllister and had no idea what had happened with the two women. And questions regarding who pulled his strings only made him tremble harder.

Around midnight, Stefanos had obtained enough to formally charge the man. But he couldn't afford to place his prisoner in the system; there was too much risk that he would alert someone linked to McAllister.

Stefanos brought Boulos back to the same airfield and locked him in the military brig, a temporary measure yet enough for the time being. Nick knew Stefanos was disappointed with how the interview had gone so far. He was after closure. Nick didn't work that way. He felt a growing sense of confidence in both his analysis and methods.

Nick was tired and knew he should doze. But what he really needed just then was a chance to think. Flying through the darkness at ten thousand feet lifted him away from himself. He could ask the questions he'd been unable to see clearly until that moment. Such as, what did he really want? Would he truly be happy with a solitary existence? No matter how grand the life of an international journalist, would he ever be satisfied as a loner? If he wanted a lasting relationship, who could possibly be better than Carey? And if this was true, why couldn't he take the steps toward the commitment she wanted? Were all the reasons he had for staying single nothing more than excuses? If so, wasn't it time he grew up?

Nick pulled out his notepad and wrote down the questions. He worked on this as he would the beginnings of an article. His fatigue actually helped, because it stripped away all the normal mental barriers. He studied the questions one by one, not looking for answers, not yet. Just asking the questions, he felt, was a move forward.

When he sensed he'd taken it as far as he could, he turned the page. On a fresh sheet he wrote the final question, the one that had drilled a hole in his brain all night long.

What do I do now?

By the time the light strengthened to where they could make out the sea below them, they were in position to begin scouting the empty islands between Kos and Mykonos. Yet this wasn't what Dimitri had in mind.

The pilot was adamantly opposed to whatever Dimitri was saying, but Dimitri matched him word for word. Nick watched them go at it as the sea turned a soft rose color below them, and the islands grew from indistinct shadows to glowing rocks. Finally he leaned forward and poked Dimitri's shoulder. "Shouldn't we get started?"

"That is exactly what I am trying to do," Dimitri replied. "If this man will only—"

"I am contracted to fly for the Greek military," the pilot said in English. "I will not risk my license and my job."

Dimitri pressed, "Two women have been kidnapped."

"I am sorry for your loss. But there are many islands for us—"

Dimitri pointed to his left. "I am certain they are there."

"You are certain. You can smell them? They call to you? Even if we knew they were there, I cannot fly over Turkish waters. And we *don't know*."

"Know what?" Nick asked.

Dimitri lifted the charts. "There are seven islands lining a deep-water channel just inside the Turkish boundary waters. They are perfect."

The pilot countered, "Looking there is extremely dangerous."

"Perfect," Dimitri repeated, shaking his head. "The currents are too strong for anyone to escape. Each island is separate from the others and the mainland. You can see nothing from any of them. The waters are fished out. This time of year there are no boats."

"Your knowledge of these waters is amazing," the pilot snapped. "And it changes nothing."

Dimitri said, "We need to do this before the world wakes up."

"You think Turkish radar sleeps? Their navy, they take naps at dawn?"

"Could we fly just inside Greek territory," Nick wondered aloud, "and at least check them out with binoculars?"

"We must go closer," Dimitri demanded.

Nick nodded and said, "We're wasting time. Let's take a quick look and then . . ."

He stopped talking because the pilot was already banking the plane.

They flew above a large island the pilot named as Samos. Ten minutes after that, they passed Agathonisi, and the pilot began descending. The sun formed a tight sliver to their left, which meant Dimitri was fighting the glare as he stared through binoculars. He continued to grouse, but Nick thought the pilot was probably right to be concerned.

The plane descended to where it flew only a few hundred feet above the water. Despite his worries, Nick found it an exhilarating experience. The Turkish mainland was a murky silhouette off to his left, cloaked by a mist that floated in the still air and turned the rising sun into a sullen orange ball. They passed one island, then another, little rocky pinpoints that came and went in a flash. Dimitri strained at each, the binoculars pressed against the windshield.

Then as they passed the third island, all three men shouted in unison.

A signal flare shot upward into the morning sky.

45

This time, the pilot made no argument at all. His name was Idas, and he had a truly remarkable voice. Nick knew this because as he circled around the island for another pass, Idas turned on the plane's stereo, and opera blasted from a dozen speakers. Nick recognized *The Barber of Seville*, and when the tenor's role opened, Idas sang along. Word for word. Flying thirty feet off the water, the wheels almost skimming the surface, circling an island where two young women danced and shrieked and hugged themselves.

Only Nick wasn't enjoying the show. Nick leaned forward between the two front seats and cut off the music. The pilot looked at him askance. "You do not like Rossini?"

Nick said, "Where are the guards?"

The pilot frowned into the sunrise. He tilted the plane and sent it around the island once again. The two women skipped about the ruined structure at the island's center, waving and shouting. They were definitely alone.

Nick shook his head. "The kidnappers are still on Patmos."

Dimitri swiveled in his seat so that his gaze remained locked on the women. "They will wait for the word to come that we have stolen the letter."

"And then they will take us out," Nick said.

The pilot asked, "All this is about a letter? What letter?"

"Very old, very valuable," Dimitri said.

"It better be. I am breaking a dozen laws. They could have missiles aimed at me right now."

"Your radio is silent, yes? So, no missiles. I must return to Patmos and get my boat and come fetch the ladies."

Nick said, "The kidnappers will have somebody watching your boat."

"I should have thought of this." Dimitri's frown deepened. "They will have eyes on the Patmos harbor, certainly."

"So how do we rescue—?"

Dimitri cut him off by asking the pilot, "Do you have a sat phone?"

"In the compartment by your knee."

Dimitri pulled out the bulky apparatus, cradled it in his hands for a moment, then turned it on and dialed a number from memory.

"Who are you calling?" Nick asked.

"The one man I can think of who will do anything," Dimitri replied, "so long as enough money is involved. His name is Stavros."

Dimitri watched as the pilot lined them up for their descent to the Kos airport. He liked how Nick was using the pilot's sat phone, talking with Manos, then with the bishop, then with Stefanos, and then doing it all over again. Making plans and keeping everyone in the loop.

Three times during their return flight, Nick asked if Dimitri wanted to speak with Manos. But Dimitri declined. Everyone involved in this rescue was focusing on the next step, working on a means to locate the kidnappers who were probably still hiding on Patmos. Dimitri liked being able to rely on others at this point. It left him free to do his job right. Which was to bring the two women home.

The Kos International Airport's main building was a throwback to a different era, when visitors sat at umbrella tables and sipped drinks while watching planes drift in and out of azure skies. There was only one other plane parked by the terminal when they landed. The pilot assured Nick the situation was very different during the high season, when jets packed with tourists landed daily from a dozen different countries.

They thanked the pilot, who didn't move from his seat. Soon as their feet hit the tarmac, the pilot revved the engines and took off for Athens.

Stavros stood by the front gate, his arms crossed, his scowl fierce. "You have the money?"

Dimitri replied, "I told you. The money is on Patmos. If I could safely go there and return, I would not need you at all."

"But you will pay me ten thousand euros for this trip, yes? One way or the other, you will—"

"Enough. We will not stain this day with threats. This is not about you and me. It is about rescuing two innocent women."

Stavros must have found what he was looking for in Dimitri's expression, for he jerked a thumb at the car and said, "Inside."

Dimitri waited until he had slipped into the passenger seat to say, "This is Nick Hennessy. He is a journalist from America."

"If you do not pay, no journalist—"

"I told you. No threats."

Stavros ground the gears and shot forward. He drove like most angry men Dimitri had known, which was badly. Stavros swerved unnecessarily. He fought the car and the road. He used the horn as a replacement for a club. Clearly other islanders knew his vehicle, for many braked and moved aside as soon as Stavros came into view.

The Kos airport was located inland from the southern town of Kardamena. As Dimitri expected, Stavros didn't take the turnoff for Kos town, but rather turned north and headed over the central highlands. The road was awful, and the drive terrifying.

They stopped in the quiet fishing village of Mastihari. The hamlet held a timeless air. Kids played a game of soccer in the middle of the main street. Fishermen sewed torn nets on the shingle beach while workers painted a newly repaired hull. A trio of black-kerchiefed women chatted by the stone embankment where Stavros parked. They offered him a friendly greeting, then chuckled as Nick rose unsteadily from the rear seat.

Nick fell into step beside Dimitri and declared, "If I wasn't in such a hurry, I would have walked."

One of Stavros's cousins was waiting behind the wheel of a decrepit aluminum boat with battered twin outboards. But as soon as the engines fired, Dimitri knew the boat's appearance was a ruse. They pulled away from the harbor and rumbled out into open waters. Then the cousin unleashed the boat's real power, and they flew.

They reached the island in just under an hour. The women were there, sunburnt and joyous and so excited that they continued dancing even as they waded into the waist-deep water.

Dimitri plucked Sofia out of the water first, because when Carey splashed on deck, Nick did what he had been thinking of ever since he'd first seen her through the plane's windshield, which was to sweep her up in an embrace that would last for the rest of his life.

46

Nick was seated on the aft bench of Stavros's over-powered craft, holding Carey's hand. Dimitri sat in the swivel fighting chair, spun around so that it faced them. He looked hard at Carey's hand in Nick's, but he didn't show any annoyance. It was more like the man was gauging the situation, taking it in deep.

Nick felt Carey's occasional tremors, both in his fingers and where her arm touched his. Sofia sat on Nick's other side, cradling the top of a thermos, the only cup Stavros had. She drained the sweetened tea and then held it out, asking Carey, "You want any more?"

"All full up, thanks." The tremors struck again just as she spoke the last word, shredding it. Nick tightened his grip on her hand. He hoped to pass on the message that she was safe now.

Dimitri asked for the fourth time, "You are okay?"

"Now I am."

They drifted in calm waters two miles off Koumana, the

Patmos headland that shielded them from view of any watchers in Skala's harbor. They needed to move in this close for Nick and Dimitri to get signals for their cellphones. Dimitri's first call was to Manos. He soon passed the phone to Sofia, then took it back to talk further.

Apparently all the fishermen knew where to moor, because just after Dimitri made his request, Stavros had steered to the stop and cut the motors.

Stavros asked, "What are we waiting for?"

Dimitri continued to alternate between staring out over the empty water off the stern and studying Nick and Carey seated together. When he didn't respond, Nick said, "We need two things to happen. First, Manos needs to confirm that the plane carrying a commander in your navy and his men have landed on Patmos."

Stavros frowned, though his words carried none of the earlier heat. "You said nothing about the navy being involved."

"They're not interested in you," Dimitri replied.

"This is about the theft you said? From the monastery? This was real?"

Dimitri sighed, shook his head, but didn't say anything.

"Very real," Nick said.

"So Manos will call, and then what?"

"Dimitri will make a call. Then you take us where we say, and leave us."

"And my money?"

"You will come to my home tomorrow," Dimitri said, "and I will pay you."

"This will be finished tomorrow?"

"Hopefully, yes."

"And if you do not survive this? What then?"

Another tremor passed through Carey's form, and Nick

resisted the urge to snap at the big man. Dimitri said to Nick, "Give me a pen and paper. I will write a note to my grandmother."

Nick fetched his pack from the deck behind the center console's windshield. Carey's hand followed him up, as though finding it hard to detach herself.

When Nick turned back, Carey's hand was still up, only now it reached toward Dimitri. Dimitri slipped from the fighting chair onto the bench Nick had vacated. Stavros grunted as he watched, and Nick assumed the big man was laughing. Nick's face burned as he settled into the seat Dimitri had given up, but he did his best to hide what he felt.

Carey said, "I wasn't scared until now."

"I feel the same," Sofia replied.

"I could keep it all down tight until you showed up. Now, I feel like one hard breeze and I'd go flying away."

Dimitri said, "You're safe now."

Carey leaned against him, and trembled.

Nick handed him the notepad. Dimitri shifted so as to free his hand, wrote swiftly, then handed the pad back to Nick. He said to Stavros, "If something happens . . ."

Stavros accepted the note, read it carefully, and then stuffed it in his pocket. "I understand."

Nick's phone rang. He checked the readout. "It's Manos."

The policeman's first word was "Sofia?"

"She's here and she's fine. Same as two hours ago."

"Let me speak with her again, please."

Nick handed over the phone and pretended not to watch as Sofia bent over the apparatus, cupping it with her entire body. When she straightened, her eyes were wet and her lips held a gentle smile.

Nick accepted the phone back. "I'm here."

"Stefanos has arrived," Manos said. "He has brought seven members of our navy's special-ops team. They worked out a strategy during the flight and did a pass over before landing. He says to tell Dimitri we will camp at Meghali Panaghia."

When Nick delivered the news, Dimitri said, "Perfect. Tell him we will moor at the Anos Kambos beach. It will be deserted this time of year."

Nick repeated the instructions, then added, "Bring food."

Dimitri walked to the bow of the boat. He kept his back to the others as he punched in the number. He knew Nick had taken his place on the aft bench. He knew Carey was not alternating between men. He knew the woman was desperate for another person's strength, that she used the proximity to affirm they had been rescued. He knew all this, just like he knew Nick had been her friend since childhood. Nonetheless, his mind tumbled with the shock of feeling jealousy for the first time in his life. He could not afford any such distractions. Their lives all depended on him getting this right. So he turned his back to the boat and stared out over the water toward the Koumana headland and the distant white dot of the church atop the ridge.

Duncan McAllister answered on the first ring. "Do you have it?"

"We're going in late this afternoon."

"The clock is ticking, boyo. Do you hear the ladies pleading for you to hurry up? Or should I have one of them sing the words loud enough for you to hear without the phone? I could—"

"The letter is not in the monastery."

The threat died unfinished. "That's not what I've been told."

Dimitri voiced the lie with a flat inflection, hoping it was enough to convince the enemy. "They've kept it safe for two thousand years. By deception."

"Where is it then?"

"The oldest church on Patmos is Meghali Panaghia. It was founded by John's own scribe."

Duncan pondered this. "The bloke who wrote the letter."

"The church was located in the island's most fertile valley, Kambos, the second largest town before Hora was built."

"Go on."

"The hills around Kambos are full of caves. The church was erected at the top of one."

"Same as the monastery."

"Exactly."

"You're sure it's there?"

Dimitri said the words that had flashed into his head the moment Nick speculated that Duncan had set him up from the very beginning. "My grandmother was once engaged to the bishop. But you knew that already, didn't you? It's why you chose me."

"I heard the rumors, sure. They made you a good fit for the job. Along with your financial dire straits."

"The bishop came through."

"You better hope so, for the sake of your lady friends."

"No threats!" Dimitri checked himself, then added, "Please."

"Sure then. You've gotten the message, you're delivering the goods, I can play the gent. For now."

"We are going in two hours before sunset. The priest will be home for his meal. We'll be gone before he returns for evening mass. When can we make the switch?"

"Hang on." Duncan cradled his phone, then came back with, "There's a beach not far from there, Anos Kambos. Did I say that right?"

"Too isolated. I want somewhere public."

"What you want doesn't hold a great deal of water just now, lad."

"I want to survive. I want the ladies alive. I want us all to walk away. Public is better."

"Well, there's no reason we can't end this as mates." Duncan sounded almost elated. "Skala harbor, midnight."

"I don't want to hold the letter one minute longer than is necessary."

Duncan McAllister became impatient. "Skala. Seven o'clock. That work for you?"

Dimitri shut the phone, took a very hard breath, turned and said, "We're on."

47

Manos was on the beach when they pulled up. Sofia leaped into the sea before the engines cut off, wading against the water as if fighting off chains. Manos moved more easily, the steady cop even now as the combination of pain and relief and love gripped him. They didn't so much embrace as clench each other. Sofia wept so hard she drew tears from Carey as well.

Stavros anchored the boat, then watched as Dimitri helped Carey down to where Nick stood to catch her. She didn't need his support any more than she needed Dimitri to assist her over the side. But she thanked them both and held on to one man's hand or the other. Needing that assurance, locked on to the fact that they were there and protecting her and caring. Both of them. Deeply.

Nick knew that now. He had no idea when the transition had taken place. But all the logic in the world could not fight against the flood of emotions that threatened to unlock his throat and force him to spill the truth. Even when there were eight naval commandos in full battle gear standing on the pebble beach, along with everyone else. He watched her step over to Dimitri, bobbing back and forth between the two men she considered friends. As safe. And for the moment, that was all it was. Two men who stood as polar opposites while Carey moved freely between them. Taking strength from both her friends.

They moved off the beach after Manos had embraced them all, even Stavros, who unbent enough to smile at the idea of having a cop in his debt. They shifted a few hundred meters up to where the commandos had set up a bivouac. The women ate a stew of lamb, pine nuts, white beans, and dates with ravenous appetites. They drank mug after mug of sweetened tea. Sofia wept a few more tears as Manos held her with an affection that forced smiles from all the battle-hardened faces. Carey continued to hold either Nick's or Dimitri's hand.

Stefanos fielded several calls, including one that reported Duncan McAllister's boat had rounded the eastern tip of Crete and was cruising straight for Patmos.

Sofia asked Dimitri, "McAllister can't make it from Crete to Skala in time for a seven o'clock meeting with you, can he?"

"He never intended to be here for the events," Manos replied.

"So the meeting . . ."

"There is no meeting," Dimitri said.

"As far as Duncan McAllister is concerned," Nick explained, "that conversation was about arranging a place where his team could ambush us."

"Or so they think," Stefanos added.

Manos had traded his police car for Dimitri's van on the way up. It was parked in a narrow ravine, next to a farm truck Manos had borrowed from an ally, who herded sheep down near the landing strip. When it was time, they loaded up as planned, the two women in the truck that would trail behind the van. Stefanos asked Nick, "Where will you travel?"

"In the van. They'll expect me to be there."

Stefanos did not object. Instead, he offered Nick a pistol. "You know how to use this?"

"I've hunted since I was a kid, and spent hours on a range."

"Officially tourists are not permitted to carry firearms in Greece."

Nick made sure the safety was on, then stuffed it into his belt. "I'll refrain from writing about this part."

The sun was into its farewell symphony by the time they reached the dry riverbed. A deep ravine traversed the island, cutting the central highlands from the northern ridges. The road followed a series of tight curves downward before straightening into a narrow valley draped in shadows.

Manos was the first to see them. "The rock by your left."

A small man and a slightly taller woman emerged from a boulder that had fallen during some long-ago storm and now partly blocked the road. He gave them a casual wave, as though he were a friend merely looking for a ride. When Manos pulled up, he strode to the driver's window and announced, "There's been a change of plans."

Dimitri leaned over and demanded, "Where are the women?"

"That's part of the change." He lifted his sweater and pulled out a pistol. "Get out. All of you."

Dimitri said, "I want to know they're okay."

"I know full well what you want. But here's how it's going to work." The small man waved without turning around, and three more men and another woman rose from positions to either side of the van. "You do what I say, everybody lives. We take you to the women. We're done. You give us trouble, we take what we want anyway. But we leave your bodies here for the vultures."

Dimitri pointed out, "There are no vultures on Patmos."

"Do I look like I care? Now get out of the van while you still have legs to carry you."

Their conversation had been long enough for the farm truck to arrive. Which was what Dimitri and Manos were after all along.

The small man gestured to the others, and all the weapons vanished. He stepped back and said, "Stay where you are. One sound and this newcomer dies."

The driver was a nondescript shepherd in tattered clothing, who responded to the man's forward gesture with a languid wave of his own. But when the truck started to pass the van, its canvas-covered rear disgorged a team of heavily armed commandos, who then swept over the rocks.

The small man said, "You'll never see the women again unless—"

He stopped when Carey jumped down from the truck and gave him a cheery hello.

Manos revealed the pistol he'd been holding below the windowsill. "You're all under arrest."

EPILOGUE

Carey stood waiting on the tarmac, on the military side of the airport. Eleni was nearby and gaping at everything around them. Eleni's aunt and mother looked very nervous. Eleni explained that standing in this place, surrounded by Greek soldiers, had brought back memories of the bad old days of the dictatorship. Even so, Carey was glad they were all there with her. They'd been instrumental to her well-being during her time in Greece.

Adriana Stephanopoulos, newly appointed director of the reopened Institute for Antiquities, stood to one side, shouting into her cellphone, trying to make herself heard above the sound of a landing jet.

The Learjet taxied over to where they were waiting. Finally, Adriana admitted defeat and put away her phone as the stairs came down and Nick stepped out. He grinned and waved at Carey.

Eleni mused aloud, "Why must the wrong ones be so handsome?"

Carey shrugged, both because she had no answer and because she was no longer certain that Nick was indeed wrong for her.

Their phone conversations had taken on a rather heated tone of late. Not heated, as in angry. Rather, heated as in, well, hot. The closer this reunion came, the more intense grew Nick's language. All about wanting to change, wanting to be who he needed to be. For her.

Just thinking about their most recent call caused Carey to shiver.

Eleni's aunt scolded Carey, and Eleni translated, "You should have brought a heavier coat."

Then Nick swept her up in an embrace, and it seemed to Carey as if she'd been waiting all her life to hear him say the words, "I've missed you so much."

He kissed her. There in front of everyone. Carey almost giggled it felt so good.

Which meant when he released her, she couldn't hold back her grin. He asked, "Are you laughing at me?"

"No, Nick."

"Okay, good." He directed her to where an elegant woman stood observing them with a smile of her own. "Phyllis Karras, this is Carey Mathers."

"My dear, how I have looked forward to this moment." Her smile was as warm as her greeting. "Although not, I admit, as much as my Nick has."

"She's offered me a job, and that gives her the right to call me her Nick."

Phyllis corrected, "But you have not accepted my offer."

"I'm thinking about it," Nick said.

She said to Carey, "Please, if you would help Nick to think more swiftly, yes? The clock is ticking rather loudly."

Carey introduced Phyllis to the others, ending with Stefanos. The young commander wore his dress uniform, which sparkled in the winter sunlight as he saluted. "Dr. Karras, an honor."

"It is I who am honored, Commander."

"Call me Stefanos, please."

"And I am Phyllis." She glanced at her watch. "We must go. The bishop will not appreciate our keeping him waiting."

But as they started toward the Learjet, Phyllis drew Carey aside. Her smile dropped away as she said, "There is a job opening as investigator in my department. I need someone with your expertise in artifacts, and I need this immediately."

"But I've only been with the Institute—"

"Yes, yes, I know. And Athens is lovely. But there are other treasures missing. You have heard of the bombing in Cairo?"

"The main museum. A car bomb, right?"

"A car bomb, but not terrorists. The museum had a hoard of secret artifacts, including several texts dating back to the birth of Christianity. Vital texts we only learned about once they had gone missing. You and Nick should be on the next plane."

Carey's lips still felt compressed by Nick's kiss. "You want me to come to work for the United Nations?"

"As a consultant based in Paris." She steered her around. "Nick will speak with you on the flight. For the sake of our world's heritage, tell him yes."

Carey allowed herself to be led down the sleek jet's central aisle and into the seat next to Nick. When they were airborne,

Nick leaned in close, though it wasn't to talk about the job. Instead, he looked her in the eyes and said two words.

"Marry me."

Carey opened her mouth to reply, but no sound came.

"I love you, Carey. I want to be the man you . . ." Nick took a deep breath, leaned back, then continued, "I've spent the past weeks thinking that the man you saw in me was the man I've fought against my entire life. Because it's scary having someone see me as being so—"

"Good," Carey whispered. "Right."

"I do want to be that man. For you. If you'll have me."

"I . . . I don't know what to say."

He nodded, his expression sad. "I know I haven't given you a single reason to accept. But I *will* change. For you. If you give me that chance."

"You want me to take the job."

"I want *you*. If that means moving to Paris, fine. But if you want me to come to Athens, I'll do that too." When she didn't respond, Carey watched him swallow the pain she saw in his eyes. "Will you at least think about it?"

"Yes, Nick. And I'll pray. Very hard."

The moment formed an intense pressure between them, not uncomfortable and yet there was no room for more words.

The flight lasted another forty minutes. They descended onto the same long stretch of empty road atop Patmos's southern highlands. Carey peered out the windows on both sides of the jet, watching the rocky island sweep in from the blue. It was as fantastically beautiful as she remembered, even in winter.

Manos was there with his wife, along with three of the island's four taxis. Somehow in the crush of introductions, Dimitri managed to separate her from Nick and draw her back to where his van sat idling. "I would tell you my grand-mother wants to have a private word, but I will not start this conversation with a lie."

Carey had spoken with Dimitri almost as often as with Nick. But the island man wasn't as comfortable with words as the journalist, especially on the phone. Dimitri had started several times to speak in ways that had left her breathless. But each time he returned to the same quiet sorrow, and in the end they had mostly talked about his time at the monas-tery—with the bishop, and on his knees.

He started the van's engine and pulled around the clutch of people, including Nick, who glared at him from the road-side. He drove in silence for twenty minutes, then when the monastery came into view, he pulled down a dirt road and stopped in a secluded area where they wouldn't be seen by others. He turned in his seat, reached for Carey's hand, and said, "Will you marry me?"

"Dimitri . . ."

"I know what they say about me. And I know it is all true. I am everything they accuse me of. But that is in the past." His pleas were so intense, his eyes glittered with unshed tears. "Give me the chance to change, Carey. For you. I want to be the man you want me to be."

"I . . . well, I don't know what to say."

"I will come to Athens. I will go to America. I will do what-ever you ask. Only, please, will you at least consider my offer?"

Minutes later, they pulled up in front of the monastery. Eleni and her aunt were standing outside the main entrance, along with Dimitri's grandmother. Carey had to tell some-body. It didn't matter that her private life should not encroach upon the reason they were gathered here. It probably wasn't a good idea to be talking about matrimony inside an ancient fortress monastery. But just then, she didn't care.

Eleni walked forward while staring back to where Dimitri matched his stride to his grandmother's. "You said he was handsome. You didn't say he was a myth."

"He's asked me to marry him."

Eleni gaped at Carey and then translated for her mother and aunt, who burst into whispering, which Eleni translated as, "This one, he is the dream made to last only one night."

"I know."

"But what a night," Eleni said, risking another glance back. "My aunt says, not this one. Not for life."

"What if he came to faith and asked God to help turn his life around?"

This froze the three women up solid. "He has said that?"

"He has been *doing* that. With the bishop's help."

This required another conference, but Carey wasn't willing to let them reach a committee decision. "There's more."

The three women did everything but climb into her lap. "More?"

"Nick's asked me to marry him too."

"Why have you not told me this before?" Eleni asked.

"Because it only just happened."

"When, today?"

"On the jet."

The translation was met with surprised silence, broken only by Eleni's mother, who started to giggle.

"Stop," Carey said, as sternly as she could manage. "If I start laughing, I won't be able to control it."

"What . . . ?" Eleni stopped because the bishop approached with his hands outstretched.

"Miss Mathers. What an honor to welcome you again."

"Thank you for inviting me."

"How could I not, when you were the one who sacrificed so much to keep this treasure in our possession?"

"In Greece's possession," she corrected, glad for his presence, his smile, and a chance to refocus on the day.

Bishop Galatas greeted each of the women, then led them back into his office. Carey did her best to smile reassuringly at Nick, but knew she would have to do better. Later. When the day wasn't quite so full.

Galatas spoke in English, then waited while Dimitri translated, "My dear friend Nick Hennessy said that the secret was out, and he was right. My associates have agreed. The treasure we have held in confidence for nineteen centuries, the scroll of the scribe of John of Patmos, must now be shared with the world."

He strode to the massive fireplace, reached inside, and pushed down an unseen lever. The rear of the fireplace rolled away, revealing stairs that descended into the dark.

The bishop turned and smiled at the gathering. "Let us go and see what the scribe had to say."

 **Davis Bunn** is an award-winning novelist and a lecturer in creative writing at the University of Oxford. His books, translated into twenty languages, have sold nearly seven million copies worldwide. Formerly a business executive working in Europe, Africa, and the Middle East, Davis draws on this international experience in crafting his stories. Davis has won four Christy Awards for excellence in historical and suspense fiction, and was recently inducted into the Christy Hall of Fame. He and his wife, Isabella, divide their time between the English countryside and the coast of Florida. To learn more, visit DavisBunn.com.

More From Davis Bunn

To learn more about Davis and his books, visit davisbunn.com.

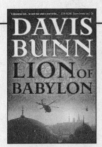

As a new coalition rises in Iraq, an ancient threat is silently amassing power. When Marc Royce's off-grid mission unearths a trail of explosive secrets, his actions could change the destiny of millions.

Lion of Babylon

Undercover agent Marc Royce is back on assignment. As war breaks out in Kenya over valuable land, how far will he go to bring peace?

Rare Earth

Investigating Iran's growing nuclear program for the State Department, Royce must rely on an old ally to help him uncover the truth before global tensions are pushed beyond the breaking point by a catastrophic blockade.

Strait of Hormuz

⬦ BETHANYHOUSE

 Stay up-to-date on your favorite books and authors with our free e-newsletters. Sign up today at bethanyhouse.com.

 Find us on Facebook. facebook.com/bethanyhousepublishers

 Free exclusive resources for your book group! bethanyhouse.com/anopenbook

an open book

You May Also Enjoy . . .

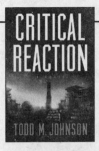

When an explosion at a closed but still poisonous nuclear facility endangers everyone in the area, how far will security guard Kieran Mullaney—and his friend, lawyer Emily Hart—go to find out what really happened?

Critical Reaction by Todd M. Johnson
authortoddjohnson.com

After Kayden McKenna discovers the body of a fellow climber, she and Jake Westin team up to investigate the death—provoking threats on her entire family.

Silenced by Dani Pettrey
ALASKAN COURAGE #4
danipettrey.com

When a group of corrupt politicians targets him for opposing reforms in freedom of speech, influential evangelist John Luther vows to expose the truth, or die trying.

Persecuted by Robin Parrish
BASED ON A DANIEL LUSKO FILM
persecutedmovie.com